The Davenport Series - Book 4

Ready to
Love Again

Judah Knight

 GreenTree Publishers

Ready to Love Again

Printed in the United States of America
ISBN-13: 978-1-944483-09-8
ISBN-10: 1-944483-09-8

Follow Judah Knight through the following media links:
    Website/blog: www.judahknight.com
    Twitter: @judahknight

Greentree Publishers: www.greentreepublishers.com

Dedication & Special Thanks

This book is dedicated to my wonderful Mother-in-Law and Father-in-Law. Warren and Fay, you gave me such a special treasure in your daughter. It is a joy to be a part of your family.

Thanks to everyone who helped bring this project to completion. I'm grateful to the host of people who are a part of my editorial team. Thanks to Adele Brinkley, my copy editor, for always making me much better than I am. I'm also grateful to those at the Trelleborg Viking Fortress Museum in Slagelse, Denmark who helped with some of the details about your wonderful museum. To everyone else who labored with me through the months to tie a bow upon this finished project, thank you.

Contents

Conclusion of *Finding My Way*

Lacy stepped aside as Meg rushed to the bed and hugged Kerrick. "I'm so glad to see you're doing okay."

"Hey, Kerrick," Jon walked to the other side of the bed and placed his hand on Kerrick's shoulder. "You scared us."

"Well, sorry about that," Kerrick said. "Any word on Randal? How's David's arm?"

"We stopped by the nurse's desk to check on Randal," Meg said. "They're working on getting him into a room. He'll need surgery on at least one of his legs, but the doctor thinks he's got a good chance at a full recovery."

"David's arm is bruised but not broken," Jon said.

"That's great to hear," Kerrick said. "I feared the worst when I saw Randal pinned under that crate. Good. Good about both of them."

"The whole thing was scary," Jon agreed, "but it looks like everyone will be fine."

"Good, 'cause I'm ready to get back to work."

"I think work can wait," Meg said. "You won't be released until tomorrow."

Kerrick crossed his arms. "That's what the nurse said, but I feel fine. I don't know why I can't leave right now."

"Yeah, right," Lacy scoffed. "I just had to help you to the bathroom."

"I was just trying to get your sympathy."

Heat rose up Lacy's neck and right up into her cheeks. *Why am I so embarrassed? Jon and Meg don't know we kissed.*

"Jon, I've been thinking a lot about the wreck's location," Kerrick said. "Remember when Mr. Phil said the island's southern end doesn't get many divers?"

"I remember."

"I think the ship dragged a reef around Double Bay but didn't sink until it was in the gap between Eleuthera and the little island to the south. Lacy and I dove there, and the depth might keep other divers away. We found a tunnel leading through the reef to the sand below."

"Interesting," Jon said, "but the only evidence we have points to Double Bay."

"That ship could have sunk anywhere," Lacy said, perching on the edge of the bed. "I don't think we have a chance in…a chance in the world to find the thing. It's like looking for a grain of sand in the desert."

"No one ever said finding treasure would be easy," Jon said.

"We don't need to worry about treasure right now," Meg said. "We've got to focus on getting you guys well."

"I've talked with a realtor about a short-term rental on the island," Jon said. "It's best to hang out here for a week to give you time to get your strength back."

"What about Randal?" Lacy asked.

"I'm not sure," Jon said. "I reached out to his mother. Surprisingly, she didn't lose it and threaten to sue. I told her I'd call her back once I know about his surgery."

"I guess he'll be in a cast for a while," Lacy said. "Does that mean we'll have to send him home?"

"Maybe," Jon said. "It's hard to imagine him wanting to hang out on the ship for the rest of the summer. Stumbling around on crutches might prove too challenging on *The Discoverer.*"

Lacy reached for Kerrick's hand, and he pulled her hand under the edge of the blanket. Her heartrate quickened. Is this what it felt like to be in love? She wasn't in love. She was just…what? Whatever it was, she didn't want it to go away.

"A little R & R on Nassau wouldn't hurt anyone," Meg said.

"We can make it fun," Lacy said. "It's too bad we had to have an accident. The summer had been unbelievable until the barge."

Kerrick tugged on her hand. Was he trying to pull her under the covers with him? What was he thinking? Jon and Meg were standing right beside the bed.

Kerrick stared into Lacy's eyes, and her cheeks glowed. This blushing thing had to stop.

"I think the summer's still unbelievable," Kerrick said, almost whispering, "and we still have a couple of months left."

Lacy heard the clock ticking but couldn't decide if it was louder than her beating heart. No one said anything until Meg cleared her throat.

"A couple of months to help five desperate boys who need a change in their lives," Meg said. "That's our focus. Right?"

Kerrick smiled while continuing to stare at Lacy. "I'm focused. We'll spend the rest of the summer searching for treasure."

"Okay," Meg said, crossing her arms. "Real treasure, as in boys with a solid future who will stay off the streets and off drugs."

Kerrick grinned and looked at Meg. "Yeah. That's what I meant. We can hang out in Nassau while we figure out what's next. It'll be fun."

"We'll go by the realtor's office to complete the paperwork and get the key to the rental," Jon said. He looked at his watch. "They might still be open."

"I want to stay with Kerrick," Lacy said.

Judah Knight

"You can't stay here overnight," Meg said. "You don't have anywhere to sleep."

"I'll sleep in the chair."

Jon handed Lacy some cash, took Meg's hand, and pulled her toward the door. "She'll be fine. We need to get to the realtor's office. Lacy, there's a cafeteria on the bottom floor."

"Just make sure you let him rest, Lacy," Meg said from the open door. "We'll have our hands full with five adventurous boys on Nassau. Kerrick needs to be in top form."

"I'll make sure he's in top form, Aunt Meg." Lacy winked. "Maybe we can get him out of here tomorrow."

"Maybe," Jon agreed, "and let's hope this is our last scare for the summer. See you tomorrow."

Chapter One
Evil Intent

Fernando raced across the villa's backyard and leaned against the back wall. Most people would be asleep, but there was always a chance someone might see him.

He pocketed the pistol and reached into his boot for the five-inch, razor-sharp knife. He loved his blade. If someone had to die tonight, he'd rather stick them. The boy? He imagined sinking his blade in deep. Why not?

His thoughts drifted to the girl. Beautiful face, long, blonde hair, perfect body...*Get your mind in the game, Fernando.*

Fernando looked back toward the bushes, where he could barely make out Miguel. They'd been partners a while. Fernando couldn't believe Miguel let him go into the house alone this time. *Why wouldn't he? I can handle it.*

His cell phone's earbud buzzed to life. "See anything?" Fernando had forgotten Miguel was waiting for a reply.

"Not yet," Fernando whispered. "Give me a sec. You haven't seen a car yet, have you?"

"No, but that doesn't mean the house is empty."

"I'll call back."

He hustled around to the side of the villa and slipped through the door they'd used the previous day. No sign of anyone. He retraced his steps to the girl's room and eased inside. Empty.

Fernando turned on his flashlight but covered the beam with his hand. The pile of clothes in the corner was still there. *The girl's not exactly a neat freak.*

He'd heard the boy call her Lacy. *Nice.* He looked at the clothes on the floor. *Yep. The name definitely fits.*

He sat on the edge of the bed and imagined Lacy under the sheets. His mind returned to the first night he'd snuck into her bedroom while she slept. He could have taken her, but patience was a virtue.

Getting the medallion was top priority. Extra fun could wait.

Spotting the medallion had been pure chance, but what a stroke of luck. If he and Miguel could get their hands on it, they'd find the pot of gold at the end of the rainbow. All their dreams would come true. Well, most of them. After seeing the girl, he now had a few new ones.

He lay back on Lacy's pillow. He breathed in and smiled. He'd soon own that girl. He'd only get her because Miguel wanted Meg, but that was fine. Why want Meg when Lacy was an option?

His phone hummed, and he looked at the text. "Girl not here. Checking rest of house," he texted back.

He hated leaving Lacy's bed, but he could come back. He checked the boy's room and worked through the house to the front bedroom. Empty.

He wouldn't mind having the redhead, either. She was a prize. Knowing Miguel, he'd call first dibs. Maybe not.

"I may just have to surprise you when you come home," Fernando said aloud, thinking of her auburn hair and full lips. He slipped the knife back into his boot. "I can handle you and Lacy once your men bleed out."

Fernando returned to Lacy's room. How had they missed them? People didn't rent expensive villas on the beach and not stay in them.

Patience, Fernando.

He'd have to hang around until Lacy and the others returned.

Fernando inspected the room and tried to imagine the best way to grab the girl. The boy might be a problem. The Latino, too. He was small but carried himself well. If needed, Fernando could shoot him. No, a gunshot could draw too much attention.

He assumed the boy would stay with Lacy for the night. Who wouldn't? He'd be distracted. Could be an advantage. An idea began forming in his mind.

He called Miguel. "The place is empty."

"I figured. Come on out, and we'll go back to the boat."

"Don't you think they'll come back sometime tonight? Why don't I hide in the girl's closet, and you stay outside watching for them? When the girl's in her room alone, I'll grab her. No one will know she's gone."

"Right. Like she'll walk out of the house quietly with you."

"Little pop on the head, and I'll carry her out quietly," Fernando said. He thought back to his plan. *Not before I have a little fun and get rid of the boy. No need to tell him that part of the plan.* He'd eventually bring the girl out unconscious.

"Headlights coming," Miguel whispered. "Hold on."

Fernando jumped to his feet and got into the closet. His heart pounded against his chest.

"False alarm. Neighbors."

Fernando took a deep breath. "I'll hide here and bring her out later. Does that sound okay?"

Miguel took in a deep breath, and Fernando thought he might nix the plan. "I think it's a bad idea."

"Come on Miguel. You let me know when they come home. I'll hide in her quiet like and bring her out after while."

He waited a long time before hearing Miguel pull in a breath on the other end. "Okay. You better not blow this. Just make sure she's got the medallion."

Fernando eased the closet door shut and walked back to the bed. He lay down and closed his eyes. This night was going to be memorable.

* * * * *

Jon started the engine of the *New Beginnings* and idled backward away from the dock. He turned the boat and eased out of the marina, heading toward *The Discoverer*.

Meg moved in close and slipped her arms around his waist. "Are you sure we did the right thing?"

"You mean not grabbing something to eat at McDonald's?"

"So funny," Meg deadpanned. "You know what I'm talking about. Lacy and Kerrick's relationship just went from zero to sixty when we returned to the car. That was a bad idea, too."

"Meg, you've got to quit second-guessing yourself. Letting Lacy have some alone time with Kerrick was the right thing to do. She's nineteen years old, for heaven's sake."

"That's what I'm worried about. I was nineteen not too many years ago, and spending the night in the same room with a boy I liked wouldn't have been a good idea."

"They're in a hospital room. What can they do?"

Meg pulled Jon's face around to look at her. "Don't you remember being nineteen? Would a hospital room have stopped you?"

Jon laughed. "Kerrick's still hurting, so they're not doing anything tonight. Besides, we've got to trust them."

"I want to, Jon," Meg sputtered, "I, I—just know how young people are."

Jon put his arm around her and lowered his lips to hers. "You're not exactly a senior adult. Quit worrying. This time will be good for them. We wanted to help Lacy, and I think Kerrick will help her."

Meg leaned her head against his chest, and Jon rubbed his hand through her hair. She was precious, but playing mother to a nineteen-year-old wasn't easy.

"Lacy's come a long way in a short period," Meg said. "I don't want her going backward."

"She'll be fine, Meg. Let's start trying to figure out our next move. We've got one lame boy and one injured intern. At least they'll be okay, but how will we go back to looking for treasure? What do we do with the rest of the summer?"

"Not to mention, what do we do with Randal's family?"

Memories of Randal trapped inside the barge seventy-five feet underwater came to Jon's mind, and he lowered himself to the captain's chair. He'd been wavering with feelings of regret since the accident. Maybe this plan of rescuing boys from the street with a salvage business wasn't a good idea. He thought he could use it to develop character and build leadership skills in the boys, but were the risks too great?

"Hello. Earth to Jon. Did you hear me?" Meg asked.

"Sorry, Honey. My mind drifted."

"No kidding. I asked when Randal's mom is coming down. You're still blaming yourself for the accident. Aren't you?"

"I'm not, Meg. Well, not really. I'm wondering whether we should keep this project going. Maybe we should give the boys a great vacation in Nassau and send them home." He shifted his gaze to her and then back out to sea, his right hand guiding the wheel.

Meg sat down beside Jon and clutched his left hand. "Jon, think back to how those boys were when we first met them on the dock in Miami. Do you remember?"

Jon smiled and laughed. "Yeah. They were something. I wondered if we'd made a mistake then, too."

"But look at them now. We're just a few weeks into this program, and their lives are already changed. Dramatically changed. How can we give up when we've come so far but still have far to go?"

Images of the boys flashed in Jon's mind. They'd gone from foul-mouthed street kids to a respectful team of young men. They'd never admit it, but they'd grown to love one another. He'd never seen a group go through a transformation like that in such a short period of time.

"You're right, Honey. I'm just struggling."

"I'd be worried if you weren't, but we have to keep the program going and finish what we started." Meg gave him a moment and then asked again. "So, what about Randal's mom?

"I'm amazed. She's not blaming us and is so grateful Kerrick saved Randal's life. I told her we'd fly her down here as soon as she can work it out to leave her other kids."

Meg patted his hand. "Sounds to me like that's the sign you need. There's too much at stake to stop the program now. Think about the power of pouring into these kids. It's only five boys, but it's five boys!"

"I know. I was thinking about a story I heard at church when I was a kid. It's about a man walking along the shore throwing beached starfish back into the ocean. Someone stopped the man, pointed to all the starfish in the sand, and said there was no way he could make a difference. The guy threw another starfish back into the water and said, 'It made a difference to that one.'"

Meg squeezed Jon's hand. "That's so good. We'll make a difference one boy at a time."

"And we'll eventually bring girls along, too."

"Whoa. Not too fast. When we go coed, we'll need twice as many interns as kids."

Jon looked at Meg and grinned. "You sure seem to have romance on your mind a lot these days. Lacy and Kerrick, and now you're nervous about a coed program."

Meg shook her head. "It's not romance I'm worried about. Technically, what I'm talking about doesn't have to be romance."

Jon pulled Meg into his lap. "I know some guys that might disagree with you."

"Jon, you're going to wreck the boat."

Jon laughed and pressed a few buttons to put the boat on autopilot. He cupped his hand behind Meg's neck and pulled her in for a kiss. "All this talk about romance is kind of getting to me."

Meg smiled and kissed him again. "Is that a fact? Too bad the autopilot's not sophisticated enough to take us to *The Discoverer* without you being at the wheel. You've been working with the boys on self-discipline; you'll have to exhibit a little of that yourself."

Jon placed his hands on her face. "Ah, the voice of reason. Another good reason I married you. Speaking of self-discipline, Kerrick's got plenty of it. He'll be an important part of the equation that helps Lacy deal with her issues."

Meg grimaced. "I sure hope you're right."

Chapter Two
A Friend Indeed

Lacy's body tingled as Kerrick's kiss deepened. Someone rapped on the door, and Lacy jerked away and dropped into the chair.

The nurse peeked around the edge of the curtain. "Your aunt wanted me to tell you the cafeteria is closing in twenty minutes, so you may want to go get something to eat."

Lacy checked her watch. "They sure close early. Okay. Thanks."

The nurse stared at her before turning to leave. Her timing was uncanny. All she and Kerrick had to do was think about kissing, and the Wicked Witch of the West appeared.

"You heard Atilla."

"Atilla?"

Kerrick laughed. "You know, Atilla the Hun?"

Lacy laughed. "He was a man."

"Doesn't matter. She looks like she could rough you up. Better do what she says."

"I was thinking of the Wizard of Oz, or rather the witch. Well, I am hungry. Will you be okay while I run down to the cafeteria?"

A young woman pushed a food cart into the room by Kerrick's bed as if on cue. She lifted the lid from the top tray. "Baked chicken, rice and gravy, and green beans." She looked at Kerrick and smiled. "And apple pie with ice cream."

Lacy crossed her arms. She wished she could kick the girl's shin. Could the girl be more obvious?

Kerrick cleared his throat. "Thanks."

The girl finally left, and Lacy made sure the door closed behind her. She came back around the curtain and saw Kerrick smiling. "What are you smiling at? That girl was moonstruck."

Kerrick looked at his watch. "You now have fifteen minutes. You need to get to the cafeteria."

"Okay, okay. I'll go by Randal's room on the way back, too. You going to be all right while I'm gone?"

"Fourteen minutes. I'll be fine. Take your time."

Lacy set a record for eating a burger and fries and headed to Randal's room. The last time she saw the boy, he'd been unconscious in the rescue helicopter. She'd been so focused on Kerrick she hadn't paid Randal much attention.

Images of the heavy crate crushing his legs filled her mind as she pushed open the door to his room. The doctor said he'd eventually be as good as new. Truly a miracle.

She entered the room and found Randal asleep. She examined his immobilized legs wrapped tight in splints. He couldn't be comfortable, but he was out like a light. Probably pain meds.

Lacy looked around for a pen so she could at least leave a note. Nothing. She'd have to get one from the nurses' station. As she turned to leave, she heard Randal clear his throat.

"Randal! I thought you were sound asleep."

Randal mustered a weak smile. "I can't believe you came to see me.

"Of course I came to see you. I've been worried sick about you and Kerrick."

"How's he?"

"He's good. How are you feeling? I see you're doing the mummy thing. Can't be too comfortable."

"It ain't too bad, except when I have to, you know, go."

Lacy grinned. "I'm sure that's rough, but your nurse sure is pretty."

Randal's face tightened.

Your nurse is pretty? Great, Lacy. She tried to imagine needing help for the most basic things like using a bedpan. She'd be horrified.

"Hey, you'll be out of here in no time," Lacy said, taking two steps to the bed. She reached out and patted his arm.

"They told me I gotta have surgery."

"I heard. Jon told me he's trying to get your mom down here. I think she's having a little challenge getting someone to take care of your little sister. Or is it brother?"

"Two brothers and a sister. The nurse told me Mom called while I was sleeping, but she's supposed to call back in an hour."

"I'm sure you'll be glad to talk to her."

Randal shrugged. "Yeah, I guess. You know, Kerrick saved my life."

Boys from where he's from didn't cry, but Randal teared up anyway. Lacy's vision blurred, and she felt tears running down her cheeks. She squeezed his hand.

"I know. I saw him. I was afraid you both would die, but here you are. You'll be as good as new after a little surgery."

"And a lot of therapy," Randal added. "At least that's what that nurse told me."

"We're all pulling for you, Randal, and we'll help you get strong again. You've got to help us find that treasure."

Randal grinned, but then his face fell. "I don't suppose I'll be getting back into the water for a while."

Lacy's heart went out to the boy. Just when he was getting the hang of scuba diving, he had to have a summer-ending accident. Maybe Jon would work something out so he could stay with the group, if his mom let him.

"I need to get back to Kerrick's room. You know how he is—big sissy."

Randal's smile covered his face. "Thanks for coming by."

"I'll be back in a while to check on you. You need anything?

"I'm good."

"I'm going to get a piece of paper and a pen and write Kerrick's room and phone number down. Be right back."

Lacy hurried to the nurses' station and got a pad and pen. She scribbled down Kerrick's room phon number, took the note to Randal, and gave him a brief but heartfelt hug. Then, she hurried back to Kerrick.

"How was he?" Kerrick asked as soon as she walked into the room.

"He's good, but I think he's more worried than he's letting on."

"He's a real champ," Kerrick said. "Maybe I can go by his room on my way out tomorrow."

"I might go by later tonight and play cards with him or something."

"Good idea. Do we know when they're doing the surgery?"

"Not yet." Lacy saw Kerrick trying to adjust his pillows. "Let me do that." She rushed to the bedside. "Lean up."

"I've been thinking I should probably milk this a bit," Kerrick said with a grin. "You know, the whole sympathy thing."

"Don't push your luck," Lacy said, adjusting his covers. "Need a blanket?"

"All I need is for you to sit beside me," Kerrick said as he patted the mattress. He slid over to make room for her.

"I want to hear all about you."

"I've told you about me."

"No, you told me what you wanted me to hear. I want to know everything there is to know."

No one had ever wanted to know her. She knew many boys who wanted other things, but Kerrick wasn't like jerks. What if she told him the truth about her past, and he decided he didn't like her?

She spent the next hour reminiscing about her childhood and surprised herself by telling him things she'd never told anyone. She even told him about what her cousin did to her when she was eleven.

Lacy jumped when the hospital intercom came to life. "May I have your attention, please? Visiting hours will end in thirty minutes."

"I can't believe it's already eight o'clock," Kerrick yawned.

"Time flies when you're having fun," Lacy teased.

She stood when she heard someone coming into the room. "Hey, uh…Debra? Is that right?"

"Hello, Lacy. You have a good memory."

"I'm so surprised to see you again."

"Well, Dear. I told you I'd come by to check in on you. I had a little trouble finding you because I didn't know Kerrick's last name. It's good I still have a little pull around here."

Debra put her arm around Lacy and gave her a squeeze.

"Debra, this is my friend Kerrick. Kerrick, this is the lady I met in the waiting room yesterday."

"Good to see you, Kerrick. Lacy sure was worried about you when they first brought you in."

"It's a pleasure to meet you, Debra. Lacy told me about you. Thanks for stopping by."

Debra pulled a chair closer to Kerrick's bed. "How's your other friend?"

"He'll need surgery on both legs," Lacy answered, "but he should fully recover."

Debra beamed. "Wonderful news! I meet with a group of ladies on Tuesday mornings. I told them all about you, and we had a special prayer for you this morning."

"Uh...thanks." Lacy faltered. "I mean, I'm sure a little prayer never hurt anyone."

"That's for sure," Debra smiled. "I've been praying all my life. Some people call the good things that happen coincidences, but I find many more coincidences happen when I pray than when I don't."

Lacy laughed awkwardly. She thought about her grandmother; her grandma prayed all the time. She went to church weekly and always told Lacy she was praying for her. Lacy smiled with the memory, but then a frown spread across her face.

"Your husband died. I'm sure you prayed for him, but he died anyway."

"That's true, dear. I prayed for him a lot, and he died. Cancer is a horrible thing."

"But, you still believe in prayer?"

"Honey, God doesn't always say 'yes' to every prayer. Sometimes his answer is 'no' or 'wait.' I had to decide long ago I'd trust God no matter what happened. You see, we live in a broken world."

Lacy reflected on being abused by her cousin. Her world still remained broken.

Debra reached out to take Lacy's hand. "I think death, sorrow, and trouble come because of the brokenness around us—and in us, for that matter. I know I'm broken and not the way I'm supposed to be. I must accept that I'm responsible for most of the trouble I've experienced, not God. I don't mean my husband died because of me, but I'm just saying things in this world are messed up."

"You can say that again," Kerrick agreed.

"I'm the chief of mess ups," Debra said. "I agree with what I heard someone say once: 'If I had to kick the person most responsible for all of my troubles, I wouldn't be able to sit down for a week.'"

Lacy and Kerrick laughed. Lacy felt Debra squeeze her hand.

"Lacy, I just wanted to stop by and check on you two. When will you be getting out of here, Kerrick?"

"I think they'll let me leave in the morning."

"My uncle thinks we'll stay on Nassau for a few days while we're waiting on Randal to get out of the hospital," Lacy said. "Randal's not going to be able to continue in our summer program, though."

"You told me yesterday you were a mentor to Randal," Debra prodded.

"My aunt and uncle started a program for troubled teens. They think the boys will change if they can get them down here in the Bahamas for the summer working with them in their salvage business."

"That sounds quite interesting. Does it work?"

Kerrick leaned forward in the bed. "In my opinion, it's a wonderful success. It has been amazing watching the transformation in these boys. They're all between fifteen and seventeen and came from some rough circumstances."

"A few weeks ago, they were at each other's throats," Lacy added, "and about every other word was a curse word. Now, they work together like a real team, and you seldom hear bad language."

"Impressive."

"My aunt has a rule about language she calls 'the potty mouth rule. She hates cursing and doesn't want her little girl growing up hearing bad language. I thought she'd never get those boys to follow the rule, but I was wrong."

"Your aunt and uncle sound like wonderful people. I sure would like to meet them one day."

"They are wonderful people," Lacy beamed. "They're the most wonderful people I know. Aunt Meg is my mom's sister, but she and my mom are nothing alike. Too bad."

Debra nodded and patted Lacy's hand. "Well, Honey. I'm going to have to go. I serve dinner downtown at a homeless shelter on Tuesday afternoons and haven't been home all day. I'd love to hear from you sometime. I've written my home address and e-mail address on this little card. Would you drop me a note to let me know how things are going?"

"Sure, Debra. You've been so kind. Thanks for coming by."

When Lacy stood to say goodbye, Debra wrapped her arms around the young woman. Lacy responded with a hesitant hug as a tear rolled down her cheek. A warmth spread through her as if she'd stepped out into the bright sunlight.

Debra pulled away and leaned over to pat Kerrick's arm. "You take care of this girl."

"Oh, I will." Kerrick smiled. "She's quite unique."

As Debra headed toward the door of the small hospital room, she turned back to the young couple. "Unique is a good thing. I look forward to hearing from you both."

The door closed behind Debra, and the two were once again alone.

"Unique?" Lacy arched a brow. "I think I'll take my unique self down to Randal's room for a bit. I'll be back."

Chapter Three

Going Home

Early the next morning, Meg tapped on Kerrick's door and entered. She stopped so abruptly Jon bumped into her.

"Sorry," he said.

"Shh," Meg warned.

Meg took in the scene and smiled. A deck of cards lay scattered on the portable table, and Lacy sat beside the bed in a black vinyl chair. Her head lay on the mattress beside Kerrick's arm, and she and Kerrick were fast asleep, their hands intertwined.

"I'd say they've had a couple of long days," Jon whispered.

"True," Meg agreed as they slipped out of the room into the hallway. "Do you remember when we were worried about their relationship escalating?"

"I remember," Jon said. "You were the one worried. I thought the possibility of them becoming an item was about as likely as me becoming Miss America."

"Miss America?"

Jon smiled. "I know. Not much of a chance. I'm married."

"You're also crazy," Meg laughed. "I'm pleased to announce I was right."

"Okay. I admit that anticipating young love is not my strong suit. If Lacy is true to form, she'll dump Kerrick by the end of the month."

"At least you're big enough to admit when you're wrong." Meg smiled and kissed Jon on the cheek. "I don't know about Lacy dumping him, though."

"I don't think I want to bet on it. I lost the last time we had a wager. Let's find a nurse to see if the doctor decided when Kerrick can get out of here."

Meg turned toward the nurses' station and felt Jon's hand slip into hers. "I'm so relieved this story has a happy ending," she whispered as they walked.

Jon nodded. "We've got to get through Randal's surgery and get him on the mend, but yeah. It could have been so much worse."

"You can say that again."

"We'll pay Randal's expenses and set up a fund for future medical bills."

Meg stopped in the middle of the hall. "I thought they said he would make a full recovery."

"They did, Honey, but you never know if he'll need further therapy or surgery."

Meg spotted Kerrick's doctor looking at a chart behind the long counter. He'd been so kind to Kerrick. They'd been fortunate.

The doctor looked up and smiled at them. When Jon asked for an update on Kerrick's condition, he confirmed his progress and that he could leave before dinner.

"He shouldn't dive for a while," the doctor admonished, "and I'd like to see him in my office next Monday."

Jon shook the doctor's hand. "Thank you, Dr. Reeves. We decided to spend a week on Nassau, so next Monday won't be a problem. Thank you for all you've done."

"Glad to help. Kerrick seems to be a fine young man. One of the nurses told me about your program for the boys. Sounds wonderful. I've talked with the hospital administrator, and he's going to wave the hospital's expenses for everything except the chamber. He was quite touched by your story. I'm not going to be sending you a bill, either."

Jon was floored. "Well, thank you, Dr. Reeves. That's very kind of you. Would you mind writing down the administrator's name so I can express my appreciation to him?"

The doctor wrote the name on a slip of paper and handed it to Jon. Jon shook his hand again and assured him they'd be at his office the following Monday.

"So, what happens to Randal now?" Meg asked as they walked toward the drink machine at the end of the hall. "He looked kind of rough when we saw him this morning."

"When you were in the restroom, he said he wants to stay with us. Let's check and see if they have surgery scheduled." They walked down the hall toward the elevator.

"How can he stay with us? He'll have casts on both legs. I doubt he can get out of bed for a while, and then he'll be confined to a wheelchair."

Jon grimaced. "Not to mention therapy and more doctor visits. I've been thinking it will be best for Randal if we rent a house on Eleuthera where he can recuperate. If he's on the island near us, all the boys can still drop in to see him. Kerrick and Lacy can stay in the house with him."

"Kerrick, yes, but letting Lacy stay with them may be courting disaster. Besides, won't Randal's mother want him to come home?"

"Think about it, Meg. He has no father in the picture. His mother works night and day to take care of three younger siblings. I think she'll be more than happy we're willing to keep him for now."

"I'm sure you're right. Too bad she couldn't leave her kids and come down today."

Jon shook his head. "It's hard to believe she doesn't have someone she can leave the kids with."

"I don't think we have any idea what her life is like, Jon. We can't relate to not being able to trust anyone with our children—certainly not the way she trusted us."

Jon pressed the call button for the elevator. "I think we should get his family out of the inner city and into a house. For one thing, Randal may have difficulty with the steps in his apartment building for a while."

Meg shuddered at the thought of their visit to Randal's home a few months earlier. When they walked into the filthy stairwell to climb to the fifth floor in the D.C. housing project, they squeezed past a pregnant girl that couldn't have been more than thirteen. Another teenager lay on the second-floor landing, stoned out of his mind. Rescuing these kids felt hopeless.

Getting back to the car that day presented the greatest challenge. Thanks to Randal, a couple of tough-looking guys let them get pass without an incident.

"A house for Randal's family would be good," Meg finally said. "Maybe we can get the whole family out of the inner city. That should change their lives. I'm really worried about his older brother; he seems like bad news."

"True. I wouldn't be interested in getting them a house if Randal's mother lived off other people, but she works two jobs to support her family.

"I don't know how she does it."

"She can make small payments so she doesn't feel like she's getting a handout," Jon continued. "I'll get Sarah to start looking for a house online from the office in Canton. I need to check in with her anyway, or she's going to feel like I don't need an assistant anymore."

"I think we should move Ann and Jose to the house on Eleu-thera too," Meg suggested, "or at least back to *The Discoverer.* We don't need to keep them at Hatchet Bay Resort."

"I thought about that," Jon admitted. "The older gentlemen might present a problem. What's his name?"

"Do you mean the old man they met at the resort?"

"Yeah. I think it's Bill or something."

"Phil."

"Yeah. Phil. Maybe if we rent a house near Rock Sound, there won't be much chance of running into Phil."

Meg crossed her arms and leaned against the wall inside the elevator as the doors closed. "If Kerrick spends a week or so in the house, I assume Lacy will be nearby. If that's the case, Jose and Ann will have to step up their babysitting skills, assuming they stay there."

"They've been getting a lot of practice the last few days," Jon said.

"Ann's not stupid. She knows what's going on, and she can handle Kerrick."

Jon laughed. "I'm not that worried about Kerrick. I'm more concerned about Lacy."

"Come on, Jon. Lacy has been as cold as the north pole for a while. I'm worried about the raging hormones in a twenty-one-year-old, single, male college student."

"I'm sure they'll be fine," Jon assured her. "Judy's available to help out, too. Besides that, I'm giving Lacy a couple of months before she returns to being the Ice Queen."

"Is that a bet?" Meg challenged.

"Uh, no. I'll stick with my prediction."

They approached the nurses' station on the fifth floor and saw Randal's doctor. The doctor explained Randal's condition again and felt positive about the surgery. It was scheduled for first thing in the morning.

When they returned to Kerrick's room, Meg heard water running in the restroom. Lacy stood at the sink washing her face, her long, blonde hair dangling from a ponytail. She looked as fresh as the morning.

"Morning, Lacy," Jon called out. "Hey, Kerrick. How do you feel?"

"Great. When can I get out of here?"

"Dr. Reeves says you can leave after lunch. We need to sign a few documents."

"How about Randal?"

"Surgery's in the morning. In the meantime, we've got a house to rent for a few days, and then we'll move over to Eleuthera."

"You mean Randal's staying with us at Hatchet Bay?"

"Maybe," Meg said. "We're going present the idea to his mother."

"We'll rent a house near Rock Sound, if we can find one," Jon said. "I don't think Randal wants to go home. We figured we could get a house on the island's southern end so the boys can spend time with him when we're not diving."

Kerrick nodded. "I like that idea."

"You'll need to stay in the house for a week. The doctor said you can't go back to diving immediately."

"I feel fine."

"I'm sure you do, but underwater pressure can do strange things."

Meg turned toward Lacy, who leaned against the wall. She marveled at her niece's beauty, even though she'd spent the night sleeping in a chair. Her make-up-free face didn't have a single blemish, and her bright blue eyes commanded attention.

"We need to step out so Kerrick can get dressed," Meg advised. "Kerrick, let us know when you're decent."

Jon pulled out his cell phone. "I need to let the realtor know we're coming by to get the key to the house we're renting."

"So, you got a house? A week on Nassau sounds like fun," Lacy said.

"Yeah, we got one," Meg said. "I guess staying here will be fun, but remember, we've got four boys with us who are not wheelchair-bound and are still rough around the edges."

"They'll be fine," Lacy insisted. "We'll be on land and all together. What could possibly happen?"

Chapter Four
Working the Plan

"Why did you kill him?" Miguel scolded. "He just came to make a repair on the villa. He never saw us."

"You can't know that for sure," Fernando insisted. "I swear he looked straight at me. He saw me through the crack in the door."

Miguel stared at the dead man on the floor. "I shouldn't have agreed to let you stay inside the house."

"I didn't have a choice. I had to kill him. Did you want him to blow the whole thing? He would have called the cops."

Miguel sat on the bed, not taking his eyes off the body. Fernando was an idiot. Why did he let him keep hanging around? Of course, something would have to be done, and he couldn't just let him leave.

An image of Fernando's knife flashed through Miguel's mind. *It's a wonder he didn't use the blade.* At least there wasn't any blood on the floor.

"I'm tired of waiting for the girl and her friends to return," Fernando whined. "We've been hiding out here watching this stupid house for days and seen nothing."

Miguel grabbed Fernando by the shirt and threw him against the wall. "You know what that girl's medallion means to us? Once we pair it with our medallion, we'll have more money than we could spend in ten lifetimes." He cursed and pressed his forearm against Fernando's throat. "Now, shut up. We've got to figure out how to get out of the mess you just made."

Miguel stepped through the girl's bedroom door into the courtyard. They were so close. No matter how stupid Fernando got, he couldn't let the idiot's dumb move ruin everything.

He thought back to the day he and Fernando found the first medallion in the cave on Conception Island. A total fluke.

They went into the cave to get out of the heat. Fernando made one of his stupid comments, and Miguel threw his lighter at him. Instead of hitting his big head, the lighter skipped further into the cave. They used their cell phones flashlight to look for it and found it on the cave floor beside a skeleton. They discovered the medallion in the bony grasp of the dead guy.

The next day, Miguel's niece insisted the scratch marks were letters. They didn't look like letters, but they decided to get some answers. That decision began a quest that gave him and Fernando the opportunity of a lifetime.

It turned out the scratch marks were Runic, and some ancient Viking must have scribbled the words on the medallion. After visiting a Runic expert who worked as a history professor at the University of Georgia, the two drug runners learned the words on the medallion said Skull Island, and at least one more medallion existed.

Miguel couldn't believe it. *If the old man had put the entire message on one medallion, we'd be living in style in Columbia.*

Half of the message would do them no good. Miguel found what had to be Skull Island and searched the island for hidden treasure. Nothing. Finding the island wasn't enough; they needed to find the matching medallion. The college professor told them the whole story, but they still had to kill the guy.

The old history professor told them the legend of a conflicted family and the father who was determined to bring peace to his home. The medallions referenced the location of the secret fortune.

The old man visited his grown children before his death and gave them each a medallion. The two sons would have to work together to obtain the fortune, and the father hoped this joint project would heal their broken family.

Miguel smiled as he thought back to Fernando's comment: "If it had been me, I would have killed my brother once I had both medallions."

The stunned professor stared at Fernando. He finally stated that most historians believed there was more to finding the treasure than just putting together the messages on the medallions. Somehow, the two sons had to work together to find their inheritance.

"Were they Vikings?" Fernando asked.

The professor leaned back in his chair. "To start with, most people don't believe the story. An old Norse clan leader, or maybe a king, wrote about this story in some diary, but many people think it was fiction.

"At least there's a story," Miguel said. "It could be true. Do we know what the other medallion says?"

"Nope. The story doesn't give details about what's on either medallion or what happened. It told of a brokenhearted father who planned to unite his family with this grand scheme. No one knew what happened or even if the family existed. Some think it was Bluetooth's family."

"Bluetooth?" Fernando laughed.

"Yes. His name was King Harald Bluetooth from Denmark."

"His real name was Bluetooth?" Fernando asked and started laughing again.

"How did a Viking king get his treasure from Denmark to the Bahamas?" Miguel asked, ignoring Fernando. "I didn't know Vikings came this far south."

"That's been debated too, but I imagine you're right. Most experts believe the Vikings never made it south of the Canadian coast, at least not as far south as the Bahamas."

"I heard Vikings went to Mexico," Fernando said. "I saw something on TV about it."

The old professor smiled and leaned back in his chair. "You hear a lot of things on TV. Bluetooth was an adventurer. We know that much from history. Some think his men uncovered an ancient city in Mexico with golden treasure, and the King left a clue as to how to find the city and the rest of her treasures."

"El Dorado!" Fernando gasped. "The city of gold? So they did go to Mexico."

The professor smiled. "Maybe, but I wouldn't bet on it. The legend's not clear if the city was supposed to be Mayan or Mesoamerican. No telling."

"Who cares what kind of city?" Fernando asked. "Gold is gold."

"I imagine the legend of El Dorado didn't come about until the Incas, but the Mayans had plenty of treasure, as did the other Mesoamericans.

"I've heard of Mayans and Incas," Miguel said, "but I've never heard of Mesoamericans."

"Mesoamerica designates a region more than a people. Technically, Mayans were Mesoamericans too. It includes groups like the Olmec, Zapotec, Mayans, and others. We're talking about ancient history that started before the Romans and lasted well into the seventh or eighth century. Maybe later."

Miguel had heard enough history to last him a lifetime. He wanted to know about the medallions. "What about Bluetooth and the medallions?"

"The legend indicates the medallions would lead the sons to some treasure, but the real treasure would be the ancient city. The sons would have to work together to find the city."

"So, two medallions point to a stash of treasure worth millions," Miguel said, "and information on how to find El Dorado—worth billions."

"Of course, that's just been a fanciful story until now," the professor said. "Finding this medallion may have proven the story true, or at least part of it. Of course, your medallion provides just half of the message if the two-medallion theory is correct."

Miguel pulled his beard. "The trick will be to find the second medallion."

Five years later, Miguel was already spending the money in his mind. He had one medallion and had discovered the island, though it wasn't called Skull Island. However, the bluff on the island's western end looked like a skull.

He and Fernando had traversed the Bahamas asking about Skull Island to no avail, but an old fisherman pointed them to a private island a couple of hours south of Great Exuma. It had to be the one.

Although he thought they didn't have a chance at finding the second medallion, pure luck placed Fernando at the drugstore when the girl walked by wearing it.

Miguel went back into the bedroom and happened to glace at Lacy's dirty clothes pile. "I think you have some sick fascination with the girl, Fernando."

"Who wouldn't? She's a babe."

Fernando was right. The girl was a real beauty–long, blonde hair and deep, blue eyes. They'd been watching the Davenport's compound, and he'd seen her several times.

In addition to the guys, he'd seen three other women. There was also an old woman, but Miguel didn't count her. All three were something. Fernando always favored younger women, but Miguel thought Davenport's wife was the real pick.

"They've got to come back," Miguel stated. "All their stuff is still here. Look, I didn't come all the way to Eleuthera to leave empty-handed. I want the girl, and I want her medallion."

Fernando grinned. "I'm all about getting the medallion, but you also promised the girl was part of the package."

"Okay," Miguel growled, "we'll get the girl, but first, we've got to get rid of this body."

"What's your plan?"

"That's your problem. You killed him. You should've stayed in the closet. That guy was not going to open the door."

Miguel looked at the young handyman lying on the floor, his neck twisted at a grotesque angle. The guy never knew what happened. His tool bag lay on its side and tools scattered across the floor.

He must have come by the villa to repair something. *Fernando's always too jumpy. He's going to get us into trouble one day.*

"The guy's golf cart is outside," Miguel pointed out. "If we're lucky, we can get him onto our boat without anyone knowing the difference. We'll dump his body out in the ocean."

Fernando snorted. "We can't take a dead body to the marina in a golf cart."

"I don't mean to take him to the marina. You take the golf cart to get our car, and we'll get the body down to the cove. That picnic area is half a mile from here. We'll hide the guy in the bushes and get our boat. We'll take the inflatable ashore as soon as it's night, get the body, and dump it somewhere."

Fernando nodded his head. "What about the golf cart?"

Miguel thought a moment. "We'll bring it to the shore, tie a rope to it, and pull it out to sea. It'll sink to the bottom."

"That should work."

"Next time, don't do anything so stupid. We're going to have to leave here for a few days now. Our luck, the girl will come back while we're gone."

"Think about it, Miguel. We know they dock at the marina. All we have to do is hang out there and keep watch. We'll grab the girl as soon as they return to the island."

"Yeah, right. Everything's so simple." Miguel flat-handed the side of Fernando's head. "I'm not going to prison over this. Got it?"

Chapter Five

Vacation in Paradise

Lacy watched the four boys walk into the luxury beachfront estate with their mouths open. Jon and Meg's home on Great Exuma shared the same elegance, except it had a more modern design. The thought crossed Lacy's mind that the boys had never gone inside the Davenports' main house.

"So how did Jon find this place," Marcy asked as she followed David into the gorgeous home.

Lacy turned to see the other female intern walk into the front foyer. "He found it on Homeaway. Can you believe that? I've used that website before with my mom. I had no idea people rented out homes like this."

"Well, it's to our benefit that they do. Did you notice how the boys walked into this place? They looked like they were walking into a church."

"I know," Lacy laughed, "though I doubt they've been in too many churches. I remember feeling that way when I walked into Jon and Meg's house for the first time."

"Me too. The boys stayed in the guest house, but I don't think they entered the main house."

"Even the guest house is much nicer than anything I've ever lived in," Lacy confessed.

"Same for me. We should follow the boys upstairs to make sure they don't do anything stupid."

The two girls hurried up the stairs after the boys. They found them inspecting the four bedrooms and the huge sitting area in the center of the second floor. Barry leaned over the railing to take in the open living area below.

"Hey, Barry," Lacy called. "You're going to fall on your head and join Randal in the hospital."

"You know his head is harder than that," Kerrick said as he walked up beside Lacy.

"What are you doing up here? You shouldn't be walking up the stairs."

"I'm not an invalid," Kerrick wheezed.

"Right. You can't even breathe after climbing the stairs. Kerrick, you need to take it easy for at least a few days. That's kind of the idea for staying on Nassau."

"Hey, guys," Marcy called to the boys. "You and Kerrick will be sleeping in the two rooms in the other wing. After today, this floor is off-limits to you."

"You know that's not fair," David whined. "Why do the girls always get the good rooms."

"You've not seen the rooms in the back of the house," Kerrick said. "You've got your own den with foosball and pool."

"You mean we've got our own swimming pool?" Aaron blurted out.

Tae punched Aaron on the shoulder. "No, you idiot. We have a pool table. This place has a huge pool out back. I saw it from the window over there."

Lacy grinned at Kerrick before turning back to the boys. "This area is for girls and the married people. The rooms in the back have a bunk bed and a twin bed in each one, so there's plenty of room."

"Kerrick can sleep up here with the grown-ups," Tae winked at Lacy. "We can take care of ourselves."

"I'm sure you can," Kerrick grimaced. "That's why I get to stay with you guys and babysit. Remember your first night at the compound? You about blew your summer."

"Oh, yeah," Lacy said. "I heard about that. You about gave up an incredible summer to go swimming at midnight."

"Come on, Lacy," Tae objected. "We were stupid. We learned our lesson. We're not going to do anything like that again."

"We know," Kerrick conceded. "We just don't want you to be tempted."

Barry looked at Lacy and raised an eyebrow. "Kerrick, I think Jon wants you to sleep with us so you won't be tempted."

The four boys laughed and headed toward the stairs. Lacy walked away from Kerrick and took in the opulence of the main sleeping area. It was beautiful. The owners opted for an antique charm that was both warm and elegant. It seemed to fit the whole atmosphere of the turn-of-the-century home.

Four bedrooms faced one another: two on each side of the house with a large den and the second-floor landing at the top of the stairs separating them. Lacy left Kerrick in the den and walked through one of the bedrooms. She ran her hand along the lace throw that covered the bedspread. Everything was so...perfect. She wondered if the people who once lived here were as perfect.

Lacy reached inside the bathroom door and turned on the light. *Why would anyone need a bathroom this large? I think our whole group could fit in here at the same time.* A claw foot tub sat behind a wicker divider, and a towel draped over an antique chair in the corner.

She walked back into the bedroom and almost ran into Kerrick.

"You scared me to death," Lacy gasped. "I didn't hear you come in here."

"You shouldn't be so jumpy," Kerrick grinned. "I'm not that scary, but I'm crazy about you."

Lacy looked up into Kerrick's light blue eyes and felt warmth flood her even as her stomach tightened. She reached up to caress his cheek and pulled him against her before she could stop herself. Their lips met with an explosion of passion as a wave of desire consumed her mind and body.

"Lacyyyyy," Marcy's voice rang up from downstairs. "Ann's on the phone for you."

Lacy pulled away from Kerrick, breathless and flushed. She wanted more.

"Uh... I need to get the phone. Ann went back to *The Discoverer* to get her clothes, and I asked her to get some of my things. I bet she can't find something."

She left Kerrick in the bedroom and hurried back through the den. She paused long enough to gawk at the newel post at the top of the stairs. It was hand-carved with what looked like flower buds starting about two feet off the floor. *Someone must have spent forever carving that thing.*

Marcy stood at the bottom of the stairs with a cell phone in her hand.

Lacy tried to look calm on the outside, but her heart was still racing from her encounter with Kerrick. "Hey, Ann."

"Lacy, I can't find your spare cosmetic bag. You said it was in the drawer by the sink in your bathroom, but it's not there. I've looked everywhere."

"Oh, Ann. I'm so sorry. Just don't worry about it. I don't need it. My main stuff is still at the resort anyway."

"That's what I've been telling you," Ann laughed. "You don't need makeup."

"Give me a break, Ann. Every old barn needs a little red paint."

"Maybe so, but you're no old barn. I'll see you in a few."

By the time Lacy rejoined the boys, they were bringing in their luggage. Kerrick winked at her from the doorway of one of the bedrooms. Lacy felt heat rush up her neck.

She walked out the backdoor and stood beside a stunning swimming pool surrounded by a tropical flower garden. She wanted to get into her swimsuit as soon as possible. It seemed like the water called her name. She looked toward the beach and saw *The Discoverer* anchored about half a mile from shore. She felt sorry for the crew, who had to stay aboard the ship.

"Hey, Lacy," Barry called from the doorway. "Jon wants to meet with everyone in the living room in five minutes."

"Okay. I'll be right in."

Lacy looked back out toward the ship. It was beautiful in its own way. It looked smaller from this distance. *How long did Jon say his ship was? 170 something. Maybe 171. Whatever, it's big enough.*

She remembered standing on the deck of *The Discoverer* when she first saw Kerrick. The ship had been docked in Pirate's Cove at Jon and Meg's compound on Great Exuma. She was painting a few spots on the railing when she looked up and saw a tall, curly-headed guy walking down the steps toward the dock. He looked like he belonged on the cover of GQ.

His shoulders were broad, and he held his head with the confidence from either being stuck up or comfortable with his own identity. At first, Lacy opted for stuck up, but now she realized Kerrick was humble and sweeter than any guy she knew.

She treated him badly that day. It was a wonder they became friends. *I suppose we've graduated to being more than just friends. I practically slept in his bed in the hospital. I suppose it was just my head that slept in his bed.*

A smile spread across her face as she remembered him holding her face in his hands in the hospital. He stared into her eyes and told her that she was beautiful. Lacy thought he was about to tell her that he loved her. She remembered the shiver that went through her body in anticipation of the "L" word, but it never came. Instead, he pulled her down toward his hospital bed and kissed her.

She almost lost control, and her resolve to avoid him had long melted. A nurse saved the day by walking in to take Kerrick's vitals. Lacy about cracked up when the nurse commented on the speed of his pulse. Lacy felt her own pulse racing.

The nurse grinned at Lacy before turning back to Kerrick. "Do you want to a cold shower before I check your pulse again?"

The awkwardness turned into all-out laughter. The nurse couldn't have been much older than Kerrick, so Lacy was sure she was cool with a little kiss. *I suppose that was more than a little kiss.*

"Hellooo," Barry called from the house. "Are you coming anytime today? Jon is getting a little impatient."

"Sorry. I'm on my way."

Lacy took an empty place on the couch beside Kerrick.

"I'm glad you could make it," Jon deadpanned.

"Sorry."

"Okay, everyone. Welcome to the Yellow Elder Blossom Estate."

Aaron laughed. "Yellow Elder?"

"That's the name of the national flower of the Bahamas," Marcy informed the group.

"The Cunningham family built this estate about fifty years ago," Jon continued. "It's now a vacation home. If the shade weren't covering that window, you could look out into Goodman Bay."

Every eye in the room turned toward the big, plate-glass window on the north side of the house. A large wooden covering extended from the window to serve as a shade.

"This bay has witnessed ships of all flags. Even the famous pirate, Blackbeard, called this island home until the new governor ran him off in 1718."

"You mean Blackbeard was a real person?" Tae asked.

"Sure was," Meg interjected. "He lived on Nassau for a while, and the pirates named him magistrate of what they called the Privateers' Republic. The museum up the road tells all about the pirates that used to be in this region."

"We've got a week here," Jon added, "so you'll have all the time you need to visit the museum. I just have a few rules."

An audible grown rose from the group of boys. Lacy smiled as she braced for the boys' complaints. She knew that deep down, these boys longed to have someone in their lives who cared enough to require them to follow the rules.

"Rule number one: Don't go anywhere alone. You must always stay in groups of at least four, and one member of your group must be one of the interns."

"Or one of the adults?" Tae questioned.

"True," Jon said. "I want to make sure that nothing happens to any of you guys while we're here. Let's use this week to regroup and prepare for the next stage of our salvage operation. Any questions?"

"When's Randal coming back?" Barry asked.

"He should be released tomorrow, but we're going to have to all work together to help him recover," Meg explained. "He'll be immobile for a while and dependent on us. We will try to find a nurse we can hire to help us out for a week or so."

David raised his hand like a schoolboy. "What can we do around here?"

"Well," Ann dragged out the word as she sat down a couple of bags at the door and joined the group. "Many people go to the straw market up the street, but I doubt you're into shopping. You'll find some interesting historical stuff around here, like an old fort and a famous staircase called the Queen's Staircase."

"Hey, Ann," Jon said. "Sorry, we didn't wait on you and Jose."

"No problem. It took us longer than we figured to get back here."

"We'll help you boys find plenty of things to do," Jon reassured the group. "I've got parasailing and wakeboarding on the agenda, as well as some other things. You'll have a blast. Any other questions?"

"Yeah," Aaron voiced from the back of the group. "What's for dinner?"

Chapter Six

Join the Party

Jon and Jose arrived at the vacation home with Randal just before lunch on Friday. Lacy watched from her bedroom window as the white, fifteen-passenger rental van pulled into the circular driveway. Before the van stopped, the other four boys in the program rushed out to help their friend into the house.

Lacy smiled as Tae and Barry tried to figure out how to get Randal from the floor of the van into his wheelchair without hurting him. Someone had removed one of the seats and prepared a comfortable spot on the floor for his ride home from the hospital. Lacy grimaced as she saw Randal's immobilized legs and taunt face.

A tear ran down her cheek as she thought about how close they'd come to losing her new friend. *I suppose that ended his summer fun. At least, he's alive.*

Randal had been so pitiful the morning of his surgery. His mother couldn't come, and he tried to shrug it off, but Lacy could tell it hurt. He'd talked to her on the phone before the nurses wheeled him away, but her absence had affected him.

"Lacy," Meg said from the open doorway, "you're supposed to be in the kitchen."

"Oh, no. I forgot I had K. P. duty today. I'm sorry, Meg."

"Marcy's taking up your slack, so I suppose you owe her the apology."

"I'll head down now. What are we having?"

"Sloppy Joes, I think. Hey, what are you planning to do during free time this afternoon?"

"I figured I'd hang around and help Randal get settled in. I'm sure he's pretty bummed about all of this."

Meg leaned against the door jam and crossed her arms.

"What?" Lacy wondered.

"I just like what I see," Meg offered. "I've noticed a change in you. It's a good change."

Lacy hurried toward the kitchen. Had she changed that much? She knew Meg was right. *I'm not sure what change Meg is discussing, but I know these boys are getting to me. Maybe she's talking about my language. I haven't cursed in days. Well, this morning didn't count. That lizard scared the...it scared the...Now, how do I keep that thought clean? So, it scared me to death.*

"Okay, everyone," Jon said an hour later from the head of the table. "Thanks for lunch Judy and Lacy."

Lacy looked out of the corner of her eye at Meg, who was smiling.

"I'm bringing the Robalo into the bay for the afternoon for skiing and parasailing. If you haven't seen her, she's a twenty-four-foot boat I picked up for quick trips around the islands, but she's also strong and fast. She's great for skiing and messing around."

The boys cheered until Barry looked over at Randal and elbowed David.

Tae cleared his throat. "We were thinking about just hanging around the house today."

"Yeah," David agreed. "We thought about playing some cards. You feel up to that Randal?"

"You guys don't have to hang around and babysit me."

"We ain't babysitting," Barry insisted. "We're just not ready to leave you in the house alone yet."

"I'm not going to be alone. Lacy's staying with me."

"Ohhh, yeah," Tae teased as he started to slap Randal on the back. He stopped himself, realizing he might hurt Randal. "I get it. You're still sweet on Lacy. I hate to tell you, Bro, but while you were laid up, Kerrick done stole her away from you."

Lacy felt her face flush. She was sure that it glowed bright red.

"I ain't sweet on Lacy. She just told me we'd hang out together today. You guys go ahead and have some fun."

"Ok, Jon," Barry declared. "It sounds like Randal wants some alone time with Lacy, so we'll get out of their hair. You might want to get a chaperone to stay behind with them."

The boys laughed, and Tae rubbed the top of Randal's hair.

"Let's spend two or three hours in the bay, and then we'll come back to prepare for dinner," Jon suggested. "What do you think about going to Clifton Heritage Park tomorrow?"

"What's that?" Barry and David said in unison.

"It's a historic park on the western tip of the island out near Clifton Bay. They have some historic home sites, just like when Nassau was first settled."

Kerrick pushed his chair away from the table and grinned. "I think these boys need a little culture."

*****

Lacy sat cross-legged on the couch in her tee shirt and gym shorts. Surprisingly, she had enjoyed the previous afternoon with Randal, and the trip to Clifton Heritage Park was quite interesting. She didn't like history much, but she found the park fascinating. She couldn't imagine living as the people did so many years ago.

As Lacy reflected on the last couple of days, she felt a deep sorrow for Randal. Growing up in the nation's capital had proven to be pretty difficult. He told Lacy all about living in the housing projects. Violence was a way of life for him and his family. His older brother was murdered in a drive-by shooting two years earlier, and one of his sisters was hooked on crack. His mother worked two jobs to take care of his family, and he didn't even know his father.

"Hey, Lacy," Ann called as she topped the stairs. "Thanks for staying back yesterday and hanging out with Randal."

"It was no big deal. He would have done it for me."

"Of course, he would've. He's in love with you."

"Give me a break, Ann. I was just doing my job."

"For the record, going the extra mile because you care for someone is more than just doing your job. It means a lot to me to see that side of you."

Lacy was feeling more uncomfortable by the minute. These boys were getting to her. The whole team was getting to her. It seemed odd that after a few weeks, she felt closer to Jon, Meg, the boys, and Kerrick, especially Kerrick, than to the rest of her family. She didn't feel close to her parents at all. They didn't care about anyone but themselves. Lacy loved Jon and Meg more than words could tell, and Ann felt like a close sister.

"Somehow, it's become quite easy to love the boys and the whole group, for that matter," Lacy admitted.

"I know what you mean. We've become one big, happy family."

*****

"So, is everyone okay?" Meg asked as Jon slipped into bed beside her.

Jon wrapped his arms around his wife and pulled her close. "Yeah, at least I think so. Everyone's in bed except for Ann and Lacy. They're having girl time or a counseling session in the den."

"Let's hope it's girl time."

"Hasn't it been interesting to watch our little team become like a family over the last few weeks? Who would have dreamed that five inner-city boys who didn't know each other and came from different cities could form such a bond?"

"That's so true," Meg agreed. "I'm also excited about what I see happening in Lacy. I think for the first time in her life she cares for other people."

"I imagine she has never been in an environment that encouraged selfless service until now. What's happening between her and Kerrick?"

"I can tell by how they look at one another that something's up."

"You used to look at me that way, too," Jon teased.

"Used to?"

"I'm just kidding you. I love the way you look at me."

"You know, Jon. I'm so glad we started this program. This decision has been confirmed over and over. Even the accident hasn't changed things. I hate it for Randal, but I think he'll somehow benefit from being injured."

"I think you're right. Remember Ron and Diane back home?"

"Uh...do I know them?"

"I'm pretty sure I introduced you to them last Thanksgiving. Anyway, Ron was diagnosed with cancer a few years ago. He and

Diane both say that cancer was the best thing that ever happened to their marriage. They said it's not that they had a bad marriage, it's just that cancer helped them find a deeper relationship. I think hard times can take people to new levels emotionally, spiritually, and relationally."

"I think you're right. I experienced that through Steve's death. Even though my husband was in the Special Forces, I convinced myself that he would always come home, and then one day, he didn't. That period was a time of deep sorrow but also brought incredible growth in my life."

"I can say the same thing about Julie's death," Jon agreed.

"Well, I hope Randal will look back at this experience one day and see it as a turning point in his life."

Jon pulled Meg closer. "This program is about life-change. It looks like we're seeing it happen."

"I'm so proud of you, Jon. The boys' school is having such a positive impact on these boys."

"We can save them one at a time," Jon acknowledged. "Well, maybe five at a time. This is at least a great start. Let's not let the accident mess up anything."

Meg snuggled her head into the crook of Jon's neck. "I agree."

"I don't want us to get too comfortable," Jon warned. "Anything can happen with these boys."

"Like what? You mean something else bad?"

Chapter Seven

The Straw Market

Over the weekend, the group did many tourist things, like climbing the Queen's Staircase and visiting the pirate museum. Swimming with the dolphins on Blue Island seemed to be everyone's favorite. Kerrick had to return to the doctor for a checkup on Monday morning, and Lacy wanted to go along. Jon, however, insisted that she stay with the boys.

Boredom began to set in while the group waited for Jon, Meg, and Kerrick to return, so Lacy tried to think of something to do. "I've got an idea. I want to go to the Straw Market. Anyone want to go?"

"The Straw Market?" David questioned. "What is that?"

"That's where they sell straw, you idiot," Barry badgered.

"Uh...not exactly," Lacy corrected. "It's a place where islanders come in to sell their crafts. Well, it's not just crafts. It's all kinds of things. Who wants to go?"

"Lacy," Barry huffed, "do you honestly think we want to go shopping?"

"Come on, y'all," Lacy begged. "I can't go by myself. You'll like it more than you know."

"All right," David consented, "I'll go."

"Anyone else?" Lacy raised an eyebrow.

"Okay. I'll go," Barry said.

Tae and Aaron both announced in unison, "I'll go, too."

Everything went well at first, though Lacy seemed to be the one who enjoyed the shopping experience the most. The smells of different foods wafting through the air caused Lacy to be a little hungry. It was an interesting environment. While people sold their goods, a man preached from an upper floor through a microphone, causing his message to be impossible to miss. A woman sang gospel songs, and Lacy thought she could be his wife. *It takes a lot of guts to stand up there and preach like that. I doubt anyone is even listening to the poor guy.*

Lacy wandered down an aisle while the boys tried on caps on a different aisle. She picked up a beautifully carved fish she thought she might buy for Randal. It looked like a parrot fish with bright colors highlighting the fish's body.

"Hey, babe," Lacy heard a voice from behind her. "We can go somewhere and have some real fun."

Lacy felt a shiver run down her spine. She turned around to see two large guys blocking the aisle. One looked like he could throw a refrigerator and was so muscle-bound that Lacy wondered how he could brush his teeth. The other guy looked like he worked out but was more toned than muscular. A side aisle to the right provided her only means of escape, but she thought that way was a dead end.

"I'm having all the fun I want to have. Why don't y'all go entertain yourself some other way?" She turned back toward the carved sea creatures and tried to ignore them.

A firm hand gripped her arm and whirled her around. The big guy pulled her within inches of his huge body. "Don't get smart with me. We'll have fun any way I want to. Won't we, Marco?"

"Sure thing, Juan."

He pulled Lacy toward him, and she could smell the stench of his breath. Although he believed in working out, he didn't favor brushing his teeth. His left hand slid down her back, pulling her against his firm body. His odor filled Lacy's nostrils, causing her to want to throw up. Fear and anger flooded her simultaneously, and she did what her father once told her to do to subdue any man: she raised her right knee hard into his groin.

Juan groaned with pain and let out a string of profanities. Marco stepped forward, took hold of Lacy, and forced her down the side aisle. Within seconds, the big guy recovered and followed them. He grabbed Lacy's throat and pulled her body back against his. He used some of the most vulgar language she'd heard to tell her what he planned to do to her.

Lacy heard a loud commotion behind the jerk holding her, and his accomplice flew into a display of tee shirts. When the big guy turned around, Lacy saw Aaron standing there with his fists balled up. Barry stood beside him, and she thought she saw David and Tae behind them. Juan screamed and went at Aaron like a middle linebacker, but Aaron hit him with such a powerful hook that the guy jerked to the side and fell to the floor.

Before Lacy could get by to safety, the little guy jumped on Aaron's back. A fierce fistfight broke out, with bodies flying into the displays, people screaming, and blood spraying everywhere. Lacy even managed to get in a few punches of her own.

Six policemen ran into the cramped space and pulled the guys apart. Lacy noticed someone with a smartphone behind the policemen videoing the whole thing. She feared for a minute that the bad guys and her four heroes might start pounding the policemen, but the brawl stopped. The police slapped handcuffs on all six guys as more patrol cars stopped at the curb outside the market.

"Ma'am," one of the officers said, "you'll need to go with us to the police station. Do you know any of these men?"

"Uh...yes...why are you putting my friends in handcuffs? They were just protecting me from these jerks."

"You can tell us all about it at the station."

The officers placed the six guys in separate cars, and a female officer held the door open to another car for Lacy. She looked behind her into the market and saw everything was a mess.

Within minutes, the police cars turned off East Street into the police compound. Passing through the gate, Lacy felt like they had entered into the walls of a fort. *If the police have to be protected by a wall, this city must be filled with really bad people.*

The ocean-green buildings loomed before her, and each seemed to follow the same design pattern. As an officer led Lacy into one building, she turned to see the boys entering another one.

"Where are they taking my friends?" Lacy pleaded.

"They'll be put in cells, ma'am," the police officer said as she led Lacy into an office.

Small cubicles lined the walls of the dank office, and it smelled of smoke. Several people typed away on computers and didn't notice Lacy passing their desks. The officer guided her to a small cubicle in the back of the room.

"Please sit down, ma'am."

Lacy called Jon before explaining the whole story to the officer. Jon and Meg appeared just as the police officer finished her questions.

"What's going on?" Jon demanded.

"Are you Dr. Davenport?" the officer stood to her feet.

"Yes, I am. Lacy, what's going on?"

"Uncle Jon!" Tears threatened to spill down Lacy's cheeks. "I was attacked at the Straw Market, and the boys rescued me.

It was ugly, and the police came and arrested the two guys who attacked me and all four boys."

The officer picked up a piece of paper from her desk. "They've all been charged with disturbing the peace and public fighting. I'm confident other charges will be forthcoming."

Jon stepped toward the police officer. "It sounds to me like you should be giving them a commendation for saving Lacy from harm. It makes no sense for you to arrest them."

"They created quite a disturbance at the market and caused a lot of damage. We won't know the cost of the damages for a while, but I'm sure it's substantial."

"Excuse me? Miss…"

"You can call me Lieutenant, Dr. Davenport."

"All right, Lieutenant. I want to speak to the Police Commissioner."

Lacy looked out the window and saw the two thugs getting into the backseat of a car. The car turned around in the parking lot and drove away. *I can't believe they're letting those guys go.*

"If you'll sit here, Dr. Davenport and Mrs. Davenport, I presume. I'll see if the Commissioner can see you now."

The officer walked away, and Lacy leaned toward Jon. "Uncle Jon, they let the two guys go who attacked me. I just saw them leave."

"Sounds like the same old police force Meg and I dealt with several years ago. We'll get it straightened out."

When the police officer returned, she asked Jon to go into the Commissioner's office alone. Meg and Lacy were led to a bench near the front door. About thirty minutes later, Jon stormed from the office toward the front door.

"So, what happened?" Meg asked. "Was he the same guy we dealt with the last time?"

"No. Different guy. They're letting the boys go."

"How did that happen?" Lacy wondered.

"I threatened him," Jon said as Lacy pictured steam coming from Jon's ears.

"Jon!" Meg warned. "You don't threaten the Commissioner."

"Well, I did. It doesn't hurt that I'm the son-in-law of the President of the United States, and we have a history with this police department. We have to pay for the damages."

"Uncle Jon, what about the guys who attacked me? Why were they set free?"

"The Commissioner said they have no proof those guys attacked you. He thinks our boys picked a fight."

"That's ridiculous," Meg said as Jon led them outside toward another building in the compound.

"Yes, it's ridiculous, but at least our boys can leave."

"I saw someone video the whole thing," Lacy remembered. "At least, I think they got the whole thing. Of course, I have no idea who the girl was."

"Well," Jon breathed, "we're getting the boys and leaving as soon as possible."

Chapter Eight

A New Family

"Hey, Miguel," Fernando called from within the galley of their boat. "Come look at this."

Miguel hurried into the galley to find Fernando sitting on the couch with a cup of coffee. A Ford truck advertisement played on the television.

Miguel filled a cup with coffee and sat down at the kitchen table. "What's up."

"I'm watching the news from Nassau, and they showed a teaser of the next story. I swear that our girl was in a brawl at the market."

The commercial ended, and the commentator began telling about a fight in the Straw Market between a group of Americans and a few local men. She told viewers that a bystander happened to video the action on a smartphone.

Fernando leaned toward the television. "Well, I'll..."

"That's Juan," Miguel interrupted. "I thought he was in prison."

"He must have gotten out. How many guys did he kill?"

"At least two, but somehow he got off. I always knew he was too strong for his own good."

"Look at the girl that just hit the other guy with Juan," Fernando advised. "That's Lacy. I know that's the girl."

"Would you look at that? The big white kid is beating Juan's face in. I would never have believed it."

"Look at our girl go at it. She's not only a babe but also a beast."

Miguel looked over at Fernando. "Okay. Wipe the drool from your face. We need to head for Nassau first thing in the morning. Did the lady say where this group was staying?"

"She just said a vacation home on Nassau."

"That shouldn't be too hard to find. It would have to be a big home. I'll bet my first ten grand of the treasure that we'll have her by tomorrow night."

*****

"Okay, gentlemen," Jon announced as the group gathered in the large den on the downstairs level of the vacation home. "We're leaving as soon as we can get packed up. Boys, I don't know if I should be angry with you or grateful for you."

Barry sat up straight on the couch. "That dude was hurtin' Lacy, and that just ain't goin' to happen."

"For the record," Jon confessed, "you did the right thing, and I'm proud of you. And Aaron, for once I'll tell you that I'm glad the big guy ran into you. I feel he's never been pulverized like that before today."

Aaron rubbed his bruised knuckles. "Nobody's goin' to mess with Lacy."

Lacy felt a tear trickling down her cheek. No one ever cared for her like this group of people. The attention embarrassed her, but she knew she would treasure this time for the rest of her life. Kerrick noticed her reaction and reached over to squeeze her hand.

"The bad news," Jon continued, "is the police have blamed all of this on us, and I'm sure the story will be plastered on T.V. tonight. When I passed the market on the way back, I saw a reporter coming out of the building. It won't be hard for them to find us, and they'll be on our front porch within the next few hours. I want us to be on *The Discoverer* by then, heading for Eleuthera."

Everyone scrambled to their rooms to pack their belongings. Before the hour was up, the boys, Jose, and Ann were in the van heading toward the marina, and everyone else piled into a smaller rental car. Lacy marveled at the speed with which the whole group boarded *The Discoverer.* Jon told Lacy and Kerrick that they would drop anchor just outside Rock Sound and go ashore in the morning to find a place to rent.

Because a wheelchair couldn't go below the main deck, Jon had the boys set up a temporary bedroom for Randal under a canopy section on the back deck. All five boys were gathered in Randal's makeshift bedroom when Lacy approached.

"Guys, I don't know how to thank y'all."

Of all the dumbest things to happen, tears began spilling out of Lacy's eyes. She walked over to Aaron and hugged him. He stood rigid at first, then wrapped his arms around her. She moved to Barry and then David, and finally Tae. She looked at Randal sitting in his wheelchair with both legs sticking straight out, and a smile spread across her face. She wiped her wet cheeks with the back of her hand.

"Randal, I do not doubt you would have been right in the middle of it."

She bent over and kissed him on the cheek. "All of you are my heroes. You are closer to me than my family, and I..." She gulped in a lung full of air. "I love you all."

All five boys looked down toward the deck, and Lacy would have sworn Aaron was crying. Tears began flowing down Lacy's cheeks again like a stream down a mountainside. She turned and headed toward her cabin.

*****

"Hey, babe," Jon said as he walked into their cabin, "you'll never believe what I just heard."

"Shh! Don't be too loud," Meg whispered. "I just got Carla to sleep. She missed her nap and was fussy. What did you hear?"

Jon lowered his voice. "To start with, I saw Lacy talking to the boys, and then she hugged them one by one. I don't think she was the only one in the group who shed a few tears. As I got closer, I heard her tell the boys she loved them."

"Wow. Are we talking about Lacy Henderson? Our Lacy?"

"Unless we picked up her twin on Nassau, she's our Lacy. I think the Ice Queen has melted."

"She's gone through some transformation," Meg concluded. "I hoped she would make some changes by being with us this summer, but I never imagined this response. I've felt for a while that Lacy couldn't feel love for someone, much less tell them she loved them. Unbelievable."

"I know," Jon agreed. "It's a miracle. Let's hope nothing comes along to mess things up."

*****

Lacy stepped through the doorway and down three steps to the passageway leading to her cabin. *I am turning into the biggest crybaby. I can't believe I just told those boys that I love them. I do, though. I really do.*

"What's up?" Lacy heard Kerrick's voice before she saw him. "Is everything okay?"

Oh brother. He's the last person I want to see me crying.

"Yeah. I'm fine."

"People who are fine don't normally cry."

Lacy stopped in front of her cabin door and turned the knob. "No, I'm fine. I was just talking to the boys. I'm tired and need to go to bed."

She stepped into her cabin, but Kerrick stepped in behind her before she could close the door. "Kerrick! You're not supposed to be in here."

Kerrick closed the door and pulled Lacy into his arms. Tears began afresh down Lacy's face, and she wondered how she had any tears left. Kerrick held her close as she sobbed. *I'm such an ugly crier. I can't believe he is seeing me like this.*

After a few minutes, Lacy regained control of her emotions. She pulled away and wiped her nose with the back of her hand. "Now that's real attractive."

Kerrick pulled Lacy back against his body and tilted her face toward his. He wiped her tear-stained cheeks.

"You're not only attractive, Lacy Henderson, you're beautiful. You're beautiful inside and out."

He bent his head down toward hers, and their lips met. Their kiss was slow and filled with passion. Kerrick pulled back and brushed Lacy's hair behind her ear.

"Lacy, I've never felt about a girl like I feel about you. I..." He held her face in his hands. "I love you."

All the blood drained from Lacy's face, and she felt her knees weaken. She knew she would have fallen out on the floor if Kerrick hadn't pulled her against his body so tightly. *I love you too. Why can't I tell him that? I told five boys I love them, and I love Kerrick more than I've ever loved anyone.*

Lacy melted into Kerrick's embrace, but she remained silent. She looked up into Kerrick's eyes and wanted him to kiss her. She wanted more than a kiss. She wanted him. All of him.

"I should leave. We know the rules, and we also know where this could lead. I love you too much to let that happen. I'll see you in the morning."

Lacy stood still as the door closed behind Kerrick. *What was I about to do? I'm such an idiot. I'm starting to act like my mother. No...no way I'll ever be like her. I do love him, though.*

She sat down on the edge of the bed and removed her shoes. She flopped back on the bed and closed her eyes. *This day has been so bizarre.*

Lacy entered the bathroom, stripped of her clothes, and stepped into the shower. The thought of sleep consumed her mind as the hot water ran down her back. Jon told the group they'd eat a late dinner, but she didn't feel hungry.

After toweling off, Lacy pulled on her favorite tee shirt, the one she'd gotten from Kerrick, and crawled into bed. As she drifted off to sleep, the light tap at the door became a part of the room's rhythm that lulled Lacy into a night of dreams and fitful rest.

Chapter Nine
Just in Time

"I don't think she's coming to dinner," Meg whispered to Jon as she sat down with a plate of food. "I stopped by her room on the way here from the lab and tapped on her door. She never answered."

"I guess she's wiped out," Jon said as he reached over to squeeze Carla's little, chubby hand.

"Dada. Boat?"

"Yes, sweetheart. We're on the boat. I love you."

Carla chattered on a bit, and Jon looked to Meg for an interpretation. Meg shrugged her shoulders. "I think that means she loves you, too."

"Today's been a rather upsetting and exhausting day for all of us, especially Lacy," Jon surmised. "I suppose it's better that I don't tell her tonight anyway."

Meg leaned forward in her seat. "What news?"

"Liz called and said she's coming down for Lacy's birthday next week."

"Oh, no, Jon," Meg gasped. "You know that'll send Lacy into a tailspin. We're finally making some progress, and Liz has to come and mess it up."

"Now, Meg. Lacy is her daughter, so she has a right to come see her."

"She may have a right, but that's still not the best thing for her to do. Liz thinks more about herself than anyone else. I'm sure her visit involves getting over her guilt for not being the kind of mother she should have been all along."

"Don't you think we should give her the benefit of the doubt?"

"I don't have any doubt, Jon. I've watched Liz's patterns for years. Her coming here has nothing to do with being here for Lacy's birthday."

"I don't see that we have any option. She told me on the phone that she planned to stay for a few days. I think she was thinking of staying longer until I told her we would stay on the boat."

"I'm sure that didn't sit well with her," Meg laughed. "She's never liked being on the water much."

Meg finished her chopped steak and cleaned Carla's hands and face. While Jon sat down beside Kerrick to go over a few things for the next day, Meg pulled her little girl out of her chair and stopped to speak to Ann and Jose before climbing the steps to her cabin. This had been a difficult day. *At least Kerrick got a good report from the doctor.* He would have to take it easy for another week or so, but he should be able to return to normal activities soon.

Meg tried to get Carla interested in putting together a puzzle, and when that didn't work out too well, she read her favorite book to her. It amazed Meg that Carla sat so still when she listened to someone read to her. Jon walked in just before Carla's bedtime, took his little girl into his arms, and swung her around. Carla giggled and begged for more.

"No, sweetheart. It's time to brush your teeth."

"Sing, Dada."

"Okay, honey. I'll sing the toothbrush song."

Jon sat on the closed lid of the toilet and laid Carla down in his lap. Meg handed him a miniature toothbrush with a dab of toothpaste on it. Jon began to sing a song about brushing teeth that he made up to the tune of Jingle Bells. He found it to be the best way to keep his little girl from squirming while he went through the ritual of brushing her teeth.

"Okay, sweetheart. Now let's say our prayers with Mommy."

Meg laid Carla in her bed in the closet-size room Jon created in their large cabin, and Jon turned off the light. Though Meg felt claustrophobic in the tiny space, it helped Carla sleep at night and gave Jon and Meg privacy.

They took turns getting ready for bed in the bathroom before Meg flipped the light switch to the small light in the wall beside the bed.

"I'm ready for this day to end," Meg sighed as she slipped under the covers. "Everything was going so well, and then the market fiasco had to happen."

Jon pulled back the covers on his side of the bed. "Remember how we talked about bad things being used for good? We've already seen how this episode helped break through some of Lacy's walls. I won't be able to call her the Ice Queen after today."

Meg smiled and kissed Jon's cheek. "You shouldn't have been calling her that to start with."

"I just call 'em as I see 'em," Jon offered with a grin. "I'm sure she has her perspective of me, too, and it can't be all glamorous."

"I'm sure she does. I could add a few things to her list that she's overlooked."

Jon looked over at his wife with mock surprise in his voice. "You mean I'm not perfect?"

"Well, you're close, but you have a few areas where improvement is needed."

"Is that a fact? Help me out by telling me one area."

Meg scratched her head as she realized this playful conversation had turned serious. "Okay. Do you remember when you and Jose talked about our change of plans earlier today?"

"Yep. Sure do. We were standing in the kitchen at the vacation home."

"Right. You turned your back to me as if I wasn't a part of the conversation. That wouldn't be a big deal, except you tend to do that sometimes when we're talking to other people. It makes me feel like I'm kind of second class and unimportant, but I know that's not true."

"I'm so sorry, Honey. I had no idea I'd been doing that. I'll try to make sure it never happens again. If it does, tap me on the back so I'll realize I'm doing it."

"Deal. So, what's something I'm doing that needs improvement?"

"Ummm. I can't think of a thing. I'd say you're perfect."

"I'd say you're a liar, and you must want something."

"You could be right," Jon whispered as he leaned on his elbow and kissed his wife."

*****

First thing on Tuesday morning, Miguel and Fernando pulled into the Marina on Paradise Island and docked their boat. They had called ahead to reserve a rental car. Miguel slipped behind the wheel while Fernando opened the door to the passenger side.

"So, how do we find them?" Fernando queried. "I know you got a text earlier. Did our boy finally come through?"

"I don't need any help from those stupid text messages. I've never trusted any of our lookouts through the years."

"You've got to be kidding me. So, you know where they're staying? How did you figure that out?"

"I Googled *vacation homes in Nassau Bahamas and* came up with a list of available homes. Only a couple of them would work for a large group. One is right on Goodman Bay, which would allow them a perfect place to anchor their ship."

Fifteen minutes later, they pulled into the driveway of the Yellow Elder Blossom Estate. Miguel parked the rental car behind a small, white pickup truck with a magnetic sign attached to the side of each door: *Island Rentals*. A middle-aged man and woman were about to walk into the house, but they stopped at the front door when they saw the two men approach.

"Is this house for rent?" Miguel asked.

"You're in luck, that is if you want it for the rest of the week. We had a group staying here, but they left in a hurry last night."

"Is that a fact?" Miguel crossed his arms and looked over at Fernando.

"Yep. I think that they got into some trouble in the market yesterday. I saw something about it on the news last night. Seemed like good people when they rented it. I think they had a diving accident and had to stay on the island for medical treat-ment."

"A diving accident?" Miguel wondered. "What happened?"

"I don't know much about that. The main guy...let's see, his name was...Davenport. Mr. Davenport called me last week and needed a place to stay. It was all last minute. I wouldn't have had room for them, but we had a cancelation the previous night. I think he runs a boys' camp or something. I also know there were more than boys in the group. He had some beautiful girls with him, too. Come to think of it, his wife was quite the looker too."

The little man's wife jabbed him with her elbow. He reached down to take her hand.

"We've been married for thirty-nine years," the maintenance man chuckled, "but just because you're on a diet doesn't mean you can't look at the menu."

"Harold," the little woman said sternly, "That's not funny. I think we've got some cleaning to do."

"I'm just cuttin' up, Sarah. You know that. You boys need a house for rent?"

"We need something for next week," Miguel lied, "and it sounds like you're booked. Thanks anyway."

As the two men returned to the car, Fernando got into the passenger seat, slammed his palm on the car's dash, and let out a string of profanities. Miguel backed out onto West Bay Street and pointed the car toward the marina.

"We shouldn't have left Eleuthera," Miguel said. "I knew we shouldn't have left."

"Hey, we did what we had to do," Fernando consoled. "We'll get 'em. All we have to do is get back to Eleuthera. On top of that, you'll owe me your first ten grand from the treasure. Remember?"

"What are you talking about?"

"Come on, Miguel. You said you'd bet your first ten grand that we'd have the girl by tonight."

"I'm not sure why I let you hang around. We'd already have the girl if it weren't for you. Let's hope they go back to Eleu-thera."

Fernando shrugged. "You know that's where they're going. Lacy left all of her stuff there. She even left her makeup in the bathroom. You know a girl doesn't get far from her makeup. Hey, let's pull through McDonald's drive-through. I'm starved."

"You better be right, Fernando. You've botched this thing up several times already. I'm tired of messing around."

"It's all going to be fine. You'll see."

Chapter Ten

The Search Resumes

Once everyone finished breakfast, Jon called the group to the conference room on *The Discoverer*. The only team members absent for the meeting were the kitchen staff, Randal, and Judy. Randal's wheelchair wouldn't fit through the passageways of the lower levels, so Judy kept him company in his temporary quarters on the main deck.

"Okay, ladies and gentlemen," Jon announced once they had taken their seats. "Playtime is over, and we're now returning to work."

Cheers rose from the group, though Lacy sensed a bit of disappointment with how their time in Nassau turned out.

"We found a rental on the island where Randal and a few others can stay while the rest of us continue using *The Discoverer* for our quarters. Meg and I will take the Robalo into Rock Sound in just a bit to check out the house. If everything is like the advertisement we saw online, then we'll rent it. In addition to Randal bunking there for now, Judy and Kerrick will stay there this week. We might rotate the group around later. It's a big place, so we can all meet there occasionally. I think Randal will have good insight into what we're doing, so he can contribute to our planning. Kerrick will still work with us during the day."

Lacy was stunned. She never considered being separated from Kerrick. Why were Jon and Meg separating them? She felt betrayed. She remembered her stupid move the night before in her cabin and realized that being split up might be a good thing.

I can't believe I was so dumb. I don't know what's come over me. Well, I do know. It's Kerrick.

"The rest of us," Jon continued, "will pick up where we left off before we started working on the barge."

"What about the barge?" Marcy wondered. "Do we have to go back to it?"

"Not right now," Jon confirmed. "So far, the insurance company just wants the measurements I sent off while we were in Nassau. They'll let us know if they want us to do anything else with it."

"So, are we going back to the bay where we found the arquebus?" Kerrick asked.

"I think we're going to split up. Kerrick, I want you, Lacy, Barry, Jose, and Ann to take the sled to Double Bay and begin mapping the area. The sled is mounted with metal detectors and sonar that will help you to trace all of the unique contours of the bay floor. It can even pick up the presence of metal that might be buried as deep as six or eight feet deep."

Aaron whistled. "Eight feet deep? That seems pretty deep for a metal detector."

"Stuff gets buried on the sea floor fast around here," Jon replied. "Kerrick, I don't want you in the water until next week. You can help supervise from the deck of the *New Beginnings*. I've rigged up a small crane for the back deck. I'd rather you lift the sled from the water and always have it covered up on the back deck whenever you return to the marina. Dismantling the crane shouldn't be too difficult. You'll be able to figure it out."

"What about all of our stuff at the resort?" Lacy asked.

"You can go back and get it tomorrow or Thursday," Jon answered. "You and Jose should drive up there and check out of the resort."

Lacy felt her face beginning to glow. *Why is Jon trying to separate Kerrick and me? Kerrick and I can drive up there and check out of the resort. Why does it have to be Jose and me?*

"On second thought," Jon added, "Ann, you should go with them."

"What about the ruse we were trying to create?" Ann asked. "Shouldn't Kerrick come along too? Lacy and Kerrick are supposed to be getting married. It might look a little odd for him not to be around."

"That's not a bad idea, but you can cover for him if anyone asks. Just say he's back on the boat."

Lacy leaned back in her chair. *He IS trying to separate us. What's up with that? One minute he wants us to act like we're getting married, and now we're supposed to act like we're divorced. I'm guessing he knows something. He and Meg aren't stupid.*

"So, what are we going to do?" Tae asked from the back of the room.

Jon pointed to the map of Eleuthera on the wall. "We'll take *The Discoverer* to the southern tip of the island, not far from here. Lacy has a theory, and I'd like to explore that angle a little. I want us in the water after lunch."

*****

Kerrick wiped some dripping ketchup from the bottle before setting it back on the table. "I thought when Jon said he wanted us in the water after lunch that we were at least going to get one more of Chef Marceau's meals."

"My hamburgers aren't that bad," Lacy huffed. "You can fix your own next time."

"I didn't mean that, Lacy. I was just commenting on how I've enjoyed the Chef's cooking. You're pretty awesome too."

"Too late. You've already complained about my cooking. You can't take it back that easily. You're going to have to earn your forgiveness."

"Oh really? I didn't know you could earn forgiveness. I thought it was all about grace."

Lacy placed her napkin in her lap. "Why is it that everyone talks about grace around here? I think you all got together to try to convince me to forgive my parents."

Kerrick looked at Lacy for a long moment. "Do you really believe that?"

"I guess not. That's pretty dumb."

"Well, we didn't get together and talk about anything, but I know that when you don't forgive someone, you're the one who gets hurt in the long run."

Lacy got up from the table and begin cleaning up from lunch. *There's no way I'm going to forgive my parents. It's not hurting me in the slightest to hate them.*

Once the galley was cleaned up from lunch, Lacy slipped into the main cabin to change into her bathing suit. The ride to Double Bay had been comfortable. The seas were as calm as the waters of Lake Sinclair. She recalled the hours she'd spent on the lake near her college town. Her friend, Caroline, had a kayak, and Lacy enjoyed spending time on the lake whenever she had a chance.

As Lacy stepped through the galley door onto the deck of the *New Beginnings*, she saw the rest of the group pulling on their gear for the dive. The sun beat down on her back, and the salty air embraced Lacy like an old friend. She was growing to love the ocean much more than the pine trees of Georgia. The thought of returning to Milledgeville for the fall semester was beginning to become unpleasant.

Lacy patted Barry on his bare, dark back. "Hey, Barry. It looks like we're diving buddies for a while."

"I guess you'll do," Barry grinned. "So, what's an arquebus? I hated to look stupid in our meeting."

"I'm sure you weren't the only one in the meeting who didn't know. It's a 17th-century rifle. They used to call them hand cannons. It had a wooden stock and a long metal tube. Jose found the metal part, but the ocean worked it over pretty well."

"Wow, that's cool. I guess that means there's treasure in this bay?"

"No telling. A Spanish sailor could have dropped his rifle over the ship's side by accident."

"That'd suck."

Lacy wondered if the word *suck* qualified as one of Meg's illegal words. "You're not kidding. I imagine those things were expensive back then, and it's not like the poor guy could run to Walmart and pick up a new one. I'd better get ready for our dive."

She pulled out her gear bag and began attaching her regulator to the yellow tank. From the last time they dove here, she knew the bay was shallow, so she decided not to wear her wetsuit. She checked the straps securing her tank to the vest and made sure the inflator hose was also connected. She sat on the bench in front of her tank and put on the vest as if she were zipping up her coat. She grabbed her mask and fins and maneuvered to the back of the boat.

"You ready?" Kerrick's wink made Lacy's stomach flip. "I'll just stay up here and try to pick up a soap opera on TV."

"Right. I can imagine you watching 'The Young and the Restless.'"

"Well, I'm young and restless, so I guess that would be appropriate."

Lacy laughed before spitting into her mask and allowing the saliva to roll around on the glass. "It seems like they'd come up with another way to keep your mask from fogging up."

"They have. Your spit, however, is free."

"True," she agreed before pulling her mask over her head and inserting her snorkel. She nodded her head and stepped into the water.

The rush she felt was like nothing else she'd experienced in her entire life. It was better than her feeling when she walked into Jack and Milly at their grand opening. It was not, however, better than being in Kerrick's arms the night before.

All right, stupid. Quit thinking like that. You've got work to do. We're supposed to take a visual of the area and then mark out our first scan area with these stakes.

She bobbed on the surface momentarily as Barry stepped into the water and came up beside her. She gave Kerrick the okay sign and dove toward the bottom. Something beyond the beauty of this underwater world intrigued her. For one thing, no one could say stupid things. Even though she always dove with a partner, she still felt alone. She preferred being alone, which made her wonder why Kerrick enraptured her so much.

Once on the bottom, she handed the first stake to Barry. He looked up to make sure he was under the back corner of the boat, and then he pushed it into the sand. She motioned for him to follow her and moved 100 kicks toward the shore. As the muscles in her toned legs flexed, she felt as giddy as a girl on her first date. She scanned the flat, sandy sea floor dotted with a few small piles of coral. *The coral shouldn't interfere with the sled.*

Lacy looked behind her for Barry as she pulled another stake from her vest pocket. When she turned to push it into the sea-floor, a sting ray dislodged from the sand and came close to hitting her in its attempt to escape. She felt as if her heart had stopped beating. She had heard that the sting from a ray could be painful. *Wasn't that how that guy died a few years ago?*

With the second stake in place, Lacy turned ninety degrees and moved another 100 strong kicks forward. In no time, she and Barry created a large square. She pulled the red twine from her pocket, and they worked together to outline a large box on the sea floor. Once completed, they swam over their box to get a visual of the area. It reminded her of the little potholder loom she had as a kid. Once Lacy was satisfied with the first stage of the grid, she and Barry headed toward the surface.

Chapter Eleven
Duty Calls

Lacy dragged her tired body into the dining area on *The Discoverer*, and her mouth watered as she smelled what must be a beef dish Chef Marceau was preparing for the team. She had no idea how Jon managed to get such a successful chef to come aboard The Discoverer as the head cook. She loved everything about this summer break: her aunt and uncle, the scuba diving, the boys, the interns—especially one of the interns. How in the world had she been so lucky?

"How was it, Lacy?" Jon's voice shook her out of a fog as thick as a fall morning.

"Great. It was great. We've scanned seven designated areas between yesterday and today, and..."

"Seven? I figured you would have done more than that."

"I'm sure y'all would have finished more, but it took us a while to get used to the sled. We also started late this morning because we had to get our stuff from Hatchet Bay Resort."

"Any luck? I mean, any luck at Double Bay?"

"We found a bunch of bottles and a nice fishing pole. Well, I suppose it used to be nice. I'm afraid the salt water did a number on it."

Jon sat down at the table, and Lacy marveled at his body's youthfulness; in her estimation, he was not a young man. *He's almost old enough to be my father. I guess he could be my father if he were twenty years old when I was born. He looks pretty good to be an old guy. Okay, so thirty-eight's not that old.*

"How did everyone do?"

"Everyone did fine, real fine."

Lacy's mind raced back to when Kerrick helped her out of the water. She handed her gear to him and took hold of the ladder that dropped from the back of the boat into the water. He reached down to grab her hand, and before she knew it, their bodies looked as if they had been grafted together. Energy surged and heat rose. If she had not realized that within moments she was going to have an audience, she would have given him a kiss that would linger in his mind until they were old enough to be in a nursing home. Instead, she offered a peck on his cheek.

"Yeah, we all did good, Jon. We left the stakes in, just like you said to do. We should finish by the time Carla is eighteen at the rate we're going."

"You'll get faster at it," Jon assured. "You'll complete the whole area in less than a week. I know you're tired. Chefs got an incredible meal ready. Sorry, we went ahead and ate without you. We'll meet in the living room at the Rock Sound house when you're done so everyone can get the whole picture of the day."

"Did y'all have any luck?"

"Not really. We picked up a few things I'll leave in the cleaning tanks overnight."

"Could it be gold?"

"I suppose it could be, but I doubt it. We went through the tunnel you and Kerrick mentioned and picked up some stones that looked to have potential. However, it's a little too deep for the boys. I'm thinking that I'm going to send the other three with you tomorrow. This should help move along your scanning project. You'll have to check behind them to make sure the squares are not some new geometric shape."

Lacy grinned. "Sounds good to me."

Forty-five minutes later, Lacy boarded the *New Beginnings* for the ten-minute ride into Rock Sound. Jon worked extra hard to include Randal in all the group meetings, so before 8:00, everyone gathered in the living room of the vacation home. It wasn't as plush as the one on Nassau, but it was adequate. Kerrick, Judy, and Randal had their own bedrooms. Lacy figured the house caught Jon's attention because it offered a large living room that she knew he planned to use as a meeting room for the whole team. Lacy sat on the couch, and a huge, unguarded yawn slipped out. *That had to be attractive.* This treasure-hunting business was exhausting.

"Okay, everyone," Jon announced from the front of the living room. "It's been quite a day. First, I'd like Kerrick to give us an update on the work of the *New Beginnings* team."

"I don't have much to report except we completed surveying seven squares of what we determined to be about 700 feet by 700 feet. We found vintage bottles and a fishing pole that I imagine was heartbreaking for someone when they lost it."

"All right," Jon breathed out slowly. "The bay is as big as six or seven football fields across, so it will take some time at this rate. I've got a new idea that I'll share in a minute. Aaron, would you like to report on our group?"

For a few minutes, Aaron talked about searching along the reef. He told how Jon and Meg went down a second time through the tunnel that dropped to about 100 feet below the surface and came back with a few rocks. "Jon says that the rocks could be something, so we left them in the tanks in the lab."

"Thank you, Aaron," Jon smiled. "I received a couple of phone calls today. One was from my assistant, and I need to make a fast trip to London to review a contract. The second call came from Cindy, who is our research friend in Spain. Before our barge accident, she told me we may need to go to Denmark."

"Denmark?" Tae questioned. "What's in Denmark?"

"It's complicated. It's not connected to our search for the sunken ship but is still intriguing. Lacy found a medallion in the cave on Conception Island."

"We know about the medallion," David interrupted. "Oh...sorry. I guess that was rude."

"You're forgiven, David. I'm glad you figured out the rude part on your own. Cindy told us that the scratching on the medallion was Runic, an ancient, Viking language. She said that it means *beneath*. Lacy and Meg found..."

"And Kerrick," Lacy added.

"...and Kerrick," Jon continued, "found writing on the cave wall as well. It, too, was in Runic. That writing said, 'Bluetooth, find the diary,' and 'Trelleborg.' Before you ask, trelleborgs were round forts the Vikings built in the 10th or 11th centuries. One of the Viking kings, Harald Bluetooth, was famous for his trelleborgs."

"Wow," Barry gasped "This treasure-hunting stuff is cool."

"Cool, indeed," Meg added. "It's even cooler when you determine what these clues mean."

"Meg and I have decided that since I need to go to London anyway, we'll take a fast trip to Denmark to do more research. We can return in a few days, so I don't anticipate our little break slowing us down much."

"Just in time for Lacy's birthday," Kerrick smiled.

"You got a birthday?" Aaron blurted out in surprise.

"Every year," Lacy quipped.

"You boys will be in great care with Jose in charge," Jon added. "We'll follow this Denmark clue, stop in London for a brief meeting, and be back when you finish mapping the bay. Any questions?"

"Yeah," Aaron raised his hand. "Where are we goin' to stay?"

Jon nodded at Aaron. "Good question. Kerrick, Judy, and Randal will continue to sleep in the house. Everyone else will stay on *The Discoverer*, which will anchor north of Double Bay near James Point. Kerrick will use the Robalo to get around to Double Bay each morning. He will meet the rest of the team, who will use the *New Beginnings* to get to Double Bay from *The Discoverer*. I suggest you try to locate a dock near the bay for the Robalo so you can just drive from the house to the dock each morning. That will save some time."

"Why don't we keep *The Discoverer* in Double Bay?" David wondered.

"Because we don't want to give anyone the idea that we're searching for treasure there," Jon replied. "I think the bay is also too shallow for the ship. I want Randal to keep a map of Double Bay with constant updates on your progress. I want you to meet here at least twice to discuss your progress so Randal can also share his insights. Kerrick, can you get Randal the materials he'll need to create the map?"

"Yes, sir."

"Any more questions?"

"Yeah," Tae raised his hand and whispered. "Anybody got any shaving cream I can put in Lacy's hand? She's asleep, and we can have some fun."

"I'm not asleep," Lacy groaned, "and that would be the last prank of your life."

Everyone laughed.

About an hour later, Lacy crawled into bed on *The Discoverer* *but* couldn't get Kerrick off her mind. He was such a paradox. The more she thought about his quirky ways, the more she felt he was hiding something. She didn't doubt she loved him; he loved her, too. Why would he be holding something back? Did it have anything to do with the picture of that girl? Could she really be his sister? Not likely. Why would he lie about it?

Lacy's weary eyes closed as the gentle swaying of the boat began rocking her to sleep. A slight scraping noise joined the common room noises that greeted her each night, and she sat bolt-upright in her bed. She made out the distinct sound of metal against metal as the doorknob to her cabin door turned.

Chapter Twelve
Denmark

Meg looked out the plane window as the pilot took a hard bank to the left. She pictured the plane making a huge U-turn as they left the tip of Sweden to fly back over the water. *Is that still considered the North Sea or the Baltic? No, maybe it's some bay.*

She looked from the wing toward the front of the plane and spotted the Copenhagen International Airport just ahead. She smiled as she noticed that the roof to the main terminal looked just like a paper airplane.

Her body felt like one big, painful throb. She didn't think her backside could stand another minute in this seat. She smirked at the thought of her body being anatomically changed from sitting so long on the flight over the Atlantic. She should have taken Jon's advice to get up and move around more.

The stop in Amsterdam had not been long enough, though she was grateful for the short reprieve. They flew out of Nassau almost twenty hours earlier, so it was 3:00 a.m. on her body clock. Thankfully, her first-class accommodations provided a comfortable place to lie almost flat at night. She remembered looking over at her sleeping husband, marveling that he could sleep anywhere at any time.

Leaving Carla had been tough. Their little girl didn't seem to mind staying with Judy, but Meg almost called the trip off at the last minute. Jon could go to London without her. He convinced her that a few days away would be okay. Carla was going on three years old, and she thought of Judy as her grandmother.

Carla placed a sloppy, wet kiss on Meg's cheek at the Nassau airport. "Wuv u, Mommy."

"I love you, too, sweetheart," Meg said as tears rolled from her eyes. "Be sweet for Grandma Judy."

They would soon be celebrating their fourth anniversary. She felt so privileged to have Jon as her soul mate, and their precious little girl was such a blessing. Meg smiled as she recalled her first transatlantic flight when she and Ann went to Spain before her wedding. It seemed like an eternity ago. She couldn't help but be excited about flying again. She felt like a kid tasting her first serving of bubblegum ice cream and couldn't keep from taking pictures out the plane's window.

Once they cleared customs, Jon led the way to the car rental counter. Weary travelers stumbled around as if they were extras on *The Walking Dead*. Meg raked her hands through her short, blonde hair, thinking she must look horrible. Everyone else looked like they had been flying all night too, so she decided that fashion was not too important for the moment.

While Jon completed the paperwork, Meg turned on her cell phone, which dinged with a new text message.

Hey, Meg. I sent you an e-mail with a ton of information that I believe you'll find interesting.

Meg held up her cell phone as Jon turned from the rental counter with paperwork folded in his hand. "I just heard from Cindy. She said that she sent us some information. I tried to look at it, but it appears to be a lot of pages."

"I suggest we head to the hotel. We can print it out in the business center."

"Sounds good. We need to call Judy and check on Carla."

"You can't right now," Jon reminded her. "While it's 9:00 here, it's about three o'clock in the morning in the Bahamas."

"That's true. It's too bad we can't take a little time to play tourists," Meg sighed.

Jon grabbed their luggage, and they headed toward the exit. "What would you like to see?"

"I don't know," Meg said as she adjusted her overnight bag on her shoulder. "I guess the one thing I've heard about is The Little Mermaid monument."

"The Little Mermaid? I've never heard of that monument."

"I assume it's to honor Hans Christian Anderson. He was Danish, you know. I heard about it when it was banned from one of the social media sites. I think someone was sensitive about having a picture of a topless statue on a site that kids might frequent."

"That's different. Maybe a little extreme, but it sure is a refreshing contrast to the rest of our culture."

"When I heard it was banned, I looked it up, but since then, the picture is back online. I think the statue is not too far from the airport."

Jon motioned toward a bench near a lane reserved for shuttle buses. "Well, if we have time on our way back to the airport, we'll check it out. Do you want to sit here while we wait for the shuttle?"

"I think I've sat enough on the plane to do me for quite a while. If I could figure out how to stand up in the car, I'd do that too."

Meg sat her small bag down on the bench and rummaged through it. She found her light jacket tucked into the bottom corner and pulled it over her goose-pimpled arms. The cool breeze blew her hair into her eyes. It appeared as if it might rain, though she remembered the forecast predicted overcast skies but no precipitation.

They climbed aboard the next shuttle, and within another thirty minutes, their sleek Mercedes Benz headed out of town on a four-lane highway. Meg watched out the window as the scenery turned from a busy seaside city to beautiful, green countryside. She loved traveling to new places. She imagined being in one of those rotating restaurants on top of a building, and the view was about to turn to a new side of town she had never seen.

She smiled as she heard Jon's stomach rumble. "The airplane food wasn't good enough?"

"Oh?" Jon raised an eyebrow. "That was food? Besides, it's been at least a few hours since we last ate. I'm starving."

"It looks like a city ahead, or maybe we're still in Copenhagen. I'm sure we can find something to eat here."

"I think this is Karlslunde. I see a Domino's Pizza ahead."

"What's that one across the street? Monarch?"

Jon turned off E20 into the restaurant parking lot. "I've never eaten at a Monarch restaurant, so let's go here."

"It looks like a chain...maybe hamburgers? I'm game."

Jon turned off the car and unbuckled his seatbelt. "A good hamburger sounds like what I need."

Jon held the door as Meg walked into a modern diner that reminded her of a restaurant on the bottom floor of Piedmont Hospital back in Atlanta. Several men sat at a bar lining one side of the place, and a hostess led Jon and Meg to a table near the window. The menu revealed that the Monarch people anticipated English tourists. Jon ordered a hamburger plate and a soda, while Meg opted for a plate with rolled pieces of ham and cheese and steamed vegetables.

"You know," Jon suggested after a couple of bites of his hamburger, "we're not far from the fort. Denmark is not very big."

"I looked at a map the other day," Meg admitted. "I was surprised at the size. Denmark is more island than mainland."

"I once read that Denmark is about a quarter of the size of the state of Georgia."

"Wow. That is small. How about this island? I mean, the one we're on?"

"I have no idea," Jon confessed. "It's called Zealand. Why don't you look it up?"

Meg pulled out her smartphone and typed a few letters into the search window. "How about that!"

"What?"

"I figured that New Zealand must be named after this island, but it's named after something in the Netherlands. Here it is. Zealand is about 1,000 square miles."

"I knew it couldn't be very big."

"Well," Meg grinned, "we'll be here at least two days. We ought to be able to see all of Zealand."

"Not if we don't get out of here. I want to get to the fort before they close. We can scope it out today and return tomorrow if we need extra time."

They finished lunch, and Jon waved for the waitress. With his hand, he made a writing motion, and Meg figured that must be the universal sign language for "bring my check, please."

The young waitress smiled a big, beautiful smile at Jon as she lay the bill before him. "Are you on holiday?" she asked with a heavy accent.

"Yes," Jon replied. "We came to visit the old Trelleborg Museum. Have you ever been?"

"Oh, yes. It is lovely. It's free, you know?"

"No, I didn't know that, but that's wonderful. Did Harald Bluetooth build the fort?"

"Yes, he did. So, you know of King Harald? He did a lot for our country. He united our people many years ago."

"That's very interesting," Meg offered as she reached across the table to lay her hand on Jon's. By the way this cute Dane was looking at her husband, it was obvious that she was flirting with him. Meg thought the cute Dane needed an overt signal of ownership. "You seem to know a lot about King Harald."

"Oh, yes, ma'am. I wrote a paper about him in school. You will like the museum. I suggest you also visit the Jelling Stones. It's like a journal on a rock, though it doesn't say much. It's intact and quite interesting."

"Jelling Stones?" Jon raised an eyebrow. "It's his journal?"

"Yes, sir. We have a brochure about it at the front door. I'll get you one."

Within a few minutes, the young, blonde waitress returned with a brochure in her hand. Her beautiful smile covered her face as she opened the folded pamphlet and pointed out the information about the stone. It was obvious to Meg that she was enjoying Jon's attention. Why wouldn't she? He was a handsome man who treated everyone like they were the most important person on the planet. Meg knew she was blessed to have him as her husband.

"Thank you so much…Gretchen," Jon said after eyeing her nametag. "You've been most helpful. I will tell your supervisor what a wonderful job you're doing."

"Thank you, sir…and ma'am," Gretchen stammered. "Thank you for visiting the Monarch. I hope you enjoy your holiday."

They headed west before noon while Meg scanned the bilingual brochure. A picture of two carved stones covered the front, along with a painting of a man Meg determined was King

Harald. She squinted at the picture of the carvings and saw right away that the writing was Runic.

"So, do you suppose this is the journal we're supposed to find?" Meg wondered aloud. She remembered the writing she and Lacy found in the cave on Conception Island and the skeleton. They made the discovery a month earlier, but so much had happened over the weeks that it seemed more like a year.

"You mean the writing on the cave wall? Maybe. Let's check out the fort today and tomorrow morning and then visit the stones."

Meg pulled up the website of the Trelleborg Fortress Museum on her smartphone. She looked down at her watch and wondered if they had time to make it there before the place closed. "Honey. Are you sure we should go to the museum today? They close at 4:00, and it's already 12:30."

"It will take us about forty-five minutes to get to the fort. Since we are closer to the fort than the hotel, we ought to visit the fort briefly and then go on to the hotel."

"Sounds good to me."

An hour later, Jon pulled into a parking place at the museum. Meg was surprised to find a gravel lot in front of a modern-looking building. She had anticipated an old rock edifice filled with ancient artifacts, but instead, contemporary architecture reminiscent of the newest public-school building in her hometown greeted them. A trail led to the left from behind the building, and Meg assumed it must go to the circular mound of the trelleborg fort.

"It's not what I thought it would be," Jon admitted as he opened the door for Meg.

"I was thinking the same thing. Oh, well. It might help us solve our mystery."

As they walked toward the entrance, Meg thought of the markings on the cave wall and the words on Lacy's medallion. It amazed her that the two were connected. She smiled as she remembered seeing the medallion for the first time.

"What are you smiling about?" Jon asked

"I was thinking back to when I first saw the medallion drifting toward the bottom of the ocean. I thought we had found another gold coin. Then I thought it was just a nice gold trinket. Lacy came to my mind immediately, and I knew I wanted to give it to her as a graduation gift. It's just interesting how it has now led us to Denmark."

"Interesting indeed. Now that we're here let's not forget the clues we know."

Meg pulled her cell phone out of her back pocket. "I've got them in here but won't forget them. The medallion says 'beneath' and the cave writings say 'Trelleborg, Bluetooth, and find the diary.'"

"The cave says 'The Trelleborg,' so whoever wrote it must have had a particular trelleborg in mind."

"I haven't thought of that. You should have been a detective, honey."

"I was a history professor, so I suppose that's close enough."

Meg reached up to brush Jon's hair with her hand. "There's no way the guy who died in the cave knew the facts of this mystery. If he did, why was he writing a note about trying to figure out the clues?"

"Good point." Jon opened the door for Meg to step into the building. He lowered his voice so no one else could hear him. "I'm also wondering who was supposed to read the dead guy's message. I feel we are about to put some pieces together that could lead us to quite a discovery."

Chapter Thirteen
Night Visitor

At first, fear froze Lacy to her mattress, but she knew she was a sitting duck under the blanket on her bed. She had almost been asleep when the scraping sound of her doorknob turning brought her fully awake.

She slid out of bed and hurried to a spot just behind the door. Clad only in a long tee shirt, she felt a shiver run down her spine. Flight was not an option. Since she couldn't run, she would fight. She scanned the room for something that could be a weapon, but it was too dark to see anything. She balled her fists up and hoped the stuff she learned in her self-defense class would work.

At first, the door opened a crack, allowing a little light into the room from the hallway. Lacy saw a man's hand on the door as the intruder eased the door open wide enough to enter the room. Whom could this be? She couldn't make out his face. Someone must have come out in a small boat and boarded *The Discoverer*. Darkness enveloped the man as he slipped into the room and closed the door without a sound. She felt as helpless as David before Goliath. *Didn't David win that one?* On a positive note, she had the advantage of surprise.

The clock's glow on the shelf beside her bed created a silhouette of the man. She knew how to stop a man, but she was unsure she could land her blow successfully. The next best spot was his nose. She swung with all her might for a spot she determined was the center of the man's face. As pain ran from her closed fist up her arm, the man gasped, and something fell to the floor.

"Lacy! What are you doing?"

The object on the floor lit up, and Lacy made out a pair of familiar shoes. Her hand throbbed. *I think I broke my hand.* She prepared to kick the guy next. She might hit his leg or his abdomen, but he was going to the hospital.

"Lacy!" the voice hissed. "It's me. Kerrick."

Lacy paused. *Did he say Kerrick?* She fumbled for the light switch and squinted as the room lit. "Kerrick? What are you doing here?"

"I came out to finish making some plans with Jose," Kerrick whispered with a muffled voice, "and you left your phone at the house. I was trying to leave it in your room so it wouldn't disappear. I tried not to wake you."

When Lacy's eyes adjusted to the light, she saw blood on the front of Kerrick's shirt. Her phone lay on the floor with a picture of her and Kerrick sitting in a chair on the *New Beginnings* on her home screen.

"Oh, my God. You're bleeding."

"Of course, I'm bleeding. I think you broke my nose."

"Well, I think you broke my hand. You shouldn't ever sneak into a girl's room. If I'd had a gun, I would've shot you."

"I'll try to remember that."

Lacy hurried into the bathroom, put a rag under the sink, and returned to Kerrick. "Here. Put this over your nose."

Kerrick obeyed, but the blood continued dripping down his shirt. Lacy got two more rags from the bathroom and rinsed out the first one.

"Lay down on my bed and tilt your head back. No...wait. You'll get blood on my bed. Take your shirt off."

Kerrick removed his shirt and Lacy pushed him back onto her bed. She pulled her pillow out from under his head and tilted his head back. She gave him a fresh rag.

"Now, pinch the bridge of your nose."

"What if it's broken," Kerrick said with a nasal tone.

"Don't be such a baby. It's not broken. I didn't hit you hard enough to break it."

Lacy wondered if it could be broken. She had hit him as hard as she could, but she felt like he had been further away from him than she had first imagined. By the time her fist connected with his face, she had lost some momentum. Her fist sure hurt like she'd just connected with a brick wall.

She hurried back to the bathroom sink and rinsed out a rag. When she returned to Kerrick with a clean, wet rag, it seemed like the bleeding was slowing. Within another few minutes, it had stopped altogether.

"Don't move while I clean out these rags."

"Yes, ma'am."

Lacy came back and began wiping Kerrick's face. He was a bloody mess. She cleaned the blood from his cheeks and nose before returning to the bathroom to wash out the rag. When she returned to the bed, she sat on the edge of the bed and cleaned up a couple of spots of drying blood that she missed earlier. She sat back to inspect her work. Kerrick's sandy blonde hair hung near his left eye, and Lacy brushed it back with her left hand. She leaned over and kissed him.

"I'm so sorry I hit you. I had no idea who it was."

"Who could I have been? We're out in the ocean, for heaven's sake. What if I had been Ann?"

"I said I was sorry. You just scared me."

"I'm sorry I scared you. You got blood on your shirt, or I suppose it's my shirt."

Lacy looked down to see several red spots on the Abercrombie tee shirt she had borrowed. Her face reddened with embarrassment as she realized she was wearing only his tee shirt. She was glad it was longer than some of her other nightshirts.

Kerrick took her hand and inspected her knuckles. "Is your hand okay?"

She looked down at her hand which was not throbbing as badly as it had been moments earlier. "It's okay. Maybe I was being dramatic when I said you broke it."

Kerrick massaged her hand and caressed her arm with the tips of his fingers. He reached up to stroke her cheek. She felt electricity course through her body as his hand slid down her neck and back. His eyes were dark, passionate, and full of desire.

He pulled her face toward his, and their lips met with an explosion of passion. Her heart pounded in her chest. She was lost in the euphoria of love, hunger, and longing.

Lacy pulled back at the sound of a knock at the door.

"Lacy? You up?"

Time froze as Lacy stared at Kerrick in horror. She pointed to the bathroom, and he stepped inside. He eased the door almost closed. She looked around her room and turned on her computer sitting on the desk near the bed. *Boot up. Please boot up.*

She opened the door to see Marcy standing in the hallway with a cup of hot chocolate and a piece of pound cake.

"I couldn't sleep so I thought I'd get a snack. I was surprised to see light coming from under your door. I supposed you'd be in bed. Everything okay? Oh, my God. What happened?"

Lacy followed Marcy's gaze to the blood on the front of her Abercrombie shirt. "Oh…I had a nosebleed earlier. I just forgot to change my shirt."

Lacy went over to her chest and pulled out a clean shirt. She wondered if she should change it now or wait. What would seem most natural? She and Marcy were close friends, but…*Kerrick is in the bathroom, and the door is cracked. The shirt stays on!*

"I have nose bleeds occasionally," Lacy stammered as she unfolded her clean tee shirt. "I used to have them a lot as a kid, but I haven't had one in a long time."

Even though her statement was not a lie, Lacy knew that her insinuation was far from true. Marcy had become such a close friend, and Lacy hated lying to her.

"Do I need to get Ann?"

"No. I'm fine. I got everything cleaned up. It must be the dry weather. It's no big deal. I was sitting at my computer, and blood started flowing."

Lacy looked over at her computer and saw that it had booted up. It was good that she'd been on her computer before bed and closed the screen without turning it off. It booted up straight to the e-mail screen she had up earlier.

So, that was a blatant lie. You are now madly in love, breaking the rules with a boy in your room and lying to your good friend. Before turning back to Marcy, she spotted Kerrick's bloody shirt on the floor.

"Do you want to go get some hot chocolate?" Marcy asked.

"I don't think so," Lacy replied, moving away from the bloody shirt. She was hoping to draw Marcy's gaze away from the condemning evidence. "Thanks, but I'm tired, and it will keep me awake. I was just about to send my mom an e-mail and then turn in."

My mom is the last person I want to e-mail right now. Why did I say that?

"Suit yourself. The cake sure is good, and gaining weight is nothing you have to worry about. I'll see you in the morning, Lacy. You sure you don't need any help?"

"Thanks, Marcy. I'm fine. Good night."

As the door closed behind Marcy, Lacy sighed her relief.

"I didn't know you have a problem with nose bleeds," Kerrick whispered.

Lacy turned and saw Kerrick coming out of the bathroom. She threw her clean shirt at him. "You about broke my hand, and then you made me lie to my good friend."

"I didn't do anything. I was hiding out in the bathroom."

"Okay, Mr. Innocent. You've got to get out of my room. Remember the rules?"

"I know. I'm sorry. I shouldn't have come in here." A big grin spread across his handsome face. "I was hoping we could pick up where we left off."

"Kerrick!"

"I'm kidding…sort of."

"Someone will find us together, and we'll be in deep weeds. Jon may have to send both of us home. Besides that, we've got an early start in the morning."

"You're right as usual," Kerrick agreed. "I still have to return to the dock and drive to Rock Sound."

"Hey, here's something to think about on your way home."

"I'm all ears."

"I predict we'll find a few objects from our Spanish galleon in the bay because I think the sailors lost stuff in the storm. The last thing they wanted, however, was to go aground. I suppose the last thing they wanted was to sink. If they still had control of their sails when they reached Double Bay and thought they would beat the storm, they'd have tried to keep the ship away from the land. I guess we'll find the mother lode below the tunnel off the southern tip of the island."

"You may be right," Kerrick agreed, "but we have our orders from Jon to map out the bay."

Lacy nodded. "I think it's the right thing to do. I'll be surprised if we find more than a few artifacts, but they could be worth a lot. I imagine that arquebus is quite valuable."

"It's at least valuable to a museum," Kerrick agreed. "Mapping out the bay will be good for the boys, and it gives us something to do while Jon and Meg are gone. They'll be back in a few days, and by then, we'll know for sure about what's in this bay."

"True," Lacy said. "I hope we'll have time to run the sled over the area. It's amazing that thing can find stuff six feet under the sand."

Kerrick took Lacy's hands. "I've got something for *you* to think about as you drift off to sleep." He pulled her close and lowered his lips to hers. The magic was there again as everything in Lacy's body responded to his touch, smell, and deep kiss.

"I've got to go," Kerrick croaked when he pulled away. "I'll see you in a few hours."

Lacy eased the door closed after Kerrick slipped out. She replaced the bloody tee shirt with her clean one, turned out her light, and closed her computer. Once she crawled back into her bed, a smile spread across her face as she relived the last hour.

What a kiss. I love Kerrick Daniels. I can't help it. I love him. I've finally found a man I can trust.

Chapter Fourteen
A Trip to the Museum

Fernando pulled away from the villa at the Hatchet Bay Resort. He cursed at a child who ran across the sandy road in front of his rental car and slammed his hand against the steering wheel. He counted in his head how many times he drove to an empty villa this week. *Now, I've come back, and her stuff is gone.*

He remembered when he first saw Lacy walking into a drugstore in George Town. Long, bronze legs. Short pants. Tight tee shirt. And the medallion. She was a babe—from her toes to her beautiful, blonde head—a certified babe. And her eyes! She had the most beautiful blue eyes.

As far as he was concerned, the girl didn't need to return for her makeup anyway. He knew for sure she wasn't wearing makeup the night he slipped into her bedroom while she was asleep. He had relived that night in his dreams many times, except in his dreams, he didn't just leave the room. She was gorgeous lying in her bed with the moonlight highlighting her body, and oh what a body! Lacy was already his. He thought about her all the time.

Someone blew a horn, and Fernando looked in the rearview mirror. He didn't realize he was still sitting at the stop sign. If he had taken Lacy back then, he wouldn't be sitting at a stop sign listening to a jerk blow his horn.

"All right! I'm going. Shut up, or I'll put a bullet in your brain."

He took a right and headed for the entrance to the resort. He was back on Queens Highway in just a few minutes, driving toward the marina. He dreaded telling Miguel that Lacy had already returned and got her stuff. Of course, Miguel assumed the girl hadn't returned because they had not seen the Carver yacht pull into the marina–the yacht that started all this insanity years ago with Miguel's uncle. Now, Miguel was going to blow a fuse.

Fernando parked the car and trudged down the dock to the thirty-seven-foot Sundancer that Miguel somehow acquired through a trade. Fernando was confident that Miguel had stolen the boat. He worked on the engine, and she could get at least forty-five knots. Speed was helpful when they had to overtake a boat on the open sea or escape quickly. Miguel was sitting behind the wheel with a can of beer.

"Let me guess. She's not there."

"If you knew that, why did you make me return to check? On top of that, they came back and got their stuff. Somehow we missed them."

"Shut up and get aboard. I imagine they had someone ship their stuff back to Great Exuma. We've got to get out of here and go do a job. Our money's running out. I'm sure we can find someone going through the Straits that would like to donate to our cause. Maybe we'll connect with one of our competitors from Columbia. They're always loaded."

"What about the girl? We've got to find her. You know the coordinates we keep getting from our boy are wrong. We need to find him and knock some sense into him."

"I'm going to assume he's sending us the coordinates of the Davenport's ship just before they set sail…"

"Yeah, and by the time we get there, they're gone. He's not much help."

"Don't worry about our boy. We'll take care of him in time, and the girl won't be hard to find when we return. We'll only be gone for a few days, a week at the most. All we have to do is ask around for a gorgeous blonde in a Carver, or they could be on their salvage ship by now. It doesn't matter. We can find her."

Filled with disappointment, Fernando shrugged and went toward the galley for his own can of beer. Lacy Henderson consumed his thoughts and dreams. That girl was messing with his mind; there was one way to deal with her. It wouldn't be long now before he felt her skin and touched that blonde hair. *You're going to be mine, Lacy. Maybe not today, but you're going to be mine.*

****

While the museum's exterior seemed simple and modern, the interior was quite impressive. People gathered in clusters around displays that covered the room; a replica of a Viking ship lined one of the walls. The ship wasn't to scale but still something to see. Jon tried to imagine sailing across the ocean from Denmark to the Bahamas in a vessel like the one before him. While it was an amazing ship, it was rather small for a voyage across the Atlantic.

Meg was drawn toward the ship too as she pulled on Jon's hand. A small group of tourists stood in front of the sign that told about the ship, and Jon noticed the sign was in Danish and English. He saw one man staring at Meg. He considered giving the man a piece of his mind, but then he thought he'd be staring at her too. He smiled as he thought about the blessing of having such a beautiful and incredible wife.

Their courtship had been fast but full of adventure. Jon thought back to the first time they were together on his boat. He wished he'd been honest then and admitted his love for this beautiful woman. He almost lost her to Alvaro Lopez and his cronies before admitting he couldn't live without Meg as his wife. He put his arm around her slim waist and pulled her against his body.

Meg leaned toward Jon. "Who do you suppose they are?"

Jon followed her eyes to see a group of young girls gathered around a display. A couple of large men stood nearby, and Jon was sure the bulge under their jackets were guns.

"There's no telling, but I'd bet my pension that those guys are bodyguards."

"I didn't know you have a pension."

"I don't, but I still bet those guys watch over those girls."

"Or at least one of them. See the cute blonde over on the right?"

Jon scanned the group of girls to see which one Meg was talking about. "They're all cute, and they're all blonde. Well, they're all blonde but two."

"The girl with the red tennis shoes."

"Oh, yeah. The big guys seem to have their eyes on her."

"Hey, let's look at that display about Harald Bluetooth."

Meg pulled Jon across the museum floor to an encased display with a large painting of the famous king. Jon scanned the items in the case and wondered how anyone could know that those things belonged to old Bluetooth.

"How about that," Meg breathed. "Bluetooth was named after our king, after all. You know. The technology. Look at that."

Jon read the paragraph about Harald Bluetooth uniting separate clans to form a stronger nation. When Ericsson Communications developed technology connecting various devices, they decided to name it Bluetooth after the king who united Denmark.

"Isn't that something?" Meg said reverently. "One of the guys on the project was reading a book about Harald Bluetooth and had the idea for a name for their new technology."

"I've always wondered what the Bluetooth symbol meant. It's King Harold's initials in Runic. Who would have known?"

"See. Coming to Denmark has solved one of life's great mysteries," Meg teased.

"We need to get on with solving another mystery. For some reason, we've been directed to check out the trelleborg and a diary. There's a trelleborg just behind this building. As far as a diary? I have no idea."

"It could be the Jelling Stone. It is like a diary on a rock."

They walked around the museum's interior and were intrigued by the information about the Vikings. Though they learned a lot about the ancient, seagoing people, nothing else seemed to reveal new clues for their search.

Jon took Meg's hand and led her toward the back door. A large sign directed tourists toward a path going from the back of the building to the old, circular fort.

Jon looked up at the dark clouds as they stepped through the door. The cool breeze blew across his face, and he wished he had gotten his jacket out of his luggage.

"We don't have long," Meg acknowledged after looking at her watch. "They're going to close in less than thirty minutes, and it looks like rain."

"At least, we've seen inside the museum. I doubt they'll force us to leave the fort. How can they lock it up?"

The mound of dirt went off in a circular direction to the right and left. Jon and Meg walked across a small bridge that spanned a deep moat. Rocks lined the opening to the fort, and Jon decided that this must have been a tunnel entrance in the past.

The main path continued north through the fort but intersected another path going east to west. Markers showed where longhouses once stood.

Meg pointed to the markers. "I guess longhouses used to be here, like the one we passed outside of the fort."

"I'm thinking the same thing. I want to go through that longhouse replica if we have time. Isn't it interesting that this path goes north and south, and that path goes east and west? If I were a betting man, I'd say it's going perfectly north."

"No doubt by design," Meg agreed. "Other than the round dirt walls and the markers for the houses, there's not much to see in here."

"True," Jon said as he squeezed Meg's hand. She smiled up at him. "Let's go see the longhouse outside and get to the hotel. I want to eat and get to our room before too late."

Meg grinned. "I'm guessing you must be tired from our long flight and all we've done today."

Jon leaned over and kissed his wife. "I'm tired all right, but that's not what I had in mind."

After walking through the longhouse replica, Jon and Meg returned to their rental car. Twenty minutes later, they pulled into the drive of the Comwell Korsor hotel and spa. Red roof tiles accenting the white, stucco building made the complex elegant. Jon thought the two-tiered covered walkway seemed extreme, but the grounds were beautiful.

The lobby area was inviting but not too plush. A gentleman sat at a large Steinway grand piano playing what Jon thought he recognized as Chopin. The staff greeted them in perfect English and directed them to a room on the third floor.

The bellhop pushed their luggage into a room on a cart. "The restaurant is just off the main lobby and open until ten o'clock tonight. The bar stays open later."

"Thank you so much," Jon said as he pressed a twenty-dollar bill into the porter's hand. He regretted not exchanging his American dollars at the airport for Danish kroner.

"Thank you, sir, and welcome to Comwell Korsor."

"This is beautiful," Meg concluded as she looked around the room.

The suite was decorated in a modern motif with white carpet on the floor and Impressionistic paintings on the wall. The furniture in the living room was simple but elegant, and a large, flat-screen television hung on the wall. The roomy bedroom offered a queen-sized bed centered on one wall. A sliding glass door opened to a balcony with a small garden of greenery surrounding two lounge chairs.

"It is beautiful," Jon agreed. "Those prints look like original Renoir."

Meg opened the sliding glass doors and stepped onto the balcony. "Do you think that huge building back there is the spa?"

Jon joined her on the balcony and wrapped his arms around his beautiful wife. "That's my guess." He noted a cart path just below their balcony and a large, white building at the back of the property that looked more like a palace than a spa.

"If you're interested in the spa, we can find out."

"I'd love to, but I doubt we'll have time for such luxuries. We're here on business. Remember?"

Jon turned back around and pulled her close. He looked into her smiling eyes. He could never decide if they were green or blue. He lowered his lips to hers and kissed her passionately. "All work and no play makes Meg a dull girl."

"Is that a fact?" she grinned.

"It is. I know you, and you are no dull girl."

An hour later, Jon stepped out of the shower, toweled off, and pulled on some clean clothes. While waiting for Meg to join him in the living room, he turned on the television to see if he could find any news in English. He was surprised when the T.V. came on to Fox News.

Meg walked into the living room, buttoning up her blouse. "I think I'll go to dinner with wet hair."

"You're gorgeous either way," Jon smiled before kissing his wife.

"So, you found Fox News. Amazing that it's everywhere."

"They are the number one cable news channel, so I'm not surprised. Let's get some dinner. I'm starved."

Ten minutes later, Jon pulled out a chair for Meg in the hotel's restaurant. He heard laughter and looked up to see the same group of girls from the museum walk into the restaurant. "I think that must be a sports team."

"I agree, and from the size of those girls, I'd say a gymnastics team."

"I see their large friends are still standing around, and there's the little blonde right in the middle of them. She seems to be the center of attention."

"She's a cutie," Meg acknowledged. "Give her a few years, and she will be a knock-out. I bet they have a gymnastics meet around here tomorrow. I wish we had time to go watch it."

"That would be nice. Too bad we've got to visit the Jelling Stone tomorrow, and we should go back to the museum."

"You're right, and we've got to be on that plane for London on Sunday afternoon. I don't want to miss that plane because then we'd be getting home later. I can't handle being away from Carla any longer."

"Let's eat and take a walk. After that, I've got to get some sleep."

"I'm tired, too. Tomorrow's going to be a busy day."

"Let's hope it's a productive one. I enjoyed going to the museum but didn't learn anything new about our mystery."

"Me either," Meg admitted. "Oh, my goodness. I forgot to print out Cindy's e-mail."

"We can do it after dinner."

"Let's not forget. I have a feeling it will provide some important information."

Chapter Fifteen
Double Bay

Lacy stared at the calm, blue water that made her feel more like she was standing beside her best friend's swimming pool in fourth grade than staring into the ocean off Eleuthera's coast. She zipped up her light windbreaker and stared at the sun slipping over the eastern horizon. She put her hands in the pockets of her jacket and smiled. She'd be burning up under the tropical sun in a few hours, but she felt as free as the seagulls flying overhead.

She pulled her blonde hair back into a ponytail and threaded it through the hole in the back of her hat. Well, it wasn't officially her hat. It was Kerrick's University of Miami hat. Just wearing it made her feel close to him. *How have I fallen so hard for this guy? I vowed never to love a guy, and here I am, neck-deep in love. Okay, so maybe that's an exaggeration. I'm not neck deep—maybe knee-deep.*

"What ya got on your mind?" Kerrick whispered into Lacy's ear as he wrapped his arms around her.

Lacy jumped in surprise, bumping her head into Kerrick's chin.

"Kerrick! You scared me to death."

"Well, you about made me bite my tongue in half."

"It's not my fault. You're the one who surprised me, and you should keep your tongue inside your mouth."

"Sorry. So…do you think we'll finish mapping the bay before Jon and Meg return?"

"If they're coming home Monday, I'd say there's not a chance in…in heaven. I can't believe I almost cursed. I haven't even said a slang word in days."

"Wow," Kerrick mocked. "That's a real record."

Lacy jabbed her elbow into his side. Kerrick recoiled but then pulled her close to him. Lacy enjoyed the feel of his hard body and thought how nicely they fit together, kind of like it was meant to be. She felt warm all over, quite different from her usual arctic state. She was secure and at peace and felt like the anchor of her heart was buried deep into something immovable. *I do have it bad.*

"So, what's up for today, Captain Henderson?"

"I'm not the captain," Lacy protested. "You are."

"I'm not in charge of this operation."

Lacy turned and put her finger on Kerrick's chest. "Yes, you are, so get used to it. You know good and well what's up for today. The same thing as yesterday and the day before that."

"I suppose you're right about what's on tap, but for the record, Jose is in charge with Jon away. I just hope we find something today." Kerrick leaned down and gave Lacy a quick kiss. "Let's get some breakfast, and then we need to meet with everyone in the conference room. Jose suggested we review a few safety precautions before we dive today. He said that he saw a few of the boys being a little careless."

"It's easy to get careless in such shallow water," Lacy admitted. "You feel like you're in a swimming pool instead of the ocean."

"Unfortunately, a twelve-foot tiger shark might be floating around in this swimming pool."

Lacy shivered as she recalled their close encounter with a tiger shark two weeks earlier. "Let's not make light of sharks right now."

"I'm sorry. I didn't mean to bring up bad memories."

"If we miss breakfast," Lacy changed the subject, "that will be a bad memory. I'm starving."

By the time they sat in the dining hall, Jose, Ann, and the four boys were already eating their meals. Lacy's stomach growled as she worked to prepare her pancakes.

"Morning, Lacy," Ann said as she carried her tray back to the kitchen.

"I'll be right back," Kerrick promised. "Gotta go to the bathroom."

"Morning, Ann. You diving with us today?"

"I don't think so. I'm not feeling so well."

"Are you okay? You sure have been sick a lot. It seems like every morning you complain…Oh, my God. Every morning you complain about being sick…morning sickness. You're p…"

"Don't say it," Ann gasped. "We don't know that's true."

"Come on, Ann. You can count to thirty. Are you afraid? Having a baby's not so bad."

"And you know that because of…"

"Okay, I don't know anything about it, but Meg seems to think it's pretty cool."

"You're right," Ann agreed. "Having children is a wonderful blessing. Jose and I want to have children, but I'm not sure I'm ready."

Lacy winked. "Well, ready or not, I think you're about to learn about this blessing."

Ann turned as white as a sheet. "I've got to go. Don't tell anyone." She rushed out of the dining hall.

"What are you grinning about," Kerrick said as he returned to his seat.

"If I told you, I'd have to kill you." Lacy laughed. "Nothing. Let's say nothing."

"For some reason, I'm inclined not to believe you. You and Ann are up to something."

"Okay, everyone," Jose announced from the front of the dining hall. "Let's meet in the conference room in ten minutes."

"Ten minutes," Lacy gasped. "I just started eating."

"You can eat that stack of pancakes in ten minutes."

"I'm not a caveman."

"You certainly are not." Kerrick grinned.

"I mean cave woman. I don't inhale my food."

"Suit yourself, but I'm getting the clean plate award and on-time award." Kerrick dove into his pancakes like he hadn't eaten in a month.

Twelve minutes later, Lacy let out a tiny belch as she sat in the conference room. She was going to regret eating so fast.

"All right, guys…and girls," Jose grinned.

Lacy looked around to find Ann, but she wasn't in the conference room.

"We've got to step it up today. We started mapping out this bay on Tuesday and are a little over halfway done. Granted, we had only half a day Tuesday, and the weather slowed us down on Thursday. We have saved some time by going ahead with the sled now instead of waiting until the whole bay is mapped. We're going to work hard today and tomorrow afternoon. I want us to finish by the end of the day Monday."

"What about Sunday morning?" Tae wondered. "We taking the morning off?"

"Yes, we are," Jose announced. "We'll visit an old friend at the Preacher's Cave."

"You mean we're going back to church?" Lacy stammered.

"Yes, ma'am. I ran into Mr. Phil Register early this morning near the marina when I went to fill up with fuel. He invited us."

"Us?" Lacy quizzed as she waved her hand toward the boys. "How does he know about us?"

"I'm embarrassed to report that I fudged a little on the truth and told him that we met the boys on Nassau and agreed to work with them on their scuba diving. He thinks we're donating some time to a boys' club."

"Going to church at the Preacher's Cave wasn't so bad, Lacy," Kerrick observed. "I think you enjoyed it."

"I'm not complaining; I'm questioning the wisdom of it."

"Thank you, Lacy, for your attention to detail," Jose smiled. "It will be fine. I thought it would give the boys a different experience. Besides, church will do everyone some good."

Lacy thought back to her previous trip to the Preacher's Cave. It was unlike any church service she had attended, not that she had been to many. The first settlers used the cave for sanctuary from the storm, but it became their church. When Lacy last went to church at the Preacher's Cave, she wore shorts and flip-flops, which would have never worked at the church she attended back home in Griffin with her best friend. The girl who sang was about her age, and Mr. Phil told her that the girl had been abused. How could she stand before that group smiling and singing about love?

"Boys, we've got to remember that even though this water seems safe, we need to show as much caution as if we were diving in one hundred feet of water. You're in as much danger of scraping coral, getting hit by a sting ray, or encountering a hungry shark here as anywhere in the ocean. We've gotten a little careless over the last few days. Any questions?"

Lacy looked around at everyone in the room. These boys had matured so fast over the last month. She recalled the day they first met on the dock in Miami. They were rough kids who didn't know how to wear a hat and were far too impressed with their underwear. She smiled as she remembered Jon telling Tae that he would wear his pants around his waist or go home to show his underwear to someone in D.C.

"Ann is not going to dive today, so I want Marcy to work with me on the sled," Jose continued.

Marcy's short ponytail bounced up and down as she nodded. She was such a sweet girl, and Lacy loved her as a sister, maybe even better than a sister. Lacy was so glad that Marcy was interning with her. She was cute and full of personality. Marcy looked at Lacy and smiled as if she knew Lacy was thinking about her.

"Kerrick, you can help with the sled from the Robalo. I'm assuming the monitor is still aboard?"

"I take it out of the boat daily for safety, but I'll get it back aboard."

"Lacy, can you lead the boys with the grid work? We need you to flag the big obstacles. The last thing I want to do is run the sled into a big piece of coral. The sonar equipment on that thing cost Jon a small fortune. Okay, everyone good?"

Grunts arose from the group Lacy assumed meant no one had a problem. She was ready to find something of value. Creating search grids on the ocean floor was about as dull as picking up pinecones for her neighbor in sixth grade. She hoped today would prove to be memorable.

Oh, no. I forgot to shave. That's what I get for taking a shower last night instead of this morning. I can't go another day with my legs looking like a forest of tree stumps. Can I shave, get into my swimsuit, and be ready to dive in twenty minutes? Why am I always rushing around and being late for everything while Kerrick doesn't seem to have a care in the world?

Lacy hurried to her quarters and began the frustrating task of making her legs smooth for…for whom? Why was she worried about how her legs looked? Guys didn't have to mess with shaving their legs. The stubble on Kerrick's face showed that he wasn't too worried about shaving, making him look sexy as… sexy as…*It just makes him look sexy.*

Once in her bathing suit, she studied her wetsuit options. She dove without her wetsuit the day before and about froze to death at one point. It's not that the water was so cold, but they dipped a little deeper for a while. They also swam through thermoclines from time to time. She was going to be prepared today. She decided against wearing the full farmer john and went with the shorty. Her legs would be fine now that they were as smooth as glass.

Once she got to the ladder, she saw everyone else aboard the Carver. *Last again.* It was a lot easier working the bay from the smaller yacht than the research vessel. The bay proved to be too shallow for the larger ship anyway. Kerrick hopped into the smaller Robalo and pulled away from the ship.

"Okay, guys," Lacy said as she joined the boys on the back of the yacht. "Tae and I will form the outside of the grid. David, you, Barry, and Aaron can run the tape on the inside of the grid. You need to keep them ten feet apart. Yesterday, we started getting them a little too close."

"It's hard to figure out ten feet, Lacy," Barry complained.

"I know. Just think of it as two body lengths."

Lacy was so relieved to drop into the water. Her wetsuit fit her like a glove, and she started sweating. She wished she could enjoy the water without the wetsuit. The rays of the morning sun lit up the sea floor, and color greeted her as she descended to the shallow bottom. She knelt in the sand to get her bearings and saw the digital readout on her computer register twenty feet deep. She and each of the boys had a bag strapped over their shoulders filled with stakes and tape. Tae had a small sledgehammer he used to drive the stakes into the sand. It looked like he was moving in slow motion when he did it, but the process worked.

The work was dull but important. Lunchtime offered a much-needed break. As Lacy peeled out of her wetsuit, she felt like a banana but looked like a prune.

Just when everyone was about finished with lunch, Jose walked into the dining area with a large grin. "Ladies and gentlemen. I've been reviewing the readouts from the sled, and we've found something."

Chapter Sixteen

Foiled

"I think we've found something." Meg looked up from the Jelling Stone.

"I don't see anything," Jon confessed, "at least nothing that has anything to do with our medallion. I see that King Bluetooth wanted the world to know that he won the whole of Denmark and made the Danes Christians."

Meg backed away a few steps from the two large stones. Though she couldn't understand the Runic letters on the smaller stone, a sign in front of the encasement translated it into several languages, including English:

Harald, the King, bade do these sepulchral monuments after Gorm, his father, and after Thyra his mother. The Harald who won the whole of Denmark and all of Norway and made the Danes Christian.

Meg looked at the artwork on the larger stone. "I see two things. First, Harald was fond of unity and family. He crafted these stones in memory of his parents. That doesn't sound like a rough Viking type to me. He became a Christian, for one thing, so maybe peace and relationships became more important to him because of his faith. He wanted Denmark to be united, and he wanted them to share his faith in Christ."

"So, he was a Christian who loved his family and wanted everyone to get along. I still don't see the connection."

"Think back to the material Cindy sent us about his children. His son... what was his name?"

"Sweyn."

"Right. Sweyn."

"He had two daughters too, but I don't remember hearing their names."

"Don't you suppose this site had to be an embarrassment to the king, Jon? Think how he felt about this place after he became a Christian. Years earlier, he buried his father here with all the pagan rituals. He even buried his father's horse and armor in preparing him for the afterlife. After Bluetooth became a Christian, he came back here to build a church and try to change the pagan focus of the site. He exhumed his father's body and buried it in a new spot. He placed the stones here as a monument to the change in his life, family, and Denmark."

"Hence the name, 'The Birth Certificate of Denmark.' He was trying to make his father a Christian after he died. Too bad it doesn't work that way."

"If Bluetooth was embarrassed about burying his father like a pagan, he was also ashamed of his son's rebellion. It disrupted peace in his family."

"I'm sure his son broke his heart."

"According to Cindy's research, Sweyn may have even killed his father."

"Or had him killed," Jon suggested.

"What Bluetooth wanted more than anything was healing in his country and his family. Look at the snake-like creature he carved on this rock. I bet Bluetooth put that there to represent evil attacking his family."

Jon thought for a moment. "It's got to represent something. Why do you think he chose a lion with a snake? Or is that a lion?"

"Isn't a lion a biblical symbol for Jesus? I'm not sure, but look over here at the carving of Christ."

They took a few steps toward the larger stone before Meg continued. "First, it's interesting he didn't include a cross but look how his body makes a cross. Here's the thing that keeps grabbing my eye, though. Do you see this circle around the middle of Christ's body? Look at the line that seems to go across his body, well, maybe behind his body. Does that remind you of anything?"

"The trelleborg! That looks like the circular fort with the intersecting roads."

"Exactly! Jesus provides the north and south portions of the path, and this line represents the east and west. That would make sense to a Viking. North was so important to them. The north star provided one of their main navigation tools, and they considered themselves to live in the north. I'm guessing that Bluetooth saw Jesus as the way home, that is the way to real peace. I may be reaching for things with that one, but that circle looks like the fort."

"So, what does it mean?" Jon asked.

"I don't know," Meg admitted. "I think it's just a few more pieces to the puzzle."

"We've got some interesting information, but I'm unsure what to do with it. I feel like we're putting a puzzle together without a picture showing the finished product."

"Oh, Jon. I just realized I never finished reading what Cindy said about a new discovery of treasure."

A smile crossed Meg's face as she remembered lying in bed the night before reading to her husband. She would have finished reading the material to him, but Jon had other things in mind. She was glad she had taken the time to read the remaining information while he was showering this morning.

"New treasure? Really? Where is it?"

"I think it was in Sweden. Something in the collection indicates that it belonged to King Harald."

"I wish we knew where that was located and how we could see it. I suggest we go back by the museum to make sure we didn't miss anything. We can ask them about this new stash of treasure. Then, I suggest we return to the hotel."

The return trip to the museum turned out to be pointless. The lady at the desk had no idea about a new discovery of King Harald's treasure. Jon insisted on it being in a museum somewhere in Denmark, but the lady seemed clueless.

The trip back to the hotel was quiet. Meg couldn't get the Jelling Stone images off her mind. She felt Jon's hand on her leg and realized he had said something she missed.

A sheepish grin spread across Meg's face. "I'm sorry, sweetheart. I've been a little consumed with thoughts about the stones. What did you say?"

"I asked if you wanted to go to the spa."

"That sounds good. I would enjoy a good massage."

They arrived at the hotel, and Meg called the attendant at the front desk. Because the spa offered more than one masseuse, the receptionist informed Meg of several openings that evening.

Because of the woman's strong, trained hands, Meg began feeling the tension of the last few days floating away. She lay near comatose and began to feel more like a jellyfish than a human.

When the session ended, the masseuse suggested Meg rest on the table until she felt ready to return to the reception area. Sometime later, Meg jolted awake at the sound of the door closing.

Familiar hands rubbed her bare back. "You okay?"

"Hey. I think I fell asleep."

"I was beginning to think you disappeared."

"I'm wiped out. I don't think I'll have any trouble sleeping tonight."

Meg stepped into the bathroom and showered. When she rejoined Jon, they walked past the swimming pool and saw the gymnastics team enjoying the water. Meg didn't notice the little blonde girl, but they all looked alike with wet hair.

As they stepped out of the elevator on their floor, Meg looked up the hallway, which made a "T" shape with an adjoining hall. They saw a man carrying a girl in his arms. He was in the far hall heading toward the other end of the building. She must have been asleep because she was much too big to be carried.

Meg touched Jon's arm. "I think that girl was the blonde from the gymnastics team. Why was that man carrying her?"

Jon took Meg's hand and quickened his pace. "And that man was the guy in the museum who kept staring at you. Something's not right. Where are her bodyguards?"

They rounded the corner, and Meg saw the door to the stairway closing. Jon headed for the door, and Meg hurried behind him. So many things were racing through Meg's mind. Who was this man? What was he doing? Is this even safe to be running after him? What if he's innocent?

Jon and Meg burst through the door to the stairway and saw the man at the top of the stairs. He was holding the girl and fumbling with his phone like he was trying to make a call. He turned and looked straight into Meg's face with a threatening look of anger and foreboding. She knew something horrible was about to happen.

The man dropped the phone and adjusted his grip on the girl, reaching under his jacket with the other hand. Jon leaped forward and punched the man right in the face. Meg gasped as the man pitched forward down the four steps to a narrow landing. The girl landed atop him, and a pistol skidded away from his limp body.

Meg hurried to the girl, who was sound asleep, but okay. The man's body shielded her from the force of the fall. She was out cold. *He must have drugged her.*

"I think this is a kidnapping," Jon panted.

Meg heard a voice that sounded like it was coming from inside a tin box. She saw the phone lying on the floor and realized the man had dialed someone before dropping the phone.

"We've got to get out of here," Meg whispered. "I'm afraid he's not alone."

Jon checked the man's neck for a pulse. "I don't think he's alive. Let's go."

Jon picked up the girl, ran back up the short flight of stairs, and hurried down the hall. As Meg ran after him, she wondered why he didn't go down the stairs. They passed a room with an open door, and one of the bodyguards lay face down on the floor in a pool of blood.

When they came to the stairwell at the opposite end of the hall, Jon stopped and looked through the small window on the door. He pushed the door open, and they stepped onto the landing.

"I'm sure that guy has a lot of help around here," Jon guessed. "We can't run through the lobby with this girl, and I don't have my cell phone."

"Maybe we should go back to our room and call for help."

Meg looked through the door window and saw a man hurrying down the other end of the hall. "Oh, no. There's another man. We're in trouble if we don't get out of here."

Chapter Seventeen
Escape

Standing in the muggy stairwell, Meg felt sweat running down her back. A dead man lay at the foot of the stairs at the opposite end of the hall, and her husband held the girl the guy was attempting to kidnap. *Since we've seen two men already, who's to say a dozen more aren't involved in this scheme?*

"We only have one choice," Jon decided. "We've got to get this little girl out of here. If we go out the door at the bottom of these steps, our car should be close."

"I think it's around the corner of the building. It's more in the front lot than the side one."

"Meg, you can go get the car and pull around near this side entrance, and I'll carry the girl to the car once you drive up."

"Okay, but what about a key?"

Jon shifted the girl in his arms. "It's in my right pocket. Can you reach in and get it?"

Meg pulled the key fob from Jon's pants pocket and hurried down two flights of steps. Before opening the door, she looked through the glass to see if any men were waiting outside. She considered the fact that at least it was dark outside. That would provide some cover. Hopefully, no one would notice her, and maybe they could get the girl in the car without drawing any attention. She didn't see any movement outside.

Meg tried not to hurry across the parking lot, and when she got to the driver's door of the rental, she noticed a white van parked on the other side of the building. Two suspicious-looking men stood near the front entrance. *I'm glad we didn't come through the lobby. I bet more of those goons are inside.*

Meg started the car and eased toward the north side of the building. Jon came out of the hotel carrying the girl, and Meg reached across the seat to open the car door for him. As soon as Jon closed the door, Meg crept out of the parking lot onto the main drive.

"Take the E20 back toward Slagelse," Jon ordered.

"Where are we going?"

"I don't know. I want to make sure no one is following us, and then we'll exit to find a phone."

Meg noticed the girl's bright pink bathing suit under her robe. She was a pretty little girl with blonde hair and refined facial features. Meg thought of her as a little girl, but she was at least twelve and becoming a young woman.

The girl stirred. "I think she may be waking up," Jon whispered.

"I sure wish she would stay asleep until we can get her to the police."

The girl's bright, blue eyes popped open and locked onto Jon's face. She screamed and began attacking him. Her fingernails scratched the side of his face, and a little blood beaded up near Jon's right ear.

Jon pinned her arms to her side. "Hey. We're trying to help you. We're not the bad guys."

"It's okay, sweetheart," Meg offered. "You're safe now. Do you speak English?"

The girl collapsed against Jon and sobbed, but Jon didn't release her arms.

"Do you speak English?" Meg repeated.

"Yes," the girl whimpered. "A little."

"Take this exit," Jon blurted. "I'm pretty sure there's a gas station on the corner."

Meg took a right and headed down the ramp.

"On second thought," Jon said, "pull into that hotel."

Meg took another right at the bottom of the ramp and pulled into the parking lot of a building that looked like a hotel. She couldn't see the name anywhere.

"Sweetheart," Meg said again. "Some bad men tried to kidnap you, but we rescued you. Do you understand?"

"Yes," the girl whimpered. "Where is Victor?"

Meg assumed Victor was one of her bodyguards. He may be the one lying on the floor in her room.

"I don't know. We're going inside this hotel and calling the police. You're safe now."

The girl leaned her head into Jon's neck and cried. Her arms went slack, and Jon released his grip on her.

"What's your name?" Jon asked.

"Astra."

"Astra?" Meg repeated. "You have a beautiful name. My name is Meg, and this is my husband, Jon."

Meg jumped out of the car and hurried to Jon's door. She figured Astra would feel more comfortable with a woman. She helped her out of the car and brushed the blonde hair out of her eyes. A tear trickled down the girl's cheek.

"Everything's going to be okay. We'll have you with your parents in no time."

Meg put her arm around Astra's trembling body, and the three walked into the hotel. Astra stumbled, so Meg slid her hand under her arm to support her. She felt the girl lean into her body.

Jon held open an inner door so Meg and Astra could enter the lobby, and the strong smell of lemon disinfectant greeted them. The décor was simple, but the place was quite clean. It didn't come close to the opulence of the Comwell Korsor, but she concluded that she would be fine with staying here. The elderly man behind the counter said something in Danish.

"Do you speak English?" Jon asked. "We're from the United States."

"Yes," the man replied with a bit of a British accent. "Good evening, and welcome to Hotel Provence. What a beautiful family. Your daughter is the spitting image of our little princess."

Meg figured the man must have a twelve-year-old granddaughter.

"What we need," Jon interjected, "is to use your phone. We need to call the police."

"Oh? Is there a problem?"

"It's a long story."

The attendant dialed a number on the phone and handed the receiver to Jon.

Meg could hear Jon's end of the conversation. "Hello. Do you speak English...My name is Jon Davenport. My wife and I are staying at the Comwell Korsor Hotel and Spa, and tonight we foiled a kidnapping attempt. We have the little girl, or young lady, with us..." Jon's face went ashen white. "Yes. Her name is Astra."

Meg saw the man behind the counter drop into his chair, and he looked as if he were going to faint. *What's going on?*

"Yes, that's right," Jon said into the receiver. "We are in the lobby of the Hotel Provence, not too far from the Comwell...Okay. Thank you. We'll be waiting here."

Jon looked at the tear-stained cheeks of the blonde gymnast. "Well, Princess; it's a pleasure to meet you. We had no idea you were the Queen's granddaughter."

Meg felt her jaw fall open. "You're the Queen's granddaughter?"

"Yes, ma'am. My mother is the Crown Princess. I'm sure that's why the men tried to kidnap me. Thank you for saving me."

"Sir," Jon said as he turned toward the stunned attendant, "do you have a small room where we can wait for the police?"

The man cleared his throat. "Yes...Yes, sir. Come this way."

As they took a side hall to a small meeting room, Meg heard the man mumbling something in Danish. She looked at Jon and raised an eyebrow.

Astra grinned up at Meg. "He's saying that Mary will never believe this. I think Mary must be his wife."

As they entered a paneled room with a large conference table in the center and a coffee service against one wall, Astra said something to the attendant in Danish. "I asked him to bring a cloth for Mr. Jon's face. We can at least wipe the blood off. I'm so sorry I scratched you. I hope it doesn't scar."

Jon smiled. "Thank you, Astra. You don't need to apologize. You thought we were the bad guys. It will be a great reminder of a brave young lady if it scars."

Meg continued holding Astra's hand as they sat in office chairs at the large oak table. The receptionist returned with a damp cloth and handed it to Jon. The young princess' hands had ceased trembling, but she didn't want to let go of Meg's hand.

"Pardon me," Astra murmured. "I need to go to the...what do you call it in the States? The loo?"

"Close enough," Meg said with a laugh. "I'll go with you and help you clean up your face." She looked at the attendant, who seemed to have regained a little color. "Sir, do you have another washcloth the Princess could use?"

The man retrieved a washcloth, and Meg took Astra's hand. "Come on, Sweetheart. I believe the restrooms are down the hall. That's what we call them in the States. Restrooms."

Astra grinned up at Meg as they headed out the door. By the time they returned to the conference room, Astra was laughing, and Meg had combed the girl's beautiful hair with her fingers. They sat down at the table next to Jon and across from the receptionist.

Within a few minutes, the police spilled into the room with weapons drawn.

"You do not need the weapons, gentlemen," Jon announced. "The princess is right here and ready to go home."

The officers maintained their positions, and a short man walked forward with his hand extended. "Dr. Davenport?"

Meg was a little surprised. *How did he know Jon's identity? Someone did some fast research, thanks to Google.*

"Yes, I'm Jon Davenport. We rescued Princess Astra but didn't know she was the princess."

Another officer said something in Danish to Astra, but she shook her head and leaned into Meg. "Isn't it okay for me to stay with you?"

Meg smiled and put her arm around the young princess. "Of course, you can, but I'm sure your parents are very worried."

"Sir," the officer in charge said to Jon, "we ask you to come with us for your safety. One of our officers retrieved your luggage from the Comwell."

"I suppose that means you didn't capture the kidnappers."

"No, sir. We did not. We found a lot of blood in one of the stairwells, and one of our officers was shot in front of the hotel. We hope to catch the kidnappers soon."

Meg remembered seeing the two men in front of the hotel. "I'm so sorry. When we left, I saw two men in front of the hotel, and I assumed they were with the man who was taking A...Princess Astra."

The princess squeezed Meg's hand and said quietly, "You can call me Astra."

"We will need a full statement from both of you," the officer asserted.

"Of course," Jon agreed. "We're happy to cooperate any way we can."

Another officer stepped forward as he slipped a phone into his pocket. "Princess Anne and Prince Erik have asked you to come to the Amalienborg Palace. They ask in part for your protection and because they wish to express their gratitude."

"We are honored to meet with Prince Erik and Princess Anne. Where is the palace?"

"The palace is in Copenhagen. Although Princess Astra and her family live at Fredensborg Palace most of the time, they've spent the week in Copenhagen, so we'll find the entire royal family there. They are quite anxious."

"I'm sure," Jon said as he pulled out his cell phone and opened his GPS. "Can you give me directions or an address?"

"We'll take you to a helipad near here and fly you to the palace. One of my agents will bring along your rental car."

Jon took Meg's free hand, and the three headed toward the conference room door. Standing in the hallway, officers surrounded them like human shields. Once at the double doors in the lobby, the officer in charge asked them to wait a moment while they secured the perimeter. A patrol car drove up as close to the entrance as possible, and the Davenports and Princess Astra hurried into the car.

"This has been the strangest trip," Meg proposed. "Who would have imagined that we'd rescue a princess and visit the palace?"

"You can say that again," Jon laughed.

"Surely nothing else exciting will happen tonight. I don't think my heart can stand it."

Chapter Eighteen
Terror in the Night

Lacy couldn't believe it. They had found something! Finally! Pulling colored tape and driving stakes in the ground had lost its glamor after about ten minutes. Searching for sunken treasure seemed exciting when Meg called her back in April, but now, the excitement took a back seat to plain old hard work.

The shallow bay allowed such a long bottom time that Lacy could stay underwater for over an hour. She had spent so much time underwater over the last few days that she began to worry about what the salt water might do to her skin.

"We've found something, and it's quite large," Jose said again.

Cheers rose from the entire group, and Lacy couldn't remove the silly grin from her face. Everyone had crammed into the galley of the *New Beginnings* to hear the news, and now the room grew warmer with the body heat. No one seemed to care. Barry gave David a high five, and to Lacy's shock, Kerrick kissed her in front of everyone.

"Ooooh," Tae shouted. "Public display of affection! I think that's breaking some rules."

"That's school," David blurted. "Kiss her again, or I will."

"I don't think so," Kerrick replied.

"You don't think what?" Barry laughed. "That you'll kiss her again or that David will?"

Everyone laughed as Jose tried to get everyone's attention. "Okay, ladies and gentlemen. Listen up! We have a sizable reading on our sonar that's got to be metal. For metal to survive in the salt water, it's either not been submerged very long or quite thick."

"So," Aaron drawled, "if it hasn't been down long, then it's not our ship?"

"Correct," Jose agreed. "Retrieving this object presents a problem because we can't get *The Discoverer* into this shallow bay. I'm also afraid we'd draw undue attention to ourselves."

"Why do we need *The Discoverer?*" David asked.

"The seavac," Jose replied. "Digging up the object without using the seavac will present a challenge."

Marcy sat her cup of soda down into the circular opening on the table that was made to keep cups from sliding around. "Can we put the seavac on the *New Beginnings*? Can't the crane lower the motor onto the back of the Carver? Dealing with that much hose might be a problem, but I'm sure we can handle it."

"We wouldn't have to coil up all the hose on the *New Beginnings*," Kerrick suggested. "We can let the part that dumps the sand float out of the back. Because it's so shallow in the bay, we wouldn't need too much hose on the other side...fifty feet at the most. The vacuum hose comes apart in fifty-foot sections."

"That can work," Jose said slowly. "The exit hose requires length to get the sand far away from the dig site, but it can drift behind the Carver. Good idea."

"The one thing we might have to worry about," Lacy added, "is someone watching us from shore. Using a massive vacuum cleaner with long hoses doesn't even come close to resembling sport diving."

"Do it at night," Barry suggested. "If you want to do something you don't want anyone to know about, you do it at night."

Tae slapped Barry on the back. "Sounds like a man with experience."

Barry grinned. "I'm just saying."

"I like it," Jose acknowledged. "It's time you boys have a night dive anyway. Let's go back to *The Discover* and prepare for a night dive. We'll have to strap down the seavac motor to the back deck so it can't slide around but using the Carver should work fine."

Kerrick and Lacy climbed to the bridge, and Kerrick engaged the motor that pulled the anchor up. Within a few minutes, the yacht headed seaward toward the larger research vessel.

The refreshing wind blew against Lacy's face, and she felt so carefree. She was sailing aboard a beautiful yacht in the Bahamas with an awesome guy. Her smile turned into a frown as she thought that the only negative thing in her life now was the sun's blinding rays. She pulled Kerrick's hat from his head and threaded her ponytail through the back before slipping it into place.

"Hey! You already have two of my hats."

"I'm not going to keep it. If I keep squinting into the sun like this, my face will be all wrinkled by the time I'm thirty. You don't want that, do you?"

"I suppose not," Kerrick grinned. "What were you smiling about?"

"I wasn't smiling."

"Yes, you were. You must be happy that your birthday is next week."

"Don't mention it. You ruined a perfect moment."

"What's wrong with having a birthday? Nineteen is a great age, full of possibilities."

"I don't want to think about it."

"Why? Oh, it's because of your mother. Lacy, you've got to come to terms with her."

"I don't have to do anything," Lacy frowned. "As far as I'm concerned, I don't have a mother. She can visit you if she wants to, but I won't be around."

"Come on, Lacy. Be reasonable."

Lacy changed the subject. "Should we call Jon and Meg? I'm sure they would want to know that we found something."

Kerrick sighed. "I'd suggest we wait to see what we've found and then call them."

"Sounds like a plan. No need to get their hopes up."

Kerrick pulled the Carver up next to the larger ship. Jose reached up to unlatch the lower part of the steps, allowing them almost to touch the deck of the *New Beginnings*. Jon had someone make adjustable steps that dropped from the deck of *The Discoverer* to the yacht. They made going back and forth between the two ships much easier.

Jose shouted up to the bridge before climbing the steps. "Kerrick, how about bringing the Carver to the back of the ship? I'll drop the seavac aboard with the crane. It will take me a few minutes to get everything ready."

"Okay," Kerrick shouted above the noise of the ship's engines. "Are we going to eat dinner here and then head back?"

Jose grinned. "Are you afraid of my cooking?"

"You've got to admit that Chef Marceau is pretty hard to beat."

"Okay. You talked me into it. We'll wait til dark to head back to the bay."

As Jose climbed and pulled the hinged section of the steps back up into place, Lacy put Kerrick's hat back on his head. "He didn't take much convincing…I mean, about eating supper here."

Kerrick laughed as he straightened his hat and pulled the yacht away from the side of *The Discoverer*. "I have a feeling he planned to eat here all along. If you reach under the steering wheel, you'll find some sunglasses for your delicate eyes."

Lacy reached around Kerrick for the glasses. She slid her hand up his chest and pulled out a chest hair.

"Hey! That hurt."

"You shouldn't be so delicate."

Lacy climbed down to the back deck and positioned herself at the back of the boat. She figured someone needed to guide the seavac into place.

Within thirty minutes, the large vacuum cleaner rested on the back of the *New Beginnings*, and Lacy strapped it down with some wide, ratchet tie-downs. Kerrick pulled the Carver back in position beside the research vessel and tied the boat snugly against the rubber bumpers near the steps. He and Lacy scurried aboard *The Discover*, hoping to take a shower before dinner.

"I can't wait to get this salt off my body," Lacy said. "It's got to be messing with my hair."

"Your hair has lightened up if that's possible."

"Really?"

"Yeah. Really."

Kerrick pulled her face up toward his and kissed her. "I'll see you at dinner."

About seven hours later, Kerrick pulled the Carver yacht away from *The Discoverer* and pointed the bow toward Double Bay. The last remnants of the sun began disappearing over the horizon behind them as Lacy pulled her wetsuit on and performed a final check on her equipment. She and Aaron planned to work the seavac while Marcy and the other boys kept the area illuminated with underwater lights. Jose intended to watch over the operation to ensure no one got into trouble.

The thoughts of another night dive filled Lacy with excitement. She had been on two night dives, and they were both thrilling. She dove the jetties at St. Andrews State Park in Panama City Beach, Florida, one night the previous summer. Diving in the ocean at night blew her mind. She saw her first octopus on that dive, and a nurse shark scared her to death. The creature that kept his head hidden under the reef all day almost bumped into her. That dive's only negative thing was her diving partner, Ben Robbins. What a jerk!

"Okay, guys," Lacy called out to the boys. "Come to the back of the boat to get your lights. Remember that we are here on business. This is not playtime. You'll be tempted to look around, but our main job right now is to dig up whatever is buried beneath us."

"Can't we look around a little?" Tae begged. "We've never been in the ocean at night before."

"I'm not sure I want to be in the ocean at night," Barry whispered.

"Don't be such a baby," David challenged. "You know that *Jaws* was just a movie."

"I've never seen *Jaws*," Barry admitted, "but I remember our dive a few weeks ago."

Lacy took a couple of steps toward the boys. "He's not a baby. We should all be a little frightened. It will help us to maintain our respect for the sea. Jose's going to keep watch over us."

Almost as if on cue, Jose walked forward. He carried a large, 44-magnum bangstick in his hand and a smaller one strapped to his leg. "We'll take the first fifteen minutes to enjoy a night dive. After that, it's back to treasure hunting. I suggest you wait to turn on your flashlights until you're in the water. You'll never forget the sensation. We may have to come back up to get fresh tanks before we uncover the…whatever it is."

"What do you think it is?" Aaron asked.

"Any guesses?" Jon queried.

"Maybe another one of the ark things?" Tae quipped.

Jose laughed. "You mean arequebus. I suppose it could be."

Marcy raised her hand like she was in math class. "My guess is a cannon. Think about it. The area was lit up on the sonar, so it's not something small. It's also got to be thick, or at least we've sort of guessed that it is."

"Good guess, Marcy," Jose congratulated. "I suppose we'll know soon enough."

Lacy sucked air through her regulator to make sure it was working properly and then stepped off the boat. The anticipation of falling into the dark sea had her stomach in knots, but she couldn't wait to see the ocean at night. She remembered from her past night dives that the underwater world was quite different at night than in the day.

As the bubbles of her entrance passed her face, she reached up to turn on the headlight she wore but couldn't find the switch. *I'll get Barry to turn it on for me.* Even though it put out only a little light, it would make her feel more secure.

As Lacy hovered about ten feet deep, waiting on the other guys to join her, Barry stepped into the water. Lacy smiled when she realized his flashlight was on before he even hit the water. The water around her glowed in Barry's light. As she turned away from him to start her descent to the bottom, her excitement turned into a garbled scream.

Chapter Nineteen
Amalienborg Palace

The drive to the helipad took longer than the flight to the palace. Meg looked out the helicopter's windows to the glowing palace below them. It appeared to be four palaces in a circle, with a statue in the middle. The pilot set the helicopter down near the statue of Fredrick V on horseback, located in the center of the massive circle. Several cars pulled forward as Jon and Meg stepped to the ground, and the strong, cold wind created by the rotor blades sent a chill down her back.

Astra jumped from the helicopter and ran into the open arms of a woman Meg knew had to be her mother. Though the young princess spoke Danish, Meg had no trouble understanding the word for mother: *Mor*. She learned the word when she watched a special on T.V. about the growing number of single women in Denmark choosing to become mothers.

"Mother, this is Meg and Jon Davenport."

With tears running down her cheeks, Princess Anne Larsen crossed the few feet between her and Meg. She wrapped Meg in her arms and held her for several seconds.

Anne's husband, the Crown Prince, extended his hand toward Jon. "Hello. I'm Erik. Thank you so much for saving our daughter. You put your lives at risk for our little girl. How can we ever thank you?"

Jon shook Prince Erik's hand and smiled. "You are very welcome. We had no idea she was your daughter or related to the

Queen. I'm so glad we happened to get out of the elevator when the man walked by with her."

Erik stepped back toward his wife, who had composed herself somewhat. "My mother wishes to meet with you inside. She is grateful for your service and wants to hear the entire story."

"We're honored," Jon said with a slight bow.

It seemed silly to get into an automobile to drive a few hundred feet to the palace's front door, but a driver held a door open for them to enter a shiny, black Mercedes. Meg looked around at Jon, but he shrugged.

The driver smiled and spoke with a heavy accent as if he had been reading Meg's mind. "It's for your safety, ma'am. The Security Service insists upon it."

Meg looked around at the massive complex as she slid into the back seat. The statue sat in the middle of a huge, open area surrounded by four identical buildings reflecting a classical style of architecture. A road lined with additional buildings came in from the west, and an opening to the east revealed a huge fountain in front of a body of water. She saw another structure on the opposite side of the water. Without thinking, she buckled her seatbelt. She watched out the window as Astra and her parents entered another car.

She felt safe in the palace complex and wondered why the Security Service still had concerns. Jon climbed in beside her and took her hand.

"Are we still in danger?" Meg whispered in her husband's ear.

"Maybe, but I doubt it. I imagine they are just taking every precaution."

The car stopped in front of the large building near the northeastern entrance to the palace complex. The driver jumped out and hurried to Meg's door. When Jon started to exit on his side of the car, the driver asked him to come out of Meg's side and to hurry into the palace.

"I'm sorry, sir. Security is on edge and has given us strict instructions. The Prince and Princess were not supposed to come out onto the plaza, but..."

"Thank you, sir," Meg bowed her head slightly. "I would have been on the plaza to meet my daughter, too. We understand."

The massive, double door in the center of the ground floor opened, and the Queen of Denmark stood inside the entry area wringing her hands. Security guards encircled her, and the room buzzed with excited attendants. Meg stared in wonder at the beauty and elegance of the wide room. The whole back wall displayed a painting of... *Is that the world? Very interesting. They've painted a map of the world along this entire wall.*

"Mormor!" Astra squealed as she ran into the arms of her grandmother.

The Queen hugged her granddaughter with obvious relief written all over her face. She looked up to catch Meg watching the intimate scene and smiled at her granddaughter's rescuers.

"We owe you quite a debt," the Queen said in accented English.

Meg noted Jon's hesitance to move toward the Queen, so she figured it best to stand still. *What is the proper protocol?*

"It's okay," Queen Ella said with a smile, sensing their hesitation. "You need not be so formal. We are now officially the best of friends."

"Your Majesty," Jon said as he lowered his head.

"Welcome to Brockdorff's Palace. You are heroes, and we want to hear all about what happened. Would you join us for tea in the parlor?"

"We are honored," Jon avowed. "We did what anyone would have done."

"Quite the contrary," the Queen said. "Sadly, too many people are too worried about their own affairs to get mixed up in someone else's problems."

Jon and Meg followed the Queen and her family from the formal entry room into the family's living quarters. As they walked, Princess Anne told the Davenports about the recent renovations. Breathtaking art covered the walls with contrasting styles ranging from the rococo style of the late 18th century to modern art that could have been painted yesterday.

The Queen led them through a tall door into what Meg assumed represented a comfortable den, but it still looked like something out of a fantasy to her. Exquisite furniture covered the light-colored hardwood floors, and a marble fireplace on one wall caught Meg's eye.

Princess Anne motioned toward the couch. "Please have a seat. We've heard from the Security Service but want to hear firsthand all that happened tonight. We'll have coffee and refreshments. We have fruit fritters and cinnamon bars, or would you rather have something else?"

"That sounds wonderful," Meg agreed.

Meg sat silently, taking in the whole experience while Jon shared their story. Astra filled in the blanks about what happened before Jon and Meg first saw her.

"I felt a little sick, so I told the other girls to go to the pool. After a bit, I decided to change into my bathing suit and join the rest of the team. When I went into the bathroom, I told Victor

I felt better and planned to go to the pool. I remember wondering what happened to Andrew."

The Queen raised an eyebrow. "Andrew?"

"Yes, mother. He was new on Astra's detail."

"Where is Victor?" Astra asked.

"So, did Andrew come back into the room?" Princess Anne changed the subject.

"Well, he knocked on the bathroom door. When I opened it, he handed me a robe to wear. I planned to put my clothes on over my bathing suit anyway. When I turned, I felt something on my…my bum? I felt something like a sting, and I remember rubbing the spot. That's the last thing I remember."

"So, Andrew had something to do with it," Prince Erik decided. "He's missing, so I assumed he was involved."

"Where's Victor?" Astra asked for the third time that night.

Princess Anne began speaking to her daughter in Danish, and Astra's eyes filled with tears. She fell into her mother's arms and wept.

The Queen leaned forward in her chair. "Dr. Davenport, you and your beautiful wife saved our little Astra. How can we ever thank you? We will pay you well for your service."

"That's not necessary, your Majesty. Meeting you is an honor; we will always consider rescuing the princess a high privilege. We came to your beautiful country to visit your Trelleborg Museum, and we had the most wonderful time."

"The museum is an amazing place," the Queen agreed. "I assume you saw the display on King Bluetooth."

"Yes, ma'am. We did. He must have been an inspiring man."

"He was indeed," Erik added. "He civilized Denmark. Before Harald was king, Denmark was a ruthless, marauding rabble of clans who murdered and plundered at will."

Meg reached for another cinnamon bar. "How did he manage to bring the clans together?"

"I think it was nothing less than a spiritual revival," Anne interjected. "Bluetooth became a Christian and determined to evangelize the whole region. Once people began to turn to Christianity, the murdering stopped, and peace settled upon the region."

"The story of Harald Bluetooth is rather interesting," Jon admitted. "We read of him back in our home in the Bahamas and decided we wanted to come to Denmark on vacation to visit the museum."

"It's too bad you didn't wait a couple of months," Erik said. "We will soon be adding to the Bluetooth exhibit."

"Is that so?" Jon raised an eyebrow.

"A couple of years ago, a little girl discovered a treasure trove that belonged to the King," Queen Ella acknowledged. "We've been working with the family to bring the items to our museum. The discovery was in Sweden, so it has taken some maneuvering to get the items released to us."

"We may have to come back," Jon decided.

"It might be best for you to wait a little longer than two months," the Queen suggested. "The girl's family is holding out on a diary that is quite fascinating. We've been told that the King recorded specific details about his family in a diary, and we want that included in the exhibit."

"How could a diary survive all these years?" Meg asked.

"The whole thing is a marvel," Queen Ella agreed. "It was originally written on animal skins and preserved in a sealed container. Someone placed the container inside a casket over 200 years ago."

Prince Erik turned to the Queen. "Mother, why can't we take the Davenports with us next week to visit with the family?"

"What a wonderful idea," the Queen agreed. "We are meeting with the family to discuss the diary next week. They will fly to Copenhagen on Friday."

"That would be an honor," Jon admitted, "but we have a scheduling problem. We run a program for boys, and I'm afraid we cannot stay away that long. We could only come on this trip because I had to fly to London for other business. Maybe we can come back after the summer is over."

Queen Ella thought for a moment. "I imagine with a little persuasion that we could get the family to come up tomorrow. If they are willing to come, would that work for you?"

A shiver of excitement ran down Meg's back as she considered the Queen's offer. Her mind raced back to the three clues on the cave wall on Conception Island: Bluetooth, find the diary, and Trelleborg. *Find the diary! Could this be it?*

"That would be wonderful," Jon conceded. "Our plane leaves tomorrow evening, but we can wait until Monday to leave if needed."

"I'll see if they will meet us for lunch tomorrow," Queen Ella decided. "That should give us time to meet and still get you to the airport on time."

"Thank you so much, your Majesty," Meg gushed. "We would love to meet this family, and I can't wait to learn about the diary."

Chapter Twenty
Discovery

Fear squeezed Lacy's heart like a dark, icy hand. As her mouth opened in terror, her regulator fell out and began floating toward her side. The strong beam from Barry's light illuminated the ocean around her, and she could see the huge open jaws coming straight toward her. The mouth of the giant shark had to be two-and-a-half feet across–maybe more.

The monster of the deep turned, and Lacy saw the creature's massive body. As she began kicking with all her strength to get away, she grabbed her life-giving regulator and put it back into her mouth. She looked back toward Barry, but he was gone. His flashlight's beam shone upward as it drifted unattended toward the sea floor.

When Lacy's head broke the surface, Jose's hands grabbed the top of her vest, and she felt her body flying. He lost his balance from pulling her aboard and fell on his back, but Lacy ended up on her side on the swimmers' landing. She crawled further into the boat and laid down trembling on the deck.

Barry knelt beside her after he dropped his tank. He put his hand on her shoulder. "What was that thing?"

Lacy had a hard time forming words. Her shaky voice filled the boys with terror. "Shark. It was the biggest shark I've ever seen. It had to be at least twenty-five feet long, maybe thirty. It was coming at me with its mouth open. I've never seen a shark with such a huge mouth."

Jose squatted beside Lacy and pulled her to a seated position. He helped her take off her vest and tank. "Could you see any teeth inside the shark's mouth?"

"That's a…that's a crazy thing to say to a girl just about eaten by a shark."

"It's not that crazy," Jose insisted. "Did you see any teeth?"

Lacy relived the horror and looked into the mouth of the shark as it swam toward her. "I guess not. I don't remember seeing any teeth now that you mention it."

"I'm guessing it was a basking shark. They swim around with their huge mouths open to catch plankton. They're harmless."

"Except they might scare you to death," Barry interjected.

"But it was coming at me with its mouth open," Lacy insisted. "I don't think it wanted to kiss me."

"I don't know why not," Tae teased, and the boys laughed.

"I bet you surprised the shark as much as it surprised you," Jose said. "It's interesting that a basking shark would be this far south, though I read an article about them being spotted in the Caribbean once. They are magnificent creatures."

"Magnificent was not what came to mind when I turned around and saw the huge mouth coming at me."

"Why don't we have coffee or sodas," Jose suggested. "That will give us a little time to calm down. We have to get into the water and dig up whatever the sonar sled has located."

"Do you have something a little stronger than coffee?" Barry grinned.

Lacy pulled off her fins and stood up. "I'm fine. We don't have to delay on my account."

"Your call," Jose said. "If you're ready to return, let's give it another shot. Maybe the basking shark will still be around. I'd love to see it."

Lacy decided to let Jose jump in first. He didn't seem to be afraid of anything. Kerrick stood behind her and helped slip her vest and tank back into place. He massaged her shoulders and put his mouth against her ear.

"You going to be okay?"

"Yeah. I'm fine. I've just got to build up a little nerve first."

"No one would blame you for sitting this out."

"No way! I'm going in."

Lacy moved in front of Tae, who was about to step down onto the swimmers' platform. She spit into her mask, rinsed it in the nearby bucket, and slipped it over her head. She looked back at Kerrick and stepped off the platform into the water. Her stomach rose to her throat, and she fought the urge to swim back to the surface and get out of the water. The water was already lit up with beams from the lights that David and Jose carried. The splash above her indicated that Tae must be right behind her.

Aaron entered the water next, pulling the long hose of the seavac. By the time they all assembled on the bottom, Jose was marking out an area with some stakes. Lacy looked around cautiously but saw no sign of the basking shark.

Jose motioned at his watch, and Lacy knew he was telling them they had fifteen minutes to explore. She grinned when she realized none of the boys wanted to venture off alone, so she kicked hard to lead the group to the coral reef.

An octopus with tentacles over two feet long squirted some ink and shot away from the approaching group. Lacy hated to see it zip away because she considered seeing an octopus a rarity. Several large fish floated around the reef as if in a trance, and a nurse shark finned by. Barry grabbed her arm, but she patted his hand. He had to know that nurse sharks were harmless because Jon made that clear to the boys early on in their training.

After making a larger circle over the top of the reef and down the other side, Lacy led them back to the dig site. Aaron took hold of the end of the seavac hose, and the other boys made a perimeter around the site. The place lit up like the football field at Griffin High School on Friday nights. While Aaron sucked up the sand, Lacy held onto the hose just behind him to better control the huge vacuum cleaner.

Lacy looked up to see Jose hovering just above the divers. He didn't seem to be paying attention to the digging process but continued to scan the sea around the group.

After sucking up sand for about fifteen minutes, Aaron pressed the red button on the end of the hose, and an eerie silence fell over the area. Lacy investigated the small pit created by Aaron's work and saw the round end of something metal. It appeared to be the beginning of a long cylinder. *I bet that's a cannon. It has to be.*

Aaron resumed his work, and within another twenty minutes, he exposed the whole cannon. Jose swam down to the bottom and inspected the find. He motioned to the gauges from his tank and pointed up to the bottom of the boat. The group started the slow ascent to the surface.

"So, what's the prize?" Marcy asked as everyone began removing their scuba gear.

Jose raised an eyebrow. "The prize?"

"Sure," Marcy laughed. "I guessed that it was a cannon."

Jose rubbed the stubble on the bottom of his chin. "Well, let's see. You get to rinse off in the shower first."

"That's not much of a prize," Kerrick challenged.

"I don't know," Marcy interjected. "This salt can get to me. I'm assuming none of us are going to shower until we get the cannon, so don't anyone forget that I go first."

"What's the plan for returning the cannon to *The Discoverer*?" Kerrick asked.

"I suggest we strap it to the bottom of the boat and haul it back," Marcy said. "We should be able to secure it enough so we won't drop it."

"That's a good idea," Jose agreed. "We can make a sling and secure it to each side of the boat. We can haul it aboard with the crane when we return to The Discoverer. Let's take a little breather, get new tanks, and go back in to get it."

About thirty minutes later, everyone stepped back into the water and finned their way to the exposed cannon barrel. The wood had rotted away many years earlier, but the barrel was in remarkable condition. Lacy swam from one end of the prize to the other, anticipating Jon's excitement when he heard about the find.

Jose dug a tunnel under the cannon barrel with a small shovel and slid a strap to the other side. Lacy and Marcy followed his lead a little further up the barrel. They wrapped the straps around the cannon once and left plenty of slack on each side so they could attach the straps to the sides of the Carver.

Aaron brought the lifting bag to Jose and attached it to one end of the cannon barrel. Marcy attached a second bag to the other end. While Barry and Tae pulled two extra scuba tanks over to Marcy and Jose to add air to the bags, Lacy pulled a rope back up to the surface.

Once her head cleared the surface, she saw Kerrick standing on the swimmers' platform. "Here you go. You've got to do something to earn your pay."

Kerrick grinned down as he reached for the rope. "I was getting a little bored up here with no T.V. or Internet."

"We're about to start the lift."

When she returned to the dig site, Lacy found that Jose had the cannon floating a little above the sea floor like a hoverboard she saw at the state fair in Perry. Jose performed a controlled lift to limit the speed of the barrel's ascent. Kerrick pulled the lead rope, and the cannon barrel started moving toward the boat. Jose and Marcy added air to the bags from the tank and tried to keep the barrel parallel to the surface.

As the cannon neared the surface, Jose guided it under the boat, and Lacy swam toward the swimmers' platform so she could get out and assist Kerrick. The boys brought the straps to the surface and handed them to Lacy and Kerrick. Fifteen minutes after beginning the process of lifting the barrel, they had the cannon tied off and ready to be taken to *The Discoverer*.

One-by-one, the divers climbed from the water with grins on their faces. Lacy felt a sense of elation and accomplishment. Though a cannon barrel couldn't be that valuable, finding it felt like they had won the lottery. To the hoots and whistles of the boys, Marcy stepped out of her wetsuit and stood under the cold shower on the back of the boat.

Lacy shook her head at the boys. "She's not taking off her bathing suit, you idiots. I swear. You boys are like animals."

"Calm down, Lacy," Tae laughed. "We're just messing with her."

Jose climbed the ladder to the bridge and started the Carver's engine. He eased the throttle forward, and the boat began going out to sea. By the time everyone had rinsed off and gotten a cold bottle of water from the galley, Lacy could see *The Discoverer* in view on the horizon. Her body ached, and the thought of going to bed helped her to move a little quicker to get her gear stowed.

Once aboard *The Discoverer*, Lacy headed straight to her cabin. She had rinsed off earlier under the cold shower aboard the *New Beginnings*, but now she wanted a real shower. She stood under the hot spray and leaned her head against the fiberglass wall. Hot water streamed down her back, and fatigue settled in her body. She regretted telling Kerrick she would meet him in the dining hall before calling it a day.

After toweling off, she looked longingly at her sleep shirt that lay folded up on the bed, but she reached for her shorts instead. She dragged herself down the hall and up the steps to the main level.

As she approached the dining hall, she noticed Jose stepping through the door.

"I figured you'd be in bed by now, Lacy."

"I thought you would be, too."

"Well…Let's say that Ann has a craving."

"I knew she was pregnant!" Lacy beamed.

"Shh! I think Ann wants to be the one to announce it to everyone."

"I'm so excited for you."

"I guess I'm excited, though this snack I'm getting for her may not survive in her stomach for long. Her morning sickness has just turned into sickness."

"Oh, I'm sorry," Lacy sobered up. "It'll all be worth it. I've heard it gets better."

"We've heard that too."

Kerrick sat at a table in the dining area as Lacy and Jose passed by into the kitchen. Lacy poured hot water into a cup for tea, and Jose grabbed a soda from the refrigerator and a jar of dill pickles.

"Any idea where I might find peanut butter?" Jose asked.

"Sure. It's in that cabinet to the right."

Jose unscrewed the lid from his drink when he sat down at the table with Lacy and Kerrick. "I just heard from Jon and Meg, and you'll never believe what happened."

"What?" Kerrick and Lacy chimed in unison.

"They foiled a kidnapping attempt in Denmark; the victim was the Queen's granddaughter."

"That's unbelievable," Lacy gasped. "I can't believe everything that happens to them."

"Do you want to know something that's even more unbelievable? They will have an audience tomorrow with someone who has King Harald Bluetooth's private diary. They said it's a really long story, and they'll fill us in on the details when they come home."

"No way!" Kerrick almost shouted. "That's crazy."

"Crazy indeed. Let's not spoil their story for the boys. I'm sure Jon and Meg want to break the news." Jose looked at Lacy with hooded eyes. "Most people like sharing their exciting news without others spilling the beans."

"Mum's the word," Kerrick said as he pretended to be zipping up his mouth.

Jose looked at the jar of pickles. "I've got to get back to my cabin. See you guys in the morning."

As Jose walked out the dining room door, Kerrick grinned at Lacy. "So...people like sharing their exciting news, like Ann being pregnant."

"I don't know what on earth you mean." Lacy feigned surprise.

"Come on, Lacy. I saw Ann puking her guts up yesterday, and she said it was nothing. I know morning sickness when I see it. And pickles and peanut butter? Who would eat that except a pregnant woman?"

"Oh? Since when did you become an expert on pregnancy?"

"I'm not an expert, but I'm not stupid."

"Okay, but you've got to promise not to tell anyone. Ann wants to make her announcement herself."

"Once you kiss me goodnight, my lips are sealed."

Lacy leaned across the table and gave Kerrick a peck on his cheek.

"I don't think that's enough to seal a guy's lips," Kerrick grinned.

He pulled Lacy to her feet and kissed her deeply. "Now, that's a little better."

Lacy started to swat him, but he grabbed her wrist. He pulled her close, and electricity once again surged through her body like the first time they touched. She wondered if they were married for fifty years, would his touch still be as exciting? Her lips melted into his again as she decided that not going to bed immediately was a good idea.

Chapter Twenty-One

Head in the Game

"Lacy? Are you okay? Lacy…"

Lacy jerked and sat up in her bed. The pounding on the door continued as she tried to wipe the fog from her mind. *What time is it? What time did I get in bed?*

"Lacy…"

"Just a minute, Marcy."

Lacy jumped out of bed and hurried to the door. "Sorry. I was..I was…"

"Still asleep. I know. We were worried about you at breakfast."

"Breakfast?" Lacy gasped. "What time is it?"

"It's almost 8:30. We finished breakfast long ago, and everyone's getting ready to return to the bay."

"Oh, my God. I overslept. I don't know what happened."

"I think what happened is named Kerrick," Marcy grinned. "He left a little bit ago to pick up Randal and told me you guys stayed up too late."

Lacy remembered their time together lying on the front of the ship the night before. Kerrick protected her from the cool night air by holding her close against his body for at least an hour, maybe two. They stared up at the stars and just talked about nothing and everything. He was so easy to talk to, and she told him things that she once vowed she would never tell a soul.

"You can say that again. We were up quite late. I'm sure Randal is ticked with him for not returning to the house in Rock Sound last night."

"Probably, but I imagine that spending the day with us in the bay will help him get over it a little. We decided at breakfast that Kerrick should get him and bring him back to the *New Beginnings*. Randal has a bad case of cabin fever."

"That's awesome. Maneuvering his wheelchair around the yacht will be a little challenging."

"We talked about that but think we can work around the problems. We want him to be in on some of our work. Kerrick thought Randal might stay in the Robalo and help him watch the monitor. He won't need his wheelchair for that."

"What about church?" Lacy gasped. "Aren't we supposed to go to church with Mr. Phil?"

"Yeah, but that's tonight. It seems they moved the morning service to this evening for some reason."

Lacy felt a little disappointed they wouldn't attend church this morning. *I can't believe I want to go back to church. I've just never experienced anything like it before, and the girl...I think I want to meet the girl who played the guitar.*

Lacy thought about Kerrick heading back to Rock Sound. "I suppose it's good that Kerrick has to go back for Randal, or you guys may have left me."

Marcy grinned. "It seems like someone said that at breakfast. I also think it's a good thing Jon and Meg aren't here. I don't know what you and Kerrick were doing last night, but it does make one wonder."

"One can quit wondering," Lacy grinned. "We just talked and looked at the stars."

"If you say so. Just remember that looking at the stars has gotten many girls in trouble. I brought you a bagel and some fruit. You can't dive on an empty stomach."

Lacy hugged Marcy, grateful for the change of topic. "You're the best. Give me a minute, and I'll join you guys at the yacht."

Lacy closed the door and put on her bathing suit. She stepped into a pair of shorts and pulled her Atlanta Braves tee shirt over her head. She slapped strawberry cream cheese on her bagel and stuffed it into her mouth. *Marcy is the sweetest person I know. Well, Meg is at the top of that list. Ann's awesome too. I'm amazed Marcy knew strawberry cream cheese was my favorite.* She brushed her hair and pulled it into a ponytail before grabbing Kerrick's ball cap.

"Good morning, Sleeping Beauty," Ann grinned as Lacy climbed down the steps to the Carver. "You're supposed to do your sleeping at night."

"I'll try to remember that."

"We decided to meet Kerrick at Double Bay, so we must get going. Everyone else is aboard."

"What about Miss Judy? Isn't she still at the house in Rock Sound?"

"She's still there with Carla, but she won't be able to join us until Jon and Meg get back. Meg doesn't want her little toddler running around *The Discoverer* until she gets back."

"Morning, Lacy," Tae said as Lacy stepped into the galley.

The four boys were seated around the table playing cards. Lacy loved these guys. It was the craziest thing. She came to the Bahamas to enjoy scuba diving and hang out with her aunt and uncle, but she now had a new family. *No. They're not family. I love them too much for them to be like my family.*

"Sorry I slept in, guys. I must have set my alarm wrong."

Barry slid over and motioned to the seat beside him. "No problem. It allowed me to teach these boys how to play cards."

"Teach us?" David laughed. "You know that you wouldn't have a chance if you quit cheating."

"Okay, boys. Deal me in, and I'll show you some serious card skills. What are you playing?"

"Spades, but I don't think we can do that with five," David said.

"Deal her in," Aaron insisted. "I'm tired of playing."

Jose guided the Carver back into Double Bay, and the boys groaned as they heard him kill the engine. He stepped through the door into the galley and told the group to get ready to dive.

"I just heard from Kerrick," Jose informed the group, "and he should be back here with Randal in the next fifteen minutes. That gives us enough time to gear up."

Barry tossed his cards on the table. "Anything new on tap for today? I'm not complaining about it, but I'm getting tired of doing the same thing every day."

Lacy shoved Barry's hat down over his face. "That sounds like a complaint to me."

"You've got to admit that it's because of our hard work over the last few days that we found the cannon barrel," Jose reminded them. "If we work hard today, we can finish up in the bay by tomorrow night. If that ship started sinking here, we'll find a distinct trail that leads to the final wreck. We've got to be patient."

"I know, I know," David nodded. "The Tortoise and the Hare."

"What?" Tae blurted out. "What are you talking about."

"Don't you have any class?" David laughed. "Are you illiterate?"

"Am I what? I'm only in ninth grade. They put me there because I'd already done the eighth-grade thing twice."

"Never mind," David sighed. "Let's just dive."

****

Fernando pulled the binoculars back to his eyes. "I see them. I knew they'd be back."

Miguel settled into the sand atop the bluff beside Fernando. "Let me see. Hmm, that's the Carver all right, but there's no way you could have known they'd be back today."

"I told you I saw them last night, but you wouldn't believe me. You've got to quit believing our stupid lookout. He had us going back to Nassau."

"We'll see about him. I've about lost my patience with that kid. What were you doing out here last night anyway?"

"Let's say I needed a little privacy. I saw lights out there and knew something was up. No one dives Double Bay at night. It had to be them, and I'm guessing they found something they didn't want anyone to see them bringing up."

"I told you we wouldn't have a hard time finding the Davenports after pulling off another job," Miguel insisted. "That little heist didn't take as long as I thought. Too bad the old man had to go for his pistol."

Fernando yawned and wished he had a drink. "You know that he and his little old lady would have gone straight to the police or Coast Guard. We had to kill 'em anyway."

Fernando sat back and leaned against the trunk of a small palm tree. The night before had been a home run, and he made plans to meet the girl again tonight. Susan was hot, and he was

ready. Spotting the Davenport group, however, could be throwing a wrench in his plans. Of course, if his new plans involved
grabbing Lacy…

"Hey," Miguel nudged him. "Did you hear me?"

"Uh…I guess not."

"Get your head in the game. You're always thinking about
the wrong thing. I said we needed to find out where they were
staying at night. We can't ride to the yacht and nab the girl."

"That's true, Miguel, but what if they stay on that research
boat? We can't very well go out to it and grab her there either."

"One thing's for sure. We won't be able to figure it out by
staying on this bluff. I'm going back to the marina to get our
boat. You stay here and keep an eye on them. I'll get as close to
the bay as possible without being obvious, and then I'll come
ashore in the raft to pick you up. I should have a cell signal, so
I'll call you when I'm in position."

"Yeah. That sounds good. You go get in the air-conditioned
car and drive back to the marina to get in the air-conditioned
boat while I stay out here and fry."

"Something like that. Quit complaining. You're about to
make a killing here. There's no telling what the treasure we'll find
with that medallion is worth. Once we've got what we want from
the girl, I promise you've got her alone for the next hour."

Fernando's teeth glistened in the morning sun. "Just an
hour? I was hoping for at least a day or two."

"I don't think you can last a day or two."

"Don't be so sure. That girl's got it coming."

"Just keep your phone handy. I'll be calling you. Come get
the cooler out of the car before I leave."

Fernando followed Miguel back to the car and opened the
trunk. The cooler wasn't very big, but it contained some drinks

and sandwiches they had picked up at the deli earlier that morning. He settled back on the bluff and tried to spot Lacy through the binoculars. He saw her standing on the deck dressed in a wetsuit. The girl beside her was wearing a black bathing suit, and she wasn't bad. *What's up with these girls and their bathing suits? Don't they wear bikinis anymore?*

As he watched the Carver through his binoculars, he remembered another time he watched Lacy from a distance. She thought that she was alone at her pool back on Great Exuma, but with his high-powered binoculars, it was like he sat in the chair beside her. She wore a yellow bikini he hadn't seen her wear since that day. He remembered inspecting every gorgeous inch of her spectacular body.

She was a dream, but her eyes were the thing that filled his memory. He had never seen eyes like hers. They were as blue as the sky. One of these days, those eyes would stare up into his. *I've got to get on her ship tonight. I don't know where to find her, but I'll find her. Somehow, I'll find her.*

Chapter Twenty-Two
Copenhagen Surprise

Meg spent the morning shopping in Copenhagen. Meeting the queen in the palace the night before had been a new and embarrassing experience, but she didn't have clothes for such an occasion. Of course, she had spent a lot of time with President Johnson, but he was family, sort of. That was different.

As she dressed for bed the night before in the guest bedroom of Princess Anne's winter home, she felt mortified about meeting the Royal Family in such casual clothes. She didn't usually give much thought to clothing, but she knew there was a time to dress up.

Before going to bed, she inspected every inch of the opulent bedroom. She didn't want ever to forget this moment. She couldn't believe she would spend the night in the Queen's palace. *I suppose this palace belongs to the Crown Princess.*

The bedroom looked like something she'd seen in a magazine. The king-sized bed had tall posts on each corner, and sheer cloth dropped down on all sides, making them feel like they were sleeping in a cave. The room was as large as half of her mother's house. It had immaculate furnishings and a beautiful tile fireplace framed with oak bookshelves covering one end of the room. She found sleeping hard, but her husband passed out when his head hit the pillow.

She would never forget walking into the elegant palace the night before wearing her New Balance running shoes, jeans, and a tee shirt covered by her fleece jacket. Her second meeting with the Queen in a little more than two hours would be different. She would be properly dressed this time.

As she pulled a possible purchase from the rack, she looked over her shoulder to see the two men from the security team standing nearby. It bugged her to have two, large men following her everywhere she went, but the Queen insisted on them. They even cleared the bathroom before she could use it. *Are we really in danger?* She pictured Jon sitting next door at the coffee shop with his bodyguard and wondered how he was faring with his new best friend. She needed to hurry up and find a dress so they could stop by a men's store for Jon.

A little over thirty minutes later, they left a store with Jon's new suit draped over his arm. Meg took hold of his free hand and said, "No one said anything about lunch this morning, so I suppose we need to grab a bite before heading back to the palace."

"I guess you're right," Jon agreed. "It may have been their oversight, but I'd rather not assume anything. We passed a café on our way over here that looked inviting. We can get something to eat and have enough time to return to the palace and change clothes before our meeting."

As Jon and Meg hurried back through the huge doors of the palace, Meg looked at the hands of her watch. *We're going to be fine. I can be ready in thirty minutes, and Jon could be ready in five.* They were led through the expansive entryway toward the staircase that led to the living quarters of the ancient building. Once in their room, Meg hurried into the bathroom.

Jon checked his watch as Meg sat beside him on the couch fifteen minutes later. "Meg, you deserve a prize for setting a record for getting dressed."

"Jon! I'm not slow. You know that."

"I'm just kidding you, Honey. But I hope you'll still get a prize before we leave Denmark."

"I've been thinking about this whole adventure. It's been crazy and mysterious."

"You can say that again. The suspense sucked me in from the beginning, but I don't think it's ever been about the treasure."

Meg noticed a tag dangling from the sleeve of her dress. "I'm sure glad I saw that. Do you have your knife on you?"

"I couldn't bring it through security at the airport, so I left it at home. I think I saw some scissors in the bathroom."

Meg returned to the sitting area with a pair of scissors. "Would you mind cutting this for me?"

"Happy to be of service."

"Back to what you were saying, Jon. I'm eager to uncover the mystery just because…because I want to know what the clues are all about. If we find King Bluetooth's treasure at the end of this search, we should do something we think would fulfill his wishes."

"That's a great idea, Meg. What do you think Bluetooth would want to be done with it? He was a Christian. Maybe we could donate it to a mission's organization."

"Possibly. One thing Bluetooth was about was unity. He wanted to unite Denmark, and he wanted to unite his family. Maybe we could do something with it to address the racial problems in the United States."

"I like that idea. We could either address racial tensions or do something to help broken families. I think many of our country's problems stem from broken homes."

"We know what coming from a broken home has done to Lacy," Meg agreed. "No doubt it's a huge problem in our country. Let's give it some thought."

Jon grinned. "I suppose we need to find the treasure first."

Dressed in business attire, Jon and Meg left the room and were directed toward a large living room in the palace. An elderly couple sat on a couch with a girl beside them in a chair. Meg guessed her to be about Astra's age.

Meg remembered reading about the girl who took the gold medallion to school and figured this had to be the girl. The couple wore simple clothes, though it appeared they made an extra effort to buy the girl a new dress.

A middle-aged woman dressed in a dark pantsuit walked toward the Davenports. "Hello, Dr. and Mrs. Davenport. I'm Sophia Jessen, and I will be your translator today. May I introduce you to Mr. and Mrs. Liam Johansson and their granddaughter, Olivia?"

Sophia turned to the couple and said something in Swedish. Meg had no idea what was said, though she recognized the words *San Roque*. Olivia's eyes widened, and she said something to the translator in Swedish.

The translator looked toward Jon with a smile. "I told the Johanssons that you own a salvage operation in the Bahamas and that you became famous for discovering the *San Roque*. Olivia wants to know if you scuba dive. She has some interest in the sport."

"Please tell her that we scuba dive about every day, and she is welcome to come to visit us anytime."

Sophia said something that Meg was sure must have been an invitation because the girl looked with pleading eyes at her grandparents. They must have replied with something akin to

"We'll think about it" because Meg saw a slight roll of the pre-teen's eyes.

Sophia spoke to the group in English and then translated it to Swedish. "Our conversation today will be in Swedish, Danish, and English. I'll translate so all parties can participate in the conversation."

The doors opened, and the group stood to their feet. Astra ran into the room and into Meg's arms. Meg hugged her, knowing she had a friend for life.

Meg kissed her young friend on the cheek. "Astra, I'd like for you to meet my new friend, Olivia. She speaks Swedish, and I have no idea how to say that in her language."

Olivia looked at Astra and said with a heavy accent, "It is a pleasure to meet you. I speak little English."

Astra beamed as she stuck out her hand. "It is a pleasure to meet you, too. How old are you?"

"Twelve. And you?"

"I'm twelve, too."

Princess Anne and Queen Ella joined the group, and Sophia introduced the Johanssons to the Princess and the Queen. Mr. Johansson bowed while his wife attempted a curtsy. It was obvious to Meg that while Mrs. Johansson may have practiced for this moment, she was still awkward with curtsies. Olivia appeared to be far more at home with the exercise.

Queen Ella invited everyone to have a seat, and servers dressed in white uniforms entered with fruit pastries and coffee. One of the servers offered soft drinks to the girls.

As the conversation began in Danish, Swedish, and English, Meg overcame the obstacle of waiting on the translation and found the story captivating. She first wondered why the Queen wouldn't just speak in English to make things a bit simpler but later realized that she didn't want to use the wrong word by accident and say something inappropriate to the Johanssons.

Queen Ella leaned forward in her chair. "So, Olivia. I understand you made quite a discovery last year."

"Yes, your Majesty."

"Will you tell us about it?"

Olivia looked at her grandfather, and he nodded his head. "Well, I discovered an old cellar on our property. It's more like an underground room. I've played there for as long as I can remember. I looked through some boxes a few years ago and found interesting things like books and vases. A long box and a few other containers were in the back corner of the cellar. Because the long box looked like a casket, I wouldn't go to the back of the cellar."

"Finding a casket must have been frightening," the Queen said.

"Yes, ma'am, I didn't know it was a casket. It resembled one, but I couldn't bring myself to look into it. That is until last year."

Astra gasped. "You looked into the casket?"

Astra looked at her mother and then down to her lap. Meg imagined a probable conversation between the young princess and her mother. The Crown Princess must have told her daughter that she could attend the meeting if she remained quiet.

"Yes. I looked into the casket. It took a while to get up the nerve. When I opened the lid, I shined my torch down into the box."

Meg thought it odd that Olivia would have a torch. It then occurred to her that the translator chose the word *torch* for the Swedish word for *flashlight.*

"Instead of finding a dead body, I found a gold medallion and several pieces of gold. I also found a sealed tube."

"What did you do?" Princess Anne wondered.

"I didn't do anything. If I told my grandparents about the discovery, I would no longer be allowed to play in the cellar. A few weeks later, I decided to take the gold medallion to school. One of the boys in my class always makes fun of me, so I decided I would show him that I wasn't..." Olivia looked at her grandfather. "That I wasn't poor."

Queen Ella nodded and smiled with compassion at the young Swedish girl. "You're not poor, my young friend. You have your wonderful imagination and a lifetime of opportunity before you."

"Yes, ma'am," Olivia lowered her head.

"I also plan to give you a finders' reward for the medallion," the Queen informed her, "and I believe the Swedish government has agreed that you can keep one of the gold pieces."

Olivia smiled with excitement at her grandparents.

Please go on with your story," the Queen urged.

"My teacher asked many questions and wanted to borrow the medallion. She and a professor from the University came to our home the next night and told us that he thought I discovered treasure belonging to King Harald Bluetooth. He said he wanted to perform some tests on the medallion."

"Indeed, you did find King Bluetooth's treasure," Queen Ella agreed and turned to Jon and Meg. "The medallion has a Latin inscription on one side that says, 'Harald Gormsson king of Danes, Scania, Jomsborg, Oldenburg.' It was determined to be authentic by a group of experts, and young Olivia has become famous in her own right. Some debate has ensued about the treasure, but it is without a doubt connected to our ancient king."

Meg was dying to see the medallion, for she had no doubt it contained a clue for their search. "What about the other side of the medallion?" she asked. "And the tube? What was in the tube? The diary?"

"We'll get to the tube," Queen Ella promised. "As to the medallion, I have a picture of it in this folder that I had printed up for you this morning. I thought you might like to have a copy."

Meg reached out with calm hands, but her insides were turning summersaults. She pulled the picture from the folder and held it for Jon to see. Once again, they saw the familiar circle, like the one on the Jelling Stone, and a cross in the middle. She remembered the picture in the museum of the trelleborg that must have been taken from a drone, and the graphic on the coin could have been a near-carbon copy.

"Fascinating," Meg whispered. "This is amazing."

"As you know, the Swedish museum is releasing the tube back to your family," the Queen informed the group. "We would like to purchase it from you. Regardless of whatever the Swedish government will pay you, we will pay you more. That diary is more important to Denmark; we want it for our museum. We are grateful that you allowed us to read it, and we've taken the liberty to have it translated."

Mr. Johansson cleared his throat. "We thought the translation would be of interest to you. The professor from the University gave us a rough translation of some of it. He said that it was written in Runic."

"May we read it?" Jon asked. "I mean the translation. I'm afraid we do not know Runic."

"I will see if we can get you a copy," Queen Ella promised.

Meg wanted to read it right then. She was certain they would find the missing pieces to their puzzle in the diary and didn't know if she could wait to go through all the proper channels. Then a cold dread settled over her. What if the Queen decided not to give them a copy?

Chapter Twenty-Three

Home at Last

"Mama!" Carla's voice cried out over the clamor of rolling luggage, laughing people, and a voice over the intercom announcing the next flight departure.

Meg dropped the handle to her carry-on bag and scooped up her precious little girl. Carla's chubby arms wrapped around Meg's neck.

"Hey, sweetheart," Jon said as he kissed Carla's cheek. "Were you sweet for Grandma Judy?"

"Yes."

"She was an angel," Judy acknowledged with a big smile. "She helped me clean the house and take care of Randal. We even made…"

"Cookie!" Carla shouted.

Meg laughed. "I hope you saved Daddy and me some."

"More, Mama."

"That sounds wonderful," Meg gushed as she hugged Carla even tighter. "We missed you so much."

"Pway?"

"Pray?" Meg wrinkled her eyebrows. "No, I'm sorry, sweetheart. You said *play*! We'll play, but Daddy and I are tired. We're going to sleep first. It's past your bedtime, too."

Jon grabbed their luggage from a conveyor belt and led his family toward the door. A taxi pulled to the curb, and Jon walked toward the opened trunk.

"The *New Beginnings* is docked at Compass Point," Judy said. "I'm glad you suggested we bring the yacht. Taking a small plane over to Eleuthera would have been such a hassle. *The Discoverer* is anchored just out of Rock Sound, too. Everyone is so excited about your return."

"We're glad to be home," Jon assured her.

"We have a little surprise for you," Judy grinned, "but I can't tell you. I promised I wouldn't mention it."

"Didn't you just mention it?" Meg laughed.

"Not exactly."

When they stepped aboard the Carver yacht, Jose greeted them with hugs. The sky burst with a brilliant pink and the beginnings of a magnificent sunset.

"Ohhh," Carla gasped. "Tank u, God."

"Thank you, God, indeed," Jon agreed as he kissed his little girl.

Judy smiled. "We've been talking about being thankful."

Meg hugged her. "You're the best, Judy. I don't know what we'd do without you."

"That goes two ways," Judy insisted. "You two have made me a part of your family, and I've never been happier. We all have a lot to be thankful for."

"I'm thankful to be home," Jon confessed as he plopped into a chair in the galley. "I'm wiped out, but we had a great trip."

Jose pulled the yacht away from the dock while Judy put the lasagna she had made in the microwave. "I figured you'd be hungry, so I made some lasagna."

"That sounds wonderful," Jon admitted. "Airplane food doesn't even hold a candle to your homemade lasagna."

Judy smiled and pulled the dish from the microwave. She spooned out the lasagna onto two plates. "I'm dying to hear about your trip to the palace. Ann told me a little about it but said you would fill us in when you returned."

"We have quite a story," Meg admitted.

"Everyone is waiting for you at the house," Judy informed them. "I'm sure the entire group is dying to hear the whole story."

"We'll have to make it fast," Meg said, "or we'll talk in our sleep. Are we going to learn about our surprise at the house too?"

"I imagine so," Judy beamed.

Jon walked through the doors of the house with a sleeping Carla in his arms. Meg followed close behind. The loud buzz of excitement ceased when Marcy announced that Carla was asleep. Jon carried his little girl to the back bedroom and rejoined the group.

"What happened?" Lacy started.

"Yeah." Tae agreed. "So, what's up with being kidnapped? I know you weren't, but you're like heroes."

Everyone sat around the large living room while Jon and Meg relayed the past few days' events. Meg yawned several times and found it difficult to focus on the conversation.

"So, did you get the translation of the diary?" Lacy wondered. "We have to see it."

"Would you believe the Queen had someone meet us at the airport with a folder just before we boarded our plane to fly home? She had the document translated into English for us."

"Have you read it?" Ann asked. "Don't keep us in suspense."

"We read it on the flight home," Meg confessed. "It's the story of a brokenhearted father doing everything possible to unite his children. It seems that the older brother had a lot of bitterness toward his family and refused to be considered the King's son."

"That is until his father was mysteriously killed," Jon interrupted. "Then he happily became the next king. Some historians think he either killed his father or had him killed."

"Wow!" David said. "That's low."

"It turns out that Bluetooth had one son and two daughters," Meg continued. "Sweyn Forkbeard was the rebellious son, leading the Vikings to sack London in 1013. This brutality would have disturbed Bluetooth had he been alive. Bluetooth tried to lead Denmark to become a peaceful country, but his son wanted the Vikings to be a ruthless people."

"How could a father and a son be so different?" Ann asked.

"Harald Bluetooth became a Christian while serving as king of Denmark," Jon replied. "His conversion led to a dramatic change in his goals and actions. Sweyn didn't share his father's faith."

Meg shuffled through a folder in her lap and pulled out a piece of paper. "According to the diary, King Bluetooth came up with an idea to force his three children to work together after his death by requiring them to work together to find part of their inheritance."

"What do you mean when you say 'find?'" Barry interrupted. "Did he hide their inheritance?"

"I'm getting to that," Meg insisted. "The diary tells the story of one of Bluetooth's most loyal men: Arne. A bit of an adventurer, Arne determined to find land for King Harald that would provide everything they needed to live well without a need for plundering. He disappeared for three years and returned with an unbelievable tale of a hidden city of emeralds and gold."

"No way," David gasped. "Where?"

"From the diary description and approximate time frame, he had to be writing about the Mayans."

Marcy leaned forward when she heard Meg mention the Mayans. "The Mayans were an amazing civilization. I've been to Tikal in northern Guatemala. The Mayan built one of their cities in Mexico around 250 A.D. that was supposed to be quite magnificent. Someone sacked it sometime around 500 A.D. or so, and the treasures disappeared."

"Where was this city, Marcy?" Ann asked.

"A little north of where Mexico City is today. Historians wondered if the Mayans took the treasure to another undisclosed place hoping to rebuild the Mayan stronghold, but no one knows."

"That's interesting," Meg maintained. "If you follow the probable timeline, it could all fit together. What was the name of the Mayan city, Marcy?"

"Teotihuacan."

"Teo what?" Aaron stammered.

"Break it into syllables," Marcy suggested, "and pronounce it like this: teo tiwa kan."

Tae shook his head. "Your brain must be about to explode out of your little head. I think you're the smartest person I know."

"Back to what I was saying," Meg continued. "Follow the timeline. One of the major Mayan cities is about to be attacked by someone in about 550 A.D. The city leaders take the treasures to an undisclosed location to rebuild another city. By Arne's arrival in about 950 A.D., this new, hidden city was completed but disserted."

"So, our buddy, Arne, takes all the gold and emeralds back to Bluetooth?" Kerrick interjected.

"Not exactly," Jon responded. "He brought back only a few samples. I think the real treasure for Bluetooth's family was more information on how to find this lost city of the Mayans. King Harald wanted his children to work together to find the first stash of treasure, but the most important discovery would be additional clues to help them find the city."

Randal spoke up for the first time. "Let me get this straight. You're saying that King Harald created medallions for each of his children with clues so his kids could discover the first pile of treasure and clues to the Mayan city, and we have one of the medallions?"

"It seems that way," Meg agreed. "We've also got a picture of a second medallion. The inscription said…let's see. Where's that quote?" She thumbed through several pages. "Here it is. It says, 'Harald Gormsson king of Danes, Scania, Jomsborg, Oldenburg.'"

"That sure is profound," David exaggerated. "But it tells us nothing."

"Doesn't seem to mean much to us," Meg concurred. "The back of the medallion, however, may be of more interest. It's just a circle with a cross, but there's more to the graphic than meets the eye."

Ann left her chair and looked over Meg's shoulder at the medallion picture. "If you say so. I think this conversation is past my pay grade."

Jon stood to his feet. "We don't know what all this information means either, but it's worth considering. Something else we need to consider is where everyone will sleep. Some of us need to head back to *The Discoverer*. Correction. Most of us need to head back, and we need to get underway before I fall asleep. Meg and I are like zombies."

Lacy stood up beside Jon. "I hoped you would bring back some definitive clues that would help us make sense of the words in the cave and on my medallion. It seems like you just added more confusion to everything."

"I agree that we're a bit confused right now," Meg agreed, "but after we think about it for a while, I believe some of the pieces will start falling into place."

"I sure hope you're right," Lacy muttered.

Meg nodded her head. "Time will tell. You'll see."

"Oh!" Jon blurted. "I almost forgot. What about our surprise?"

Lacy nearly leaped out of her chair. "Oh, yeah. While you two have been globetrotting, we've been here working. We found a little treasure of our own."

"Is that a fact?" Meg mused. "Judy told us you went to a church service and big dinner at the Preacher's Cave with Mr. Phil. That doesn't sound like all work."

Lacy grinned. "That's true, and believe it or not, I enjoyed going to church."

"Who wouldn't like all that food," Tae said.

"So," Jon tried to return to the topic. "What about the surprise? What did you find?"

"We'd rather show you," Jose confessed, "but I have a feeling you won't be able to take in the whole experience because you're so tired. So, we'll tell you."

"We found a cannon," Barry blurted.

"More like a barrel to a cannon," Kerrick added. "Our Spanish ship either threw off cargo to lighten the load, or the storm took a cannon overboard. Nevertheless, we found a cannon."

"Finding a cannon is a great start. Did you find anything else around it?"

"Doesn't appear to be," Jose admitted. "It's like the thing fell overboard and got covered up by the sand where it landed."

"I wouldn't be surprised if that happened," Jon agreed. "Did you finish mapping out the bay?"

"Almost," Lacy said. "We lack a spot about the size of a football field. So far, the cannon is the only thing we've found."

"If you didn't find a debris trail, then I'd say the cannon went overboard accidentally," Jon said. "If they were trying to lighten the load, you'd find more than just a cannon. Great job, team. I'll look at it in the daylight tomorrow. In the meantime, let's return to the ship and go to bed."

"Jon, why don't you and Meg stay here tonight in my room with Carla?" Judy suggested. "I'll go back to *The Discoverer.*"

Ann grinned. "I bet Lacy would like to sleep in a bed that doesn't move tonight. You can think of it as a birthday present a few days early. You can stay in the second bedroom, and Kerrick can sleep on the other bed in Randal's room."

Meg followed Ann to the door as the rest of the group began filing out. "And just why are you insisting that Lacy sleep in the room next door to Kerrick? Do you realize how easy a little mishap would be? I'm not going to be able to sleep a wink."

"I thought it would be a nice thing to do," Ann grinned mischievously. "I wasn't just thinking about putting her close to Kerrick. I'm not playing matchmaker. I thought it might give you some time for a little one-on-one in the morning. She needs you."

Chapter Twenty-Four
The Wrong Place at the Right Time

Fernando pulled his head up above the side rail of *The Discoverer* and looked around the deck. Thick clouds covered the night sky, and the small LED lights along the superstructure's bottom lit the deck. Climbing up the anchor chain had been harder than he'd imagined.

He pulled himself over the rail and landed on the balls of his feet without a sound. When he looked down toward the water, he made out the shape of his raft tied to the chain. *Sure is convenient that they don't have a lookout posted. I wonder why it's so quiet.*

Fernando considered it a miracle that he had found *The Discoverer*. Funny how things work out. He and Miguel had lost sight of the Davenport's crew earlier that day when Miguel's boat stalled out, and they figured they may have lost their opportunity. Their boat trouble almost caused Fernando to miss his second date with Susan. She was something. *I'm certain that she doesn't hold a candle to Lacy.*

At dinner, Susan told him about seeing a big research boat out from Rock Sound. She went fishing that afternoon with her old man, and they wondered what a boat like that was doing around Eleuthera.

The darkness of the night surrounded him, and he pulled out a small penlight. He scanned the surface of the deck with short bursts of light. *Maybe, no one's home except for the crew. What if they decide to come to this side of the boat and see my raft? They won't do that, you idiot. The stairs are on the other side of the ship.*

Fernando worked to stay out of the light as he eased toward the door leading below. He knew Lacy's room wouldn't be above the deck. *I'll surprise her in her room if I can figure out which on'is hers.*

He opened the door leading below and stepped down the few stairs to the passageway lined with doors. He put his ear to the first door on the right and listened, but when he tried the knob, it was locked. He started to pull out his pick but decided to eliminate the rooms first based on which ones were unlocked. The door to the third room was open, and he slipped inside. Using his penlight, he scanned the room and could tell it wasn't Lacy's. He saw dirty clothes in a basket that belonged to a man and a woman. He knew Jon and Meg lived in style in their apartment above, so this one must have been the other couple's room. *The redhead is a doll, but I'll pass.*

Fernando started to open the door, but he heard faint footsteps outside. He pinned himself against the wall and prepared to attack anyone who entered. The footsteps continued past the room and back out to the main deck. He opened the door a crack and listened. Nothing.

The next room was open, too, and it was a girl's room. His light hit the open door to the bathroom, and he saw a blue-striped bathing suit drying on a hook. *That belongs to the other girl.* He remembered seeing the shorter girl wearing that bathing suit at the Davenport compound. She, too, was worth looking at. *She's not bad, but I'll save her for next time.*

When Fernando tried the room across the hall, the door was locked. He thought for a moment about the layout of the sleeping quarters. He'd put the two girls across from one another if he were assigning rooms. This room had to be Lacy's. He pulled out his pick and went to work.

The door was open in less than a minute, and Fernando stepped into the room. He breathed in deeply and smiled. *This is it.* His mind returned to the wonderful night he stood in her bedroom on Great Exuma. He watched her sleep that night and deserved an award for not touching her. She was sound asleep and wearing only a tee shirt. He trembled at the memory. He tiptoed to her bed and put her pillow to his nose. Electricity coursed through his body as her memorable scent filled his nostrils.

Won't Miguel be surprised when I bring you home tonight? I'll give you a little smell of my dream juice, carry you down the stairs, and pull you around to my raft while you dream about all the fun we'll have together. That shouldn't be too hard. We might have to take our time getting home, too. You'll enjoy getting to know old Fernando.

When he heard the door across the hallway open and close, he stepped into the bathroom and glued himself against the wall. He knew Lacy would be joining him in just minutes. *Don't girls shower before going to bed?* He stepped into the shower and pulled the curtain closed. He didn't hear another sound, except for his heart pounding. He waited a full thirty minutes before deciding she must not be coming back. *I bet she's spending the night somewhere with that boy. I'll kill him.*

He left the bathroom and walked without a sound to the cabin door. When he cracked it open, he saw the door across the hall. *I suppose me and the striped bathing suit girl could have some fun.* He stepped into the hallway and put his left hand on her doorknob. He grabbed his knife with the other hand.

Wait a minute, you idiot. She'll scream. She could be in the shower, which would be perfect, but what if she's not? I can't blow this.

He crept down the passageway and returned to the deck. He considered climbing back down the anchor line but chose to go down the stairs on the other side of the boat.

I'll have to paddle for a while, or they'll hear my motor. It's a good thing I thought of that earlier. I'll tell Miguel that me and Susan went out for a ride.

Close to an hour later, Fernando pulled the string to the small motor on the back of his raft and sped back toward the marina on the other side of the island. He was frustrated but holding Lacy's pillow to his nose lit a fire in his gut. She was going to be his. It was just a matter of time.

****

Lacy lay still in bed as the first hint of dawn peeked through the windows. She needed to go back to sleep, but she was wide awake before the sun rose for some reason. Jon had ruined her. She'd never be able to sleep in again.

She padded to the bathroom to begin her morning routine. Once she dressed, she decided to figure out how to make some coffee in the kitchen. The thought crossed her mind to fix breakfast for everyone.

When she entered the kitchen, she saw Meg making coffee. "Hey, Meg. I didn't expect to find you here."

"Good morning, Lacy. Aren't you the early riser?"

"I guess Jon has made me into a morning person. I woke up before 6:00 and couldn't go back to sleep."

"You want some coffee?"

"Thanks, Meg. I may as well. Why are you up so early?"

"Carla woke up at about 5:00, and I was wide awake by the time I got her back to sleep. So, what's up with you and Kerrick? It looks serious."

Lacy took a cup of coffee from Meg's hand and sat at the kitchen table. "It's not serious. I mean, we're not getting married next week or anything."

"I'd hope not," Meg laughed as she sat across from Lacy. "He's a great guy, and I approve of him."

"But...?"

"But you're young. You're only nineteen."

"Eighteen. I won't be nineteen until tomorrow, so don't rush it."

"Okay, so you're eighteen. I have seen some strong signs, though."

"Like what?"

"Well, like the way you look at each other. He also seems free to touch you. Not that I mean anything inappropriate. I just noticed that he feels comfortable touching you."

"I'll admit he's special. We have something between us that's pretty strong. It's the craziest thing, Meg. I wanted to hate the guy, and I now...I...uh...let's say I like him–a lot."

"I see. How did that happen?"

"I don't know, but he's the most sensitive, compassionate person I've ever met. He likes me for me. He's not a jerk, like most guys. He looks into my eyes when we talk, and I feel like he's looking into my soul half the time. He seems to understand me better than I understand myself."

"Wow. He sounds special. Most guys are all about themselves."

"You can say that again. He's the most honest guy I've ever met. I ran from guys because I didn't want to be disappointed. I decided that all guys were jerks and miniature versions of my dad. They'll all run off to another woman in a few years, so why bother?"

"Not all guys are like that," Meg insisted. "I've found two that were the cream of the crop. I guess I've just been blessed. Steve was special, and Jon is amazing too."

"Do you still miss Steve?"

"I'll always miss him. It's strange how Steve's death made it possible for my heart to be open to Jon. I can't explain it. Steve loved me and would want me to love Jon with all my heart."

"You're right. That sounds weird. I suppose Kerrick falls into the unique group of guys that every girl wishes to meet. I just somehow got lucky."

"I agree that he's unique," Meg said slowly, "but don't go too fast. Even good guys can hurt you."

"I've been a little afraid of that, but I can't imagine Kerrick hurting me. He's so sensitive and caring. He treats me like a princess. It's funny."

"Funny? How?"

"Not funny. Sad. My father called me Princess, but Kerrick treats me like one."

"You're right. That is sad. Lacy, you'll have to let your anger toward your parents go. You can't spend the rest of your life hating them. Hate will destroy you."

Lacy's face tightened, and her fists clenched. She didn't know if she wanted to hit something or cry. "I know you're right, but I can't let it go."

"I wish I could help you, but I think it's something you're going to have to choose in your own heart. You could start tomorrow when your mom comes."

"I don't want to see her. Didn't you tell her that?"

"I did, but she says she'll come to see you anyway."

"Let me guess. She says she's my mother and can come to see me if she wants to."

"Something like that. You'll never work through your feelings for her until you begin seeing her as the broken person she is."

"She's broken all right. She doesn't need to see me; she needs to see a shrink."

"Probably, but you can help her too. I've found that if I can see people as broken, I can look past some of the stupid things they do. The truth is that we're all broken, and we want everyone to give us…"

"Let me guess," Lacy interrupted. "We want people to give us grace and space. Grace to mess up and space to grow up."

Meg laughed. "Am I that predictable?"

"Let's say I've heard that sermon before. I know I'm broken too, and I'm so glad to have an aunt like you. You've helped me so much, Meg. Not just this summer. You've helped me my whole life. I've always wanted to be like you."

"Oh, my," Meg choked on some coffee. "Trust me. I'm broken too."

"If you are, you hide the cracks well. I'm thankful that you're in my life. I'm a different story than you. I've been broken my whole life, and it's apparent to everyone around me. I'm not sure I can even love someone. Maybe deep down, I'm like my mom. I've never loved anyone except myself."

"Everyone's broken in one way or another, and I think you can love someone. Since you were a little girl, I've felt your love for me."

"You're easy to love."

"No. Your love for me shows you can love."

"It's kind of sad that the last time I loved someone, I was a little girl," Lacy sighed.

"I didn't mean that you only loved me or anyone else when you were little. I think you've been a little emotionally scarred by some of the bad stuff that's gone on in your life, and you've never worked through your struggles."

Lacy leaned back in her chair. 'You know, Aunt Meg. I'm tired of being angry all the time. I think I'm ready to love again."

"Do you want to know what I think?"

"Sure."

"I think you're in love with Kerrick."

Lacy sat her mug on the table and crossed her arms. A single tear trickled down her cheek. "I," she paused, grabbed a napkin off the table, and dabbed her eyes. "I am. I love him so much."

"Lacy, you have such a bright future. I believe in you and think you'll be an outstanding woman. I'm confident you'll work through your issues and do the right thing with Kerrick."

Tears began rolling down Lacy's cheeks. These little talks were turning her into a crybaby. Meg and Ann seemed to know how to bring things out in her that somehow turned her into a sniffling loon. She bowed her head.

"You don't have to be embarrassed. Tears are good. Sometimes we must be broken before we can be remade."

"So, you think I'm being remade?"

"Are you?"

"I suppose so, but I'm quite a project. Thanks for being so patient with me. I love you, Meg, and I love Jon. You two are the best thing that's ever happened to me. I think I'm going for a walk down to the sound."

"Okay. Make sure to be back for breakfast. I'm going to get everyone going in about an hour."

Lacy stood up from the table and moved toward the kitchen door.

"Lacy, please be careful. There are weirdos out there, even this early in the morning."

Lacy paused with her hand on the knob and grinned. "Careful is my middle name."

Chapter Twenty-Five

Back to the Bay

Meg finished cooking the sausage and started on pancakes. She marveled at how her conversation with Lacy just fell right into place. Ann told her last night that she might have an opportunity for one-on-one time with Lacy, and everything happened as she predicted.

Meg went to Randal's room and knocked on the door. "Guys? Breakfast is ready." She opened the door to the room she and Jon had slept in the night before to see Jon reading a book to Carla. "Good morning, Sweet Pea."

"That's a first," Jon teased. "You've never called me Sweet Pea."

"Not you, goofball. You're not a sweet pea. You're a…"

"I'm a hunk of burning love."

Meg laughed. "If you say so. Speaking of burning love, I've got pancakes on the stove."

She hurried back to the kitchen in time to flip the pancakes. She set the table and wondered why Lacy hadn't returned. It wasn't that far to the sound.

"Good morning, Meg," Kerrick said, pushing Randal into the kitchen in his wheelchair.

"Good morning," Randal echoed.

"Hey, guys. Kerrick, Lacy went for a walk to the water. I told her to be back for breakfast. Would you mind seeing if you can find her? "

"Sure thing."

"Mama," Carla toddled into the kitchen as Kerrick left to find Lacy. "Book?"

"After breakfast, sweetheart. We'll read a book until Grandma Judy gets here."

Jon poured a cup of coffee and sat down at the table. "We didn't talk with Judy last night about plans to get her back here."

"True. We were all so tired that those details didn't cross our minds."

"Let's send Kerrick out in the Robalo to get her, and then we can put Randal in the boat for another day in the bay." Jon turned toward Randal. "Kerrick told me how much you enjoyed being a part of the group yesterday. I'd love for you to return with us if you're up to it."

"I'd love to."

Meg walked over to the table and picked up Jon's plate. "How many pancakes do you want, Honey?"

"I'll take three. Is there any milk left in the refrigerator?"

"We have another gallon."

Jon got up and headed toward the refrigerator. "Randal, do you want any milk?"

"Sure. Thanks, Mr. Jon."

Meg's back was turned to the conversation, but she grinned at Randal's response. For some reason, he was Mr. Jon, but she was just Meg. The boys feared Jon, so she assumed the mister would always be a part of his name.

Meg placed plates of pancakes in front of Jon, Randal, and Carla. "Randal, I assume you want three, too."

"Thank you. Three's great."

"Pway, Mama."

"Okay, Sweetheart. You can pray."

Carla bowed her head and balled up her little fists. She babbled for a minute with words Meg couldn't understand, but she was sure God knew what she meant. Meg did, however, understand the final word: "Amen."

The kitchen door opened, and Lacy entered, followed by Kerrick.

"Girl, where have you been?" Meg demanded. "I was about to call the Royal Police."

"Really?" Lacy gawked.

"No. Not really," Meg admitted, "but I started to get a little worried."

"I'm sorry. I was watching the seagulls and lost track of time. The water is so peaceful this time of day."

"You're right about that," Kerrick agreed. "I love being on the water first thing in the morning."

"Then you're just the guy for the job," Jon insisted. "How about finishing breakfast and going out to *The Discoverer* to pick up Judy? We need her to come back here to watch Carla so we can get to work."

"I'll go with you," Lacy insisted.

Meg sat plates of pancakes and sausage in front of Lacy and Kerrick. "You both need to eat first."

Fifteen minutes later, Kerrick and Lacy hurried out the door.

"She seems to be happy," Jon observed.

"I think she is," Meg confessed. "Maybe for the first time in her life."

****

Kerrick handed the keys to Lacy as they stepped onto the dock. "You want to start her up, and I'll untie the ropes?"

"Yes, sir, Captain," Lacy saluted.

"So, we're back to the Captain stuff?" Kerrick stopped Lacy before she stepped off of the dock onto the swimmers' platform at the back of the boat. "So, if I'm the Captain, does that make you my mate?"

Lacy stared into his smiling blue eyes with a grin, "That's about the corniest thing I've ever heard."

He put his hands on her hips and pulled her to him. "I can be worse, but I'll save it for later."

He placed his lips onto hers, and she wrapped her arms around his neck. Lacy could feel her heart pounding and her stomach turning summersaults. Opening her eyes, she noticed a fisherman in a nearby boat staring at them.

"I think we have an audience," she whispered.

Kerrick nipped her ear. "He's just jealous."

"I don't know about that, but I do know that Meg will have my hide if we don't get Judy back here."

"So, are all women part of the cold-water committee?"

Lacy pulled back a little and looked up into Kerrick's eyes. "The what?"

"You know. The cold-water committee. They're always pouring cold water onto every good idea."

"You're saying that making out here on the dock in broad daylight is a good idea?"

"It's one of the best ideas I've had today."

"In that case, I'm the chairman of the committee."

Lacy stepped backward off the dock, missed the swimmers' platform on the boat, and fell into the water. When she came up sputtering, Kerrick doubled over laughing.

"Yes, ma'am, Madam, Chairman," Kerrick howled. "I'll get these ropes untied right away."

"That wasn't funny," Lacy huffed while trying to hide the growing grin on her face.

She pulled herself into the boat and started the engine. "Are you going to get aboard, or will you stand there laughing your head off?"

Kerrick jumped aboard and fell backward into the seat as Lacy jammed the throttle forward.

"That fisherman's not going to like the wake you're leaving him," Kerrick said as he gasped for air.

"He won't notice," Lacy grinned, "'cause he's laughing so hard."

Lacy pointed the Robalo toward the opening of the sound and had the little boat out in the open water in record time. As they bounced across the still ocean, she felt Kerrick's mouth on her neck and his arms wrapped around her.

"Don't think you can make up with me now after laughing at my demise," Lacy shouted.

"You've got to admit that was one of the funniest things I've ever seen."

"I can't admit it because I don't know what you've seen."

"Trust me. It was pretty funny. Okay, I've got an idea to make up for it."

"It's going to have to be good," Lacy cooed.

"Let's go to dinner tonight. My treat. For your birthday."

"I'm not celebrating my birthday this year."

"Okay. Then let's just go out to dinner."

"Are you asking me on a date, Mr. Daniels?"

"Yes, I am, Madam Chairman."

"It's Madam Chairwoman, and yes, I'd be honored to go on a date with you. Where will we go?"

"I saw a brochure for a cool-looking restaurant at Governor's Harbour. It's called Pascal's."

"Sounds good to me. Will Jon let us use the boat?"

"I'm sure he will. You're his favorite niece, and I'm his favorite male intern."

"I'm his only niece, and you're his only male intern."

"Then it's settled. He'll let us."

Once Judy was back at the house with Carla, Jon, Meg, Kerrick, and Lacy headed toward Double Bay. Jon pulled the Robalo beside the *New Beginnings*, and Kerrick tied the two boats together. Meg and Lacy stepped out of the Robalo and hurried aboard the yacht.

"It's about time you guys got here," Barry jabbed.

"Y'all are too anxious to get started," Lacy insisted. "I suppose that's a good sign."

"Lacy, you and Kerrick go ahead and suit up," Jon ordered, "and I'll review a few things with the boys."

"I can dive?" Kerrick felt like shouting.

"The doctor said a week, and it's been a week. It's about twenty feet deep here, anyway. You should be fine."

"After you, Madam Chairwoman," Kerrick said as he opened the door to the galley.

"Enough with the Madam Chairwoman," Lacy demanded.

Kerrick grinned and pinched her cheek. "Yes, ma'am. You sure are getting ornery in your old age."

Lacy rolled her eyes and hurried through the galley into the back cabin. She slipped into her bathing suit and stepped back into the galley to put on her wetsuit. Kerrick walked past her into the cabin to dress, but when he passed her, he let his hand slide across her bare belly. His touch was electrifying. Thankfully, he continued into the cabin and closed the door.

"Any questions?" Jon was saying as Lacy joined the group.

"Yeah," Lacy raised her hand. "What will Kerrick and I be doing?"

"I'd like you to guide the sled while we scan the last three sections you mapped out yesterday. The boys are confident they can finish mapping out the last area of the bay, and they'll be ready for us when we get to them. Jose is going to supervise."

"Why isn't Ann diving with us anymore?" David asked.

"She wanted to spend the day with Judy and Randal," Jose replied.

"I thought Randal was coming with us," Tae said.

"He was at first, but we decided that two days in a row might be a little much," Meg answered. "We don't want to set him back."

Everyone was suited up and in the water within ten minutes. While the boys followed Jose toward the end of the taped-off section, Lacy and Kerrick began to guide the sled toward an orange post that marked where they had stopped scanning the previous day.

They completed the job by 4:00. Lacy dragged her body aboard the Carver and stripped out of her wetsuit. When she stepped out of the freshwater shower on the back of the boat, she swapped places with Tae and gave him a high five.

"Well, today's dive was an exercise in futility," Lacy mumbled.

Tae looked at her before turning on the water. "An exercise in what?"

"Never mind. I left you some hot water."

"I didn't think this shower had any hot water."

Lacy grinned. "It doesn't."

Kerrick walked toward Lacy on the back deck. "Hey, Gorgeous. Your generous uncle has agreed to let us take the Robalo to Governor's Harbour tonight."

"Awesome. The problem is my clean clothes are on *The Discoverer*, and yours are at the house."

"That's not a problem," Kerrick asserted. "We'll get your clothes and then shower at the house. I'll bet $25 that I'll be ready first."

"You're on. I hope you've got some money."

Chapter Twenty-Six
A Night Out

Lacy sat on the couch with a day-old copy of USA Today and scanned through the opening pages. She wanted to find the sports section and see how the Braves were doing.

Kerrick burst through his bedroom door into the den. She looked up from the paper and held her hand out as she returned to the article about the Braves' most recent loss.

"You should have lowered your bet a little," Lacy grinned while still looking at the paper. "Twenty-five dollars is mighty tempting to a starving college coed."

Kerrick dug in his pocket and pulled out some bills. "Starving coed? You don't look starving to me."

"So, are you calling me fat?"

"No! You're not fat, but you're not a normal girl."

Lacy pulled her hand back before he gave her the money. "I'm not taking your money, and what is that supposed to mean?"

"I mean that most girls are slow, and yes, you are taking my money. You beat me fair and square."

Lacy ignored the cash. "You sound like a chauvinist. Some girls are slow, just like some guys are slow. Granted, girls have more to do to make themselves presentable."

Kerrick pulled Lacy to her feet. "Lucky for you, you're presentable all of the time." He kissed her and led her to the door. "Maybe we can beat the dinnertime rush."

"I doubt that," Lacy said, looking at her watch. "It's almost 5:30, and it'll take us at least thirty minutes to get to Governor's Harbour."

"Okay, so let's hurry to get there before they close."

"Isn't that Front Porch restaurant where we went with Mr. Phil close to Governor's Harbour?"

"I think that place was on Hatchet Bay, but that's not far from Governor's Harbour."

"Didn't Mr. Phil say he lives somewhere in Governor's Harbour?"

"Maybe. I don't remember. Let's get going."

****

A beer commercial plastered the screen halfway through the evening news. Fernando got up and headed toward the refrigerator. He grabbed the last can of beer and returned to his chair as Miguel walked into the galley.

"The power of suggestion," Fernando motioned toward the television.

Miguel opened the refrigerator door. "Hey, you got the last one."

"You snooze, you lose. We can get more when we go to dinner. I'm starved. How about a burger?"

"Sure. We can go over to Mark's. Woah. Look at that jerk flying into the marina."

Fernando got up and looked out the window. "I'll be…"

"Is that who I think it is?"

"Right into our hands," Fernando grinned. He pictured the research vessel at Rock Sound but didn't want to admit to Miguel that he went aboard it last night. "I heard there was a research boat down at Rock Sound."

"Maybe. Who cares where their ship is? The girl is tying their little fishing boat off fifty yards away from us."

"I bet they're going to eat somewhere close by."

Miguel pulled out his phone as they watched Lacy and Kerrick walk into Pascal's. "I've got an idea. We've been texting our boy asking for the exact location of the Davenports. We know they're at Rock Sound, or at least nearby. That little Robalo came from the south, and they wouldn't take something that small too far from the main ship."

"If he gives us the wrong location, we'll know he's screwing with us."

"If he's screwing with us, the game's up."

Miguel typed a text into his phone and hit send. He had to wait almost ten minutes before his phone buzzed with a reply. "He says the whole group returned to Nassau—even the girl."

"Right! And we just saw Lacy get out of her fancy little red boat and waltz into Pascal's. Didn't you hear from Freddy this morning? Is he still in Jacksonville?"

"Yeah," Miguel confirmed. "He said Kelsey's parents are out of town, and she's alone. I think it's time 'ol Freddy pays our little girl a visit."

"I wish I were there. I'd love to visit her."

"Shut up and get your gun. Get the drug and a rag, too. I like this new stuff much better than the needle."

Miguel punched in a number and held his phone to his ear. After a few rings, Freddy answered. "Hey, Freddy. It's Miguel."

"Put him on speaker," Fernando insisted. "I want to hear."

Miguel pulled the phone away from his ear and tapped a button. "Are you near the girl's house?"

"What do you think?" a gruff voice sounded through a cracking speaker.

"Okay, stupid question. You're staying in the apartment across the street. Listen. We need some pictures, and it may be time to ratchet this thing up a bit."

"She just came in from a run, and I'm positive she's alone."

"Send me a convincing picture, and stand by."

"You know my fee, and if this thing goes to the next level, we're talking about some serious money."

"I know. Just do it."

Miguel and Fernando headed for Pascal's porch. They found a couple of chairs in the outside dining area that gave them a good view of the front door and ordered drinks. Miguel's phone buzzed as the waiter returned with something from the bar.

"It took him long enough," Fernando grumbled.

Miguel looked at the text message. "He says the girl did some stretching exercises in her house before she got in the shower."

"He watched her stretch and get in the shower?"

Fernando's mind raced back to Jacksonville, Florida, where he first met this girl. Almost a year ago, he pretended to be selling subscriptions to the Jacksonville Herald Newspaper and knocked on the front door of her small home. He had waited across the street until her parents drove away and knew she was alone.

"Hi. My name is Juan, and I'm selling subscriptions to the Jacksonville Herald. Would you be interested?"

"We already get the newspaper," the dark-haired beauty said with a soft, sexy voice.

"Oh. Well, in that case, can I ask you some questions? If you let me ask you a few questions, the newspaper will give me ten dollars, and you'll get a ten-dollar Starbucks gift card. You'll also be entered to win an all-expense cruise for four."

Fernando pulled a gift card from his pocket that he had purchased at Walmart earlier that day.

"Uh...Sure. I guess so."

"Okay," Fernando said as he uncapped his pen. "What's your name?"

"Kelsey."

Though he already knew it, Fernando asked for her last name and began rattling through questions about the paper. He asked about the girl's personal habits and schedule. He learned a lot about Kelsey's class schedule, shopping preferences, and favorite places to hang out. He learned that because she had just started her freshman year at Jacksonville University, she chose to focus on school and not get a job.

She stayed home most mornings this semester and spent her spare time at the library on campus when she wasn't at home. She didn't have a boyfriend, and she didn't read the paper.

The girl was a babe. She wasn't quite as tall as Lacy and didn't have the spunk Lacy had, but she was still hot. He would have given anything to be the one at her house right now. Well, maybe not anything. Lacy was the chick he wanted most.

The phone buzzed again, and Miguel whistled as he looked at the picture. Fernando reached out and grabbed the phone.

"Whoa," Fernando blurted out. "She doesn't have..."

"Would you shut up?" Miguel said under his breath. "The last thing we need is for someone to hear us."

Fernando lowered his voice. "He's in the house. He's got to be inside to take a picture like that."

"How else would he know she was stretching and then got in the shower, you fool?"

"Good point."

"Let's make our boy squirm."

******

Lacy leaned back and placed her hands on her stomach. "I'm about to explode. I shouldn't have gotten the platter."

"I told you the reviews said they had huge portions," Kerrick reminded her. "Of course, it's your birthday, so you can have whatever you want."

She stared into Kerrick's light blue eyes. "Don't remind me. I think I have everything I want right here."

Kerrick smiled as he took Lacy's hand. "This has been the best summer of my life. Deciding to work with the Davenports will be the second-best decision of my life up to this point."

"What's the first best decision.?"

"Diving into the water after your medallion when you broke the chain."

Lacy laughed. "I'm glad you did it, but why was it your best decision?"

"Because that was the first time you smiled at me, and I think my impulsive act caused your heart toward me to thaw."

"That's interesting," Lacy said as she sat back in her chair. "You may be right. I suppose saving my medallion started something, and before you knew it, I was spilling my guts to you about my screwed-up life and messed-up family."

"I'm glad you opened up to me. The fact is that we all have messed up lives to some extent."

"Mine wins the prize."

"Lacy, you know I care about you a lot. Because I care, I'm worried about how you will handle your mom tomorrow."

"Don't ruin a perfect evening by bringing her up."

"You just can't ignore your mom."

"Yes, I can. She may be coming to see me, but I won't see her."

"Lacy…"

"I don't want to talk about it or her. Period!"

"If you say so," Kerrick mumbled. "I've got to go to the bathroom. I'll be right back."

Kerrick slipped away from the table and headed across the restaurant. Lacy couldn't believe he had to be so stupid as to bring up her mom. *If he wanted to ruin my evening, he sure picked the right way to do it.*

Lacy heard a funny noise coming from the other side of the table and noticed that Kerrick's phone vibrated once against his plate. He left it lying on the table. *Who would be sending Kerrick a text message?* After a minute, the phone vibrated again.

Lacy looked toward the bathroom doors, and there was no sign of Kerrick. She picked up his phone and turned it over. She saw on the screen that a text with an attachment came in from some phone number that was not on his list of contacts. *If this were from his family or a friend, it would have a name on the screen and not just a phone number.* When she pressed the button, it went straight to the home screen. It surprised her that he didn't have his phone protected with a password. With trembling fingers, she tapped the screen over the text message icon.

A picture of a beautiful girl appeared on the screen, and she appeared to have just gotten out of the shower. Lacy's mouth dropped open as her world seemed to stop. The message said, "Miss you," followed by a series of X's.

A chasm opened in her heart, and she fell into a black hole. Lacy laid the phone down on the table and stood to her feet. She bumped into a chair at the empty table next to theirs as she turned to head toward the front door. She didn't know where to go but had to get out. As she reached for the door, another buzz-ing sound came from the direction of her table. It didn't matter. Nothing mattered anymore.

Chapter Twenty-Seven
Missing

Meg stopped her rocking chair and cleared her throat to get Jon's attention. Jon looked up from the map he was pouring over on the small table in the corner and saw Meg nodding her head toward the light switch. He winked at her and padded toward the switch.

"Hold on just a second," he whispered. "I'll turn on the lamp."

Once the tiny lamp beside the bed came on, Meg tiptoed into Carla's small bedroom and laid her down in the bed. Jon watched from the main part of the cabin as his heart swelled with gratitude for the wonderful gift of his wife. She was a treasure.

His thoughts were interrupted by the light chirping sound of the ship's phone system. "Hello."

He heard on the other end of the phone. "Hey, Jon. It's Jose. We've got a problem."

"What's up?"

"Kerrick just called and said Lacy's missing."

"Missing?" Jon gasped.

Meg closed the door to Carla's room and walked toward Jon. "What's missing?"

"You'd better come on up to the bridge, Jon."

Jon hung up and headed toward the door.

"What is it, Jon. What's missing."

"Lacy's missing. I've got to get up to the phone."

"Oh, my God. I'll come up with you."

Meg turned on the baby monitor and followed Jon up one flight of stairs to the bridge. Jon saw Ann coming up from the main deck as they topped the stairs.

"When did he call?" Jon asked as he and Meg burst through the door.

Jose reached for the phone. "He called Captain Buffington about ten minutes ago and asked him to get a message to either you or me to call him back. I came up to call, and I just got off the phone with him when I buzzed you."

"What did he say?"

Jose looked up as Ann came through the door to join the group. "He said he and Lacy were having dinner together at Pascal's, and he brought up her mother. She got upset about it, but he didn't think it was a big deal. He went to the bathroom, and when he came back, she was gone. The waitress said that she just walked out the door."

"Lacy's got a temper," Meg confirmed. "I can imagine her getting angry and walking out."

"Where would she go?" Ann wondered. "It's not like she even knows her way around."

"She's just blowing off some steam," Jon said. "My guess is that she'll be back at the restaurant by the time I get up to Governor's Harbour."

"I'll go with you," Jose insisted.

"Call us as soon as you know something," Meg called to the two men as they hurried toward the steps.

As the *New Beginnings* sped toward Governor's Harbour, Jon's mind raced back to all that had happened over the last few weeks. The accident on the barge was a close call, but other than that, things were going well. Lacy had become a different person.

When she arrived at the compound on Great Exuma over a month ago, she was bitter, rude, and resentful. This morning, she was a different girl: laughing, sensitive, and compassionate. Meg warned him several days ago that her mother's insistence on coming to visit could send her into a tailspin.

Jose pointed starboard as they slowed to enter the marina. "There's an open slip two down from that Chris Craft."

"Thanks. I think I see the Robalo a little further up."

Jon pulled his cell phone out of his pocket and dialed. "Kerrick. Where are you? Has she come back?" He listened for a minute. "Jose and I'll be there in a few minutes. We're docking now."

After securing the Carver, Jon and Jose hurried toward Pascal's. As they approached the restaurant's porch, Kerrick stood and walked to meet them. His face was ashen.

Jon put his hand on Kerrick's shoulder. "We'll find her, Kerrick. Don't worry. I assume you have a picture of her on your phone you can show people."

"Uh…yeah," Kerrick mumbled. "I have one."

"I imagine she's upset and took a walk. You know how she can be. Let's split up and search the area. We can stay in touch by phone. Kerrick, it would be best if you stayed around here. I'll start by going down the street along the bay. Jose, you can go down Queen's Highway. We'll meet in the middle."

As Jon and Jose turned to leave, Kerrick called out. "Jon. There's more. I think I know why she left."

The two men turned back toward Kerrick. Jon had never seen Kerrick look so forlorn. "What's up? Did you guys fight?"

"Jon. Please forgive me."

"I don't know what you're talking about."

"It's a long story," Kerrick began, "but I'm afraid we don't have much time. You know my dad is sick."

"I know. Colon cancer. Right?"

"Right. He began struggling to pay the bills and made some risky investments. He borrowed money from some guys because his investments didn't pan out. These guys are pretty bad, and they started giving him a hard time. I think he decided to die and not worry about what he owes them."

"We can help your dad," Jose promised.

"Well," Kerrick continued, "the guys he owes the money to realized my dad didn't plan to pay them. A man with an accent contacted me back in the fall and told me I had to help them or face the consequences. While we talked, I received a text with a picture of my sister at the beach. He told me he had men following Kelsey around, and if I didn't get him some information, I would attend her funeral before my dad died from cancer."

Jon crossed his arms. "Helping them out has something to do with us?"

Kerrick hung his head. "I'm sorry, Jon. They were going to kill Kelsey if I didn't help them. I didn't get back to them immediately, and they sent me another picture of her in her bedroom. They used a telephoto lens to make it look close up."

"What did they want you to do?" Jose asked.

"They said I just had to get a job with you and let them know when you would be away from home. They planned to break into your house on Great Exuma and bust into your safe. I played along, and when I learned that you didn't have much in your safe, I felt it would be okay. It seemed to me that my sister would be okay in the long run, and you wouldn't lose out on much."

"How did you know I didn't keep much in my safe?"

"You told me once that you didn't trust safes and that yours was only to hold things until you could get them to a securer location."

"I remember that now that you mention it. I told you I only had a few legal documents in the safe."

Kerrick nodded. "For some reason, those guys didn't break into your house. They've continued to harass me over the last month, saying I had to inform them about your location."

"Did you?"

"At first, I did. I'm sorry. I figured they were delaying the break in for some reason. Then, I quit replying to their texts right away. A couple of weeks ago, they sent me a picture of Kelsey. It was close up, and she wasn't fully dressed. They told me I'd better reply to their messages."

"I'm assuming you began to cooperate."

"Not exactly. I sent them messages telling them where we had been instead of where we were going. I need also to tell you that Lacy saw that picture a couple of weeks ago—the one of Kelsey...not fully dressed. She thought a girl was sexting me. She got mad, but we worked through it."

"Did you tell her what was going on?"

"No, but I told her the picture was my sister. I don't think she believed me. When I went to the restroom tonight, another picture came through. My sister was...well...coming out of the bathroom. After taking a shower. The message said something about her missing me. They sent me two, and I'm confident the guy taking the picture had to be in the house. There's no way he could have gotten that shot otherwise."

"Maybe they hid a remote camera in her room," Jose suggested.

"Well, I know Lacy saw the first picture because I left my phone on the table at the restaurant when I went to the restroom. The picture had been opened. I'm sure she thinks Kelsey is my girlfriend. She saw the picture, got mad, and ran away."

"That's possible," Jon nodded.

"I can't handle this thing with these guys anymore," Kerrick confided. "I need help, Jon."

"You should have told me a long time ago. Your sister could be in danger. Let's find Lacy, and then we'll figure out how to get help for your sister. You still need to stay around here so when Lacy comes back, you'll see her. We'll follow my plan and see you back here in an hour or so."

"Okay. Jon, I'm sorry."

"I know you are, Kerrick. We'll talk more about it later."

****

Kerrick watched as Jon hurried off toward Bay Street and Jose turned toward Queens Highway. Sorrow and regret flooded his mind as he considered the deception over the last seven or eight months. His shame wrapped him up like a blanket. He should never have gone along with those thugs. Why didn't he report them right away to the police? He had been so frightened for his father, and now, his sister could be in trouble.

Ignoring their threats would have been easier if they hadn't shown him the other picture in December. *I didn't even tell Jon and Jose about the picture of the dead guy.*

Miguel never told Kerrick who the dead man was in the picture, but he was sure they'd kill his father if he didn't cooperate. Now, Kerrick wondered if Kelsey was safe. Were they messing with him, or were they threatening his sister? They sent so many pictures to him over the last few months, but this one was different. *They must have a remote camera in her bedroom.*

Confessing everything to Jon brought him some relief. Jon would know how to handle all this mess.

Kerrick had made things a lot worse by trying to handle the situation himself, and now, he'd betrayed Jon. A pain stabbed his heart as he thought about the fact he had also betrayed Lacy. *She'll never forgive me.*

Kerrick walked back toward Pascal's and looked around the dining room again for the 100th time. People crowded the main dining area, but he saw no sign of Lacy. He tried to imagine what she would have done, and several possibilities came to mind.

She may have stomped around Governor's Harbour, which meant Jon or Jose would find her. She could have gone somewhere secluded to sulk.

He walked back onto the front porch and tried to imagine what his sister would have done. *Kelsey would call a friend. She would pour her heart out to someone who would listen. The problem is that Lacy doesn't have any friends on Eleuthera. The only person she knows is Mr. Phil Register; she wouldn't call him.*

Chapter Twenty-Eight
Perfect Catch

Miguel couldn't believe it when Lacy stumbled out the restaurant door. He nudged Fernando and nodded toward the girl walking toward the steps. When they got up to follow her, she stopped at the corner to talk to an old guy crossing the street. She seemed to know the man. He joined Lacy as they walked down the street toward the bay.

Miguel and Fernando hurried down the steps toward Lacy and worked to catch up with them without being conspicuous. They got close enough to where they could hear their conversation.

"I didn't recognize the girl, Mr. Phil. It had to be his girlfriend. Her message said she missed him."

The old man patted her shoulder. "She could just be a friend."

"Friends don't send pictures of themselves like that. Mr. Phil, she was…" Lacy began to cry.

"Honey. It will be okay. I've thought about you and Kerrick a lot and hoped we could meet again soon for dinner. I'm sure you'll be able to work through this."

"Seeing you crossing the street surprised me," Lacy sniffed.

"I think it was providence that we met here tonight. I live a few miles from here and often come to Pascal's."

"I'm sure you need to eat dinner. I'll be okay."

"Nonsense. I can eat dinner any time. I'll help you sort through everything. When's your wedding?"

"Oh, Mr. Phil. We're not getting married."

"Uh…Lacy. I'm sure there's a reasonable explanation for the picture. Kerrick's a nice young man. Why don't we talk about it? We can sit on a bench in the park. Would you like that?"

"Sure, but our relationship is hopeless. I should have known better."

Miguel motioned to the next street. He and Fernando took a left and strolled up a block before taking another right. They saw Lacy and the man walk into a small park and sit on a bench on the far side near a fountain.

"Let's come in from behind them," Miguel ordered. "With the noise from the fountain, they'll never hear us."

"We can't just take them right here, Miguel. Someone might see us."

"Calm down, Fernando. It's getting dark, and there aren't many people around. We'll give it a few minutes."

"You going to knock off the old man? I'll grab the girl."

"I'm sure you will, Fernando. I'll get the girl, and you take care of the old man. You'll get your turn, but not until we've got the medallion."

"You always have the fun."

"Right. You go through the park and stop to ask the old guy for directions or come up with something. I'll come out of the bushes and grab the girl. We'll need a car to get the girl down to our boat. Carrying her would not be a good idea."

"I'm sure the old man has a car," Fernando guessed.

"Good point. He uses a cane, so he wouldn't have walked far. We'll get his key and find his car. He probably has a key fob, and you can press the button and watch for lights to come on. I'll stay here with the girl while you find the car."

Miguel watched as Fernando strolled down the street to the other side of the park. He couldn't believe the girl was 100 yards away. He didn't see the medallion, but it didn't matter. The Davenports would happily trade a small piece of gold for their precious niece. Too bad Lacy would never live to see them again.

Miguel had almost given up on finding the other medallion, and now it was as good as theirs. He would soon be richer than the Davenports. The only loose end was Fernando, but he wouldn't be a problem. Once they found the treasure, Fernando would be history.

When he saw Fernando approaching the fountain, Miguel moved toward the palm tree behind Lacy. He uncapped the bottle of isoflurane he bought from his supplier in Nassau and poured the liquid on a rag.

"Excuse me," Fernando cleared his throat as he approached the bench. "I'm supposed to meet a friend at Pascal's. Do you know where it is?"

When Phil Register stood to point up the street to the restaurant, Miguel stepped around the palm and through the bushes. As Lacy turned toward the noise behind her, Miguel grabbed her and covered her mouth and nose with the rag.

"Hey, what are you doing?" Phil blurted as he raised his cane to strike Miguel.

Fernando punched the old man so hard that his head jerked hard, and he fell backward. His head hit the corner of the bench, and he collapsed onto the ground. Lacy slumped into Miguel's arms.

"That worked well," Fernando said, rubbing his right fist. "Why don't I wait with the girl while you get the car."

"Just do what I said," Miguel growled. "You're not thinking with your brain."

Twenty minutes later, Fernando pulled the old man's Cadillac up to the dock while Miguel held Lacy in the back seat. He saw a jacket on the floorboard, picked it up, forced Lacy's limp arms through the sleeves, and pulled the hood over her head.

"That should keep anyone from identifying her," Miguel said. "Let's get aboard. If we pass anyone, she's just drunk, and we have to get her to bed."

Miguel looked down the dock toward their boat and didn't see anyone. He got out of the car and pulled Lacy out behind him. "Fernando, you'll have to get on her other side. We need to make it look like she's been walking to the boat but passed out."

They wrapped her arms around their necks and dragged her down the dock. Miguel saw the *New Beginnings* beside a large Chris Craft fishing boat.

"That's the Davenports' yacht," Miguel said. "They must be here looking for Lacy."

As they approached the Chris Craft, a couple stepped onto the dock from the fishing boat and started toward town. The man eyed Fernando and Miguel.

"I told her not to drink anymore," Miguel insisted. "My old lady can't handle her liquor."

Miguel looked at Lacy and saw her head facing down toward the dock. No way the couple could identify her. He looked up and saw that the overhead light was out. *They won't be able to identify any of us.* The woman shook her head as she and her husband walked up the dock toward town.

****

Kerrick headed toward the marina and noticed a couple walking toward him. "Excuse me. I'm looking for a friend of mine." He held out his cell phone to the couple to show them a picture of Lacy. "Have you seen this girl?"

The man looked at the picture. "She's a beautiful girl, young man. You shouldn't let her get away. We've just pulled in from Nassau, so we haven't seen anyone."

"Honey, we saw a couple of guys on the dock," the woman reminded her husband. "They had a drunk woman with them. It was dark, though, and I couldn't see them very well."

"Any chance the guys had an accent? Like maybe English wasn't their first language?"

"They were Hispanic," the man said, "I'm sure of that. The guy who spoke to us used perfect English but had an accent. I'm pretty sure their skin was darker than mine, though there wasn't much light on the dock."

Kerrick looked toward the dock and saw two men helping a third person onto a large cruiser. *That's got to be Lacy, and I'd bet money on those men being Miguel and his lackey.* One of the guys climbed up to the bridge while the other one untied the boat. Kerrick began running toward the dock.

By the time he got to the slip, the boat was already heading out of the marina. He looked around for the Robalo but realized he'd never be able to take a boat that small out to sea. He jumped aboard the Chris Craft docked in the next slip, climbed to the bridge, and reached under the steering wheel. Sure enough, there was a key box. He pulled the spare key out and started up the engine. *I'm going to be in trouble for taking this boat. I don't have any choice. They've got Lacy.*

As he pulled out of the marina, he dialed Jon's number. He knew Miguel was taking Lacy to their island, but Kerrick didn't know how to get there. Miguel took him there in December, but they'd covered his head with a bag before leaving Nassau. When

Jon's phone went to voice mail, he left a message and raced out of the marina into the night.

****

Jon said Jose's name into his phone and waited for his phone to call his friend. "Hey, Jose. Any sign of her?"

"No, I haven't seen many people at all."

"I've seen a few people here, but they were in groups. Let's continue walking, and I'm sure we'll meet in a bit. Have you heard from Kerrick?"

"No. Ann called a minute ago, but that's been my only call."

"All right. I'll see you in a few."

About thirty minutes later, Jon waved to Jose at the other end of the street. They met in the middle and walked back to Pascal's.

"I called Kerrick after we talked," Jon began, "but his phone went straight to voice mail. He must not have a good signal here."

"That's odd. His voice was crystal clear when we talked to him on the phone earlier."

"Maybe his battery died. I assume he'll be around Pascal's."

Jon was quite concerned about Lacy. He couldn't imagine her leaving Governor's Harbour, and it would be a long hike either up or down the Queen's Highway to get to the next community. He had a feeling deep in his gut that something wasn't right.

"Let's cut through the park," Jose suggested as he pointed. "Pascal's is a few blocks that way."

"Is that someone sleeping on the ground?" Jose wondered aloud as they walked across the street toward the park's edge. "I haven't seen any homeless people on this island."

When they rounded the bench, Jose gasped as he recognized his friend. "It's Phil Register. We've had dinner with him and visited his church several times."

Jon knelt and placed his fingers on his neck. "I'm afraid he's dead. Call the police."

"Does 911 work out here?"

"I'm not sure, but I think that's a patrol car that just turned toward Pascal's. I'll stay here with the body."

A few minutes later, a patrol car pulled up, and Jose exited the passenger side. A police officer got out from behind the wheel, and they walked toward Jon.

"I'm Officer Sanders," he said as he took in the scene. He knelt and placed his fingers on Phil's neck. "Have you touched anything?"

"I felt for a pulse, and that's it," Jon admitted. "Those are our footprints in the sand."

"I know the man," Jose offered.

"Most people around here do," the officer replied as he turned on his flashlight. "Everyone considers him the patriarch of the island. It looks like he hit his head on the bench. He probably had a heart attack."

Jose looked at Jon, who shook his head slightly. The officer pulled a device off his shoulder and called for help.

"Officer," Jon began. "We need to meet up with one of the interns who works for us, and I'm sure you need a formal statement. Can I give you my phone number, and we can talk later?"

"I'm sorry, sir, but I need some information now. I'm sure Mr. Register died by natural causes, but I at least need to ask you a few questions."

"Can Jose go up to Pascal's? He can be back in a few minutes."

"Sure. I'll ask you some questions while he's gone."

By the time Jose returned, the officer was through questioning Jon. He opened his notebook to another page and asked for Jose's full name. After another ten minutes of questions, Jon and Jose left the park. As they walked away, an ambulance pulled up to the curb.

"Phil didn't die of natural causes," Jose whispered as they left the park.

"I didn't think so," Jon said. "That bruise on the side of his head came from something else."

"I'm sure his jaw was broken," Jose added. "That officer will be calling us back soon. I didn't see any sign of Kerrick."

"I'll try to call him again." Jon turned on his phone and saw he had a voicemail. "He's called. That's odd I didn't hear it ring. I must have been dialing you at the time."

Jon put his phone on speaker. "Hey, Jon. It's Kerrick. Those guys have Lacy, and I'm…" The message ended abruptly.

Jose stared at the phone. "He's what?"

"I bet he's going after them. What else could it be? Let's go to the marina and see if the Robalo is gone."

They got to the Robalo, and Jon climbed aboard. He placed his hand on the motor. "It's cold. If he's following them, he's either running or in a car."

Jose stepped aboard. "Or he's on their boat. He could have hidden on their boat and called us as they pulled out of the marina. Maybe he lost signal before he could complete the message."

"Good point. That makes the most sense. All we can do is hang out and wait for him to call back."

Chapter Twenty-Nine
The Chase

Kerrick stayed far enough behind Miguel's boat so as not to be seen but close enough to keep up. They didn't seem concerned that someone might follow because they ran their lights as their boat headed south. Kerrick thought to turn his off as soon as he started the engine, but he knew the danger of traveling on the sea at night without lights. He also knew that the couple in Governor's Harbour wouldn't keep silent about their missing boat, and he would be in serious trouble.

Small islands began appearing on the right, turning into longer stretches of land. *This must be the Exuma Islands.* After another twenty minutes, Kerrick recognized Pirates Cove, where the Davenports' home was located. He wondered why Miguel traveled so close to land. He also remembered that when he went with them to the island in December, Miguel made a big deal to Fernando about ensuring the tanks were topped off before leaving George Town.

They'll fill up at the marina. That seems to be their habit. Maybe I should pull into Pirate's Cove and top off at Jon's pump. He'll at least have enough to fill this tank.

Kerrick knew he was taking a risk to stop, but if he waited to get gas at the marina after Miguel, he would surely lose them. He didn't need to risk running out of gas somewhere south of the Exuma Islands.

He pulled into Pirate's Cove next to Jon's personal supply of fuel. Jon never kept much fuel in the tank on the dock, but it would be enough. He filled up and headed for the marina, but he decided to turn on his lights like a typical fishing boat.

He started pulling into the George Town marina but saw Miguel's boat still tied next to the pump. Kerrick decided he should stay out of the marina so Miguel couldn't identify the Chris Craft. He turned off the lights and let the boat idle on the dark water south of the marina. He heard his phone ding with a text message. *I should have already thought that I would have a signal here. I need to call Jon.*

He looked at the message and froze in horror as he saw another picture from Miguel. Someone had Kelsey tied up with tape over her mouth. She sat on a bench next to a building, and he could see water behind her. He dialed Jon's number.

"Hey, Jon. It's Kerrick."

"Where are you, Kerrick? I got part of your message, but most of it didn't come through."

"I saw the guys putting Lacy on their boat, so I borrowed someone's Chris Craft and followed them. We just stopped at George Town for fuel, but I filled up at Pirate's Cove."

"Someone let you borrow their boat?"

"Well, not exactly. I think it belongs to a couple that I passed on my way to the marina. I felt like I didn't have a choice. Listen, I got another text with a picture. They have Kelsey."

"Who has her? Is she on the boat?"

"I don't know. She's tied up with tape over her mouth but sitting on a bench somewhere."

"Send me the picture while you have a signal, Kerrick, and I'll get some help."

"Okay. I'm sending it now. I see Miguel coming out of the marina, so I'll lose you in a minute. I think we're going to their island, which I heard Fernando call Skull Island back in December. I looked for it on a map once, and there's no such thing as Skull Island. I'll try to call you when we get there, but I may not have a signal. I'll try to locate their satellite phone. I'm sure they have one."

"Okay, Kerrick. You be careful. We're headed back to *The Discoverer*, and then we're coming your way."

"Please find Kelsey," Kerrick's voice broke. "This is all my fault."

"We'll find her, Kerrick."

Kerrick saw Miguel's boat pull out of the marina, and he eased forward on the throttle. "They're leaving, so I've got to go. I'll try to call again soon."

His mind raced back to that fateful trip back in December. He felt forced to come, or those thugs would kill his father and maybe his sister. He met Miguel in George Town and agreed to go with them to their "center of operations." Miguel took him to a cabin in his boat, and a guy covered his head with a bag.

Kerrick couldn't determine their direction last time, so he had pressed his stopwatch to time the trip. Wherever their island was located, it took them an hour and forty-five minutes to get there from the George Town marina. He remembered having the sensation of turning to the right at one point, so they must have gone south from the tip of Great Exuma. He figured he was about to find out.

****

Jon pocketed his phone as he and Jose hurried toward their boat. They passed a couple on the dock who appeared distraught. "Excuse me. Do you own a Chris Craft?"

"Yes," the man blurted, "and someone's stolen it."

"I know about your boat and will guarantee its safe return. If something happens to it, I'll replace it. My niece has been kidnapped, and one of my employees took it to follow the kidnappers. My name is Jon Davenport, and here's a card with my contact information."

The woman, whom Jon assumed was the man's wife, stepped toward him. "I'm sorry about your niece. Are you going to the police?"

"Yes. I was just about to call them when we spotted you. We've got to get back to our ship. I'll take care of your expenses while waiting for our return. What's your name?"

"I'm Matt Evans, and this is my wife, Barb. I hear what you're saying, but I still want to speak with the police," Matt asserted.

"I'll tell them to find you at your hotel. I know of a nice place here called Pineapple Fields. I'll have my wife call them to make the arrangements. Thank you for bearing with us. Will you give me your number so I can stay in touch?"

Matt scribbled his cell number on a scrap piece of paper. "If what you're saying is true, I understand your urgency, but this could be a scam."

"Honey, the girl's been kidnapped, for heaven's sake."

"We don't know these people," Matt replied as he looked at Jon's card. "Dr. Davenport? Why is your name familiar?" He looked at Jon and pointed his finger. "You're the guy who found the treasure!"

"Yes, sir. I did. We found the *San Roque* a few years ago."

"I remember watching a special about it on television. Okay. We'll go to the hotel. Just have the police come to our room."

Jon called Meg as he ran toward the marina and told her to arrange for Mr. Evans and his wife. "Meg, I'll fill you in when we get back. I don't have time to talk right now." He hung up the phone and told Jose to follow him in the Robalo. Jon jumped aboard the Carver and headed toward Rock Sound.

When Jon and Jose boarded *The Discoverer*, Meg and Ann stood at the top of the stairs, anxious for news about Lacy. Meg hurried to Jon's open arms as he stepped onto the deck.

"Oh, Jon. Where's Lacy? Do you think she ran away to avoid her mother?"

"I'll tell you the whole story in a minute, sweetheart. I've got to get up to the bridge to see the captain."

Jon climbed the steps to the bridge, followed by Meg, Jose, and Ann, where they found Captain Buffington at the ship's controls. Jon told the captain to head south toward Pirate's Cove and grabbed the satellite phone off the shelf. He dialed the police department on Eleuthera to report the kidnapping and to ask them to stop by Pineapple Fields to see Matt Evans.

The officer on the other end of the line insisted that Jon come to complete a report. He told the officer he would be there as soon as possible, but Jon knew he had no intention of returning to Eleuthera immediately. He figured he would contact the Coast Guard as soon as he knew Kerrick's location.

He pulled out his cell phone to show Meg the picture of Kelsey. She gasped as she looked at the poor, frightened girl. They'd tied her hands, and the unmistakable look of fear covered her face. Duct tape sealed her mouth.

"I think I know where that is," Meg insisted. "It's in Jacksonville. Look at the edge of the picture."

Jon looked past the frightened girl and saw water to the right of the building. He could see another building across the water from where Kelsey sat.

"How can you tell anything from that picture?"

"I recognize the sign on that building across the water. I've been there. And Kerrick's from Jacksonville."

Jon zoomed in on the picture and read the words, *Marine Salvage*.

"Do you remember when hurricane Alice came through before Carla was born? We went to Jacksonville to help with the clean-up."

"I remember," Jon agreed. "I didn't want you to go because you were seven months pregnant."

"A relief organization stored supplies in a warehouse on the docks. I helped sort through everything before we sent trucks out to groups rebuilding some of the houses along the coast."

Jon looked at the picture again. "It certainly looks like it could be at those docks."

"Why don't I go to Jacksonville?" Meg said. "I can work with the police to find her."

"I'll go with you," Ann insisted.

"Okay," Jon agreed. "Take the Robalo back into Rock Sound and leave Carla with Judy. She can take you to the airport. Keep me informed as to what's happening."

Jose touched Meg's arm. "It's very important that whoever has Kelsey not be allowed to contact Miguel. We must surprise him on his island."

Jon asked the captain to stop the ship so Meg and Ann could get aboard the Robalo, which was tied to the larger ship along with the *New Beginnings*. Jon contacted the police department in Jacksonville and told them the whole story. He also informed them that Meg and Ann would be chartering a plane to Jacksonville and should arrive shortly.

"Captain, you should take the boys back to Pirate's Cove. Jose and I will take the Carver. Hopefully, we'll meet you there with Kerrick and Lacy. I'll stay in touch."

While Meg and Ann raced off toward Rock Sound, Jon pointed the bow of the Carver toward George Town. He had no idea where Miguel was taking Lacy, but the kidnappers' island had to be south of the Exumas.

As he pulled away from *The Discoverer*, Jose joined him on the bridge. "What if Kerrick calls your cell phone before we have a signal?"

"He'll leave a message." Jon held up the satellite phone he had taken from *The Discoverer*. "I hope he'll think to call us on the sat phone. Think about it, Jose. If they filled up with fuel at George Town, they must still have some distance to travel. For some reason, they stopped at George Town instead of going over to Long Island. That must mean they're going around the tip of Great Exuma and then heading south. I remember seeing several islands south of Great Exuma and north of Flamingo Cay. I wouldn't be surprised if this Skull Island were somewhere in that direction."

"It's possible," Jose agreed. "Do you think we'll be able to find them?"

"We'll find them. I hope we're not too late."

Chapter Thirty
Prisoner

Lacy's eyes sprang open as the boat bumped against the dock. Fog filled her mind as she looked around the dark cabin. She didn't recognize anything about her surroundings. At first, she thought she was asleep in Jon and Meg's cabin on the *New Beginnings*, but the smaller bed and blank wall where Jon had a flat screen T.V. indicated this was a different boat. *Where am I?*

She tried to brush the hair out of her eyes, but her hands were tied behind her back. She lay still in the darkness, trying to organize her memories. Her mind returned to the restaurant with Kerrick and sitting on the bench in the park with Mr. Phil.

That guy! I remember. The guy walked up to ask Mr. Phil a question. Someone grabbed me from behind and covered my mouth and nose. That's all I remember. He must have used...whatever that stuff is called that makes people pass out. I've been kidnapped! Where's Mr. Phil?

Lacy heard someone approaching the cabin, so she closed her eyes again. The bed creaked as someone lay on the bed beside her. She felt a hand brush the hair out of her face. *Is that Kerrick? It doesn't smell like him.*

She opened her eyes a crack to see a strange man moving toward her to...to kiss her. She moved her head back and rammed her forehead into his face as hard as possible. Blood splattered all over her, and the man cursed as he rolled back. He got to his knees and slapped her face. Lacy's cheek burned as if it were on fire.

"Fernando!" a voice said from another part of the boat. "What are you doing in there?"

The man got off the bed, holding his nose. He left the room cursing and spitting blood. "She broke my nose. I just went in to check on her."

"How could she break your nose if you were just checking on her?" The other guy laughed.

Lacy saw a different man look through the door. He grimaced as he took in the bloody sight and then looked back out the door. "Fernando! You fool. You've messed up my bed." He turned back to the bed and looked at Lacy. "Well, well, well. So, you're a fighter. I'm not surprised."

Lacy rolled over on her back and tried to sit up. "Who are you, and where are you taking me?"

"You'll find out in time. I suggest that you stay away from my friend. He's got it out for you."

"I don't even know your friend."

"Oh, but he knows you. Trust me."

The man stepped back into what Lacy thought was the boat's galley and returned with a wet cloth. "Let's get this blood off your face. Ol' Fernando might have a disease or two."

After cleaning off her face, Miguel offered her a bottle of water, but Lacy spit on him. "You might need a friend, and I promise Fernando won't be one. He has plans for you. I'm the only thing between you and him, so I suggest you not do that again. If you don't cooperate, I'll let Fernando fulfill his wildest imagination. Do I make myself clear?"

Lacy glared at the man until he turned and left the cabin. She heard him laughing as he walked away. Her arms hurt, and she had no feeling in her hands. She decided the washcloth man must be in charge, and Fernando was the flunkey.

She heard the guy call out to Fernando, "I'm going inside to get us something to eat. I'll get the girl something, too. Get the boat ready, and I'll return in a few minutes."

About fifteen minutes later, Lacy felt the boat begin to move. What could she do? Kerrick must be worried sick about her. Kerrick. The last thing she remembered was him going to the restroom, and a girl sent her picture to his phone. Lacy's heart broke. She vowed never to love a man, but she fell for Kerrick. Now, she was paying dearly for her mistake. She guessed Kerrick was off with the beautiful brunette by now. *Don't be stupid, Lacy. He's searching the island for you.*

The washcloth guy appeared again with a ham sandwich and a bag of chips. "You hungry?"

"No."

"Fine. I'll hold onto this sandwich until you're ready for it. My name is Miguel."

Lacy cringed when he said his name. In every movie she'd seen about bad guys, it was never a good sign when you knew their names. Did this slip mean Miguel was going to kill her?

"Can you untie me? These ropes are hurting my wrists."

"I would have, but you've proven to be a fighter. I think you'll be fine until we get to where we're going."

Once Miguel left the cabin, Lacy drifted off to sleep again. She awoke with a start as the engine turned off. *We must be here, wherever that is.* She lay still, waiting for one of the men to show up, hoping it would be Miguel and not the other guy.

The door swung open, and Fernando stared at Lacy through the gloom. "You think busting me in the nose was funny? Just remember that you've got it coming."

He pulled out a long, sharp knife, and Lacy felt a chill run down her back. He took two steps toward the bed and cut the rope that had her legs bound together. "Now, get off the bed, and let's go."

Lacy stood on wobbly legs. She needed her arms for balance, but they were still tied behind her back. She waited for him to cut the rope around her hands, but he made no move to do so. Determined not to fear the creep, she walked up to him and stared into his face the whole time. When she passed him, he pushed her hard, and she fell to the floor. She'd have smashed her face, but she turned in time to land on her side. A pain shot through her right shoulder.

"You having trouble walking? That'll be your least concern when I'm done. Now get up."

Fernando pulled her onto her feet and held her arm as he led her off the boat. Lacy saw several boats tied up as they walked up a long dock. This was not a deserted island. She could see a few houses scattered along the hillside leading down to the water. A jeep awaited them at the end of the dock. Fernando pushed her into the back seat before sitting down beside her.

Miguel got into the driver's seat and turned on the car. They drove for less than fifteen minutes up a dirt road and passed through a gate guarded by two men. She noticed a round, blue pond that reminded her of the Ocean Hole on Eleuthera, and a small house sat in front of the pond. The road began a climb to the high point of the island beyond the house.

The jeep stopped before the house, and Fernando pulled Lacy out behind him. She saw another jeep parked beside the house and wondered who was inside. He opened the front door and guided her through a small den filled with a couch and a couple of chairs. She saw a kitchen to the right where a man poured coffee into a cup, and a hallway led off to the left. Fernando guided her down the hall to the last room and opened the door.

He followed her into the room and pushed her against the wall. He pressed hard against her and tried to kiss her. She bit him when his lips were on hers until she tasted blood. She remembered Miguel saying something about Fernando having a disease, but now she didn't care. He screamed out in pain.

Miguel came into the room and told Fernando to leave. Miguel took out a pocketknife and cut the rope off her hands. "I'm telling you that you're not scoring points with Fernando; however, I find your spunk entertaining." He motioned with his head to the right. "You'll find a bathroom through that door. You can't get out of the windows, so don't waste your time. If you manage to escape from your room, you'll find a guard in the den that will either be Fernando or Ray. If you think Fernando is rude, you'll be amazed at what Ray likes to do to women. I suggest you stay put."

He walked out of the room and closed the door. Lacy hurried into the bathroom. It was small with a tiny shower on one end and a toilet beside it. On the other end was a small sink with a window on the wall above it. She tried the window, but it wouldn't budge. She had drunk a lot of soda at dinner with Kerrick, and it had been hours since she had used the bathroom. She was so thankful to have her hands free and access to a toilet.

A few minutes later, she returned to the bedroom and collapsed. She had to figure out a way to get out of this place.

****

As Kerrick approached the island, he immediately saw why it was called Skull Island. One end of the island rose to a cliff that dropped around 100 feet into the water. He could see in the growing moonlight that the face of the cliff looked like a human skull.

He knew Miguel wasn't too far ahead of him, and the last thing Kerrick needed was to be seen. He remembered being brought to this island in December. When they passed the cliff, his head was covered with a bag, so he never saw the skull.

When they docked, Miguel pulled the bag off his head so Kerrick remembered the jeep ride to the compound. He figured it would take a few minutes for Miguel and Fernando to get Lacy into the Jeep, so he idled for five minutes near the base of the skull before moving toward the dock on the other end of the island.

He saw Miguel's boat tied to the dock but didn't notice a jeep anywhere. Kerrick pulled the Chris Craft to the dock and shut down the engine. Once he tied it up, he ran down the dock and started the jog toward the compound. He had to figure out how to get inside the fence and rescue Lacy.

After running hard for about forty-five minutes, Kerrick saw the lighted entrance to the compound ahead. He slowed down and eased into the small brush on the side of the road. He worked his way through the brush to the fence that separated the private land of the compound from the rest of the island. He followed the barbed wire-covered fence away from the gate and found a place where an animal must have dug under the chain-link fencing. He managed to squirm under the fence on his belly.

Kerrick remembered being taken to a small house in front of a pond. The memory was etched into his mind because he remembered thinking how fortunate to have a fresh-water pond on the compound. Miguel informed him the water was salt. He spotted the pond ahead, and a few lights from the house punched holes into the darkness. Now, he just needed to figure out in which room he'd find Lacy.

He eased up behind the house and looked through the kitchen window. He saw Fernando and the other guy he'd met in December but couldn't remember his name. The next window revealed an empty bedroom. Someone had painted over the windows, but a few scratches in the paint revealed an empty bed in a room with little light. Next, he came to a couple of smaller windows he figured opened into bathrooms. The final room must be where they held Lacy. He heard a sound at the front of the house and dropped to the sand on his belly.

After a few still moments of silence, he moved toward the final window at the back of the house. These windows were also painted, so he put his ear to the glass. He could hear someone on the other side who seemed to be straining to... straining to do what? Raise the window? He pulled out his pocketknife and removed the spackling holding the glass in place.

The spackling was old and cracked, so the task wasn't too difficult. Whoever was straining on the other side must have stopped. *I wonder if she heard me?* Kerrick stopped whittling on the spackling when a noise behind him broke the stillness of the night. He turned to determine its source and felt an explosion of pain in his head before blackness enveloped him.

Chapter Thirty-One
Enemies

Kerrick felt like he had been hit by a Mack truck. He reached up to touch his throbbing head and jerked his hand away when it grazed the painful knot. He tried to remember what happened. Someone hit him from behind. That was evident, but who? Miguel? It's possible that one of the other guards attacked him.

A door cracked open, and light poured into the small bedroom. Kerrick saw the surroundings of the first empty bedroom he had glimpsed through the scratched, painted glass earlier that night. The dirty bed creaked under him as he rolled over to look toward the source of the light. The dark, ominous outline of a man filled the open doorway.

"Well, look who we have here," crooned Miguel's familiar voice. "I'm surprised you could find my little island, but I suppose you followed us. It's obvious I need to post more guards along my fence."

"What have you done with Lacy? That wasn't part of the deal."

"The deal is that you are my partner, my friend, so you'd better start acting like it. If I go down, you go down."

"I'm not your partner. You know as well as I do that you blackmailed me so you could rob their home. That's all."

"That was all until we had the most wonderful discovery. I suggest you get a cup of coffee and prepare to call the good doctor. You're going to be my spokesman."

"I'm not doing anything for you."

"You will if you want Lacy to live until morning."

Kerrick stood to his feet, and pain shot down his neck. "Who hit me?"

"Your new best friend: Ray. I'm surprised he didn't kill you."

Kerrick staggered to the kitchen sink. He splashed cold water on his face and once again ventured to touch the pounding knot on his head. He collapsed into a chair at the kitchen table as Miguel set a cup of coffee in front of him. He looked up as he heard a gasp coming from the adjoining den.

"Kerrick!"

Kerrick looked up toward Lacy like a deer caught in the headlights. She was standing just inside the den, and Fernando held onto her arm.

Miguel moved toward the girl. "Good morning, Lacy, or is it good night? It's time to learn that your boyfriend's on our side. He's been helping us all along."

"Kerrick? What does he mean?"

"Lacy..." Kerrick began.

"I mean," Miguel continued, "that you are here because Kerrick helped us kidnap you."

"Don't listen to him, Lacy."

"You!" Lacy shouted. "You..."

Fernando pulled Lacy toward the bedroom as she let out a string of profanities. She screamed at Kerrick, and though he couldn't see her now, she must have punched Fernando. Kerrick heard a groan come from that direction. He jumped to his feet when he heard the sound of Lacy being slapped. Her cursing ceased and turned into weeping. The bedroom door slammed closed, and Fernando returned to the kitchen. Kerrick knew Miguel staged this scene so Lacy would turn against him.

Miguel folded himself onto the couch and grabbed a coffee from the end table. "The only way she gets out of here is if you call Jon and give him my demands. Once he comes through with what I want, you and the girl leave."

Kerrick knew what Miguel meant. They would leave all right…in body bags. "What if Jon doesn't meet your demands?"

"Then you both die."

"We're going to die anyway, so why should I cooperate."

"You don't know that you're going to die. If you don't cooperate, however, you will watch me do things to Lacy that will make her want to die. Before I allow her beautiful life to end, you will die by the slowest means imaginable, and she will be forced to watch. You will both beg me to end your miserable lives. Are you getting the picture?"

Kerrick knew Miguel was a psychopathic killer and wouldn't think twice about killing them. Fear and dread filled his heart.

"What if I can't get hold of Jon?"

"Oh, you will. I suggest you call him right now."

"What do I tell him?"

"Tell him the only way the girl lives is if he delivers her medallion to me by noon tomorrow."

"Her medallion? Why do you want that?"

"It's none of your business. Your business is to call Jon. Right now!"

Kerrick jumped as Miguel screamed the last two words. He slid a satellite phone over to Kerrick and repeated his command in a calm tone. "Right now."

Kerrick picked up the sat phone and dialed the phone number to Jon's phone. "Hey Jon. It's Kerrick? Where are you?"

"We're south of Great Exuma, and we may have discovered your island. I'm pretty sure we passed the boat that you…that you borrowed."

"Why are you still in Rock Sound?" Kerrick asked, looking at Miguel. "I figured you'd be in Pirate's Cove."

"Did you not hear me, Kerrick? Oh…I get it. They can hear you, but they can't hear me. Yes. Let them think we're on Eleuthera. We will be on the other side of the island south of your location."

"Jon, listen. Some men have Lacy. You can have her back if you'll give them her medallion."

"Her medallion? So, the message on that little disc holds a valuable secret, and they must have the other medallion."

"He said you need to bring it to him before noon tomorrow. I'll call you back to tell you where to take it. Do you understand? You have to do it before noon tomorrow."

"You're saying you'll do something before noon tomorrow."

"Right. As soon as possible. Jon, these guys aren't playing. I'll call you back."

"Good job, my boy," Miguel sneered. "Now, back to your room. I've got work to do."

****

When Meg and Ann's private charter landed at Jacksonville Executive Airport and taxied to a nearby hangar, a man in a dark suit stood near the door that led inside. Meg leaned over to whisper into Ann's ear. "I'll bet you five dollars that guy is with the FBI. Another five says he has sunglasses in his pocket."

"I'm not betting because I know you're right."

When the two women exited the plane and walked down the stairs, the man in the dark suit came out to greet them. "Mrs.

Davenport? I'm FBI Special Agent Mike Fitzgerald. I've been briefed about the operation and have a team of men standing by to assist us."

Meg wondered about his briefing because she didn't know what was happening. "Good evening, Agent Fitzgerald. This is my friend, Ann Garcia. What have you been told about this situation?"

"Let's go into the break room in the hangar. I have four men waiting on us there."

Meg and Ann followed the FBI agent through a metal door. They found four men sitting around two round, plastic tables in a small room. Agent Fitzgerald introduced Meg and Ann to the group and asked Meg to update them on the circumstances behind their urgent phone call.

"Hello, gentlemen. Thank you for coming to help us. We believe a young woman has been kidnapped and is being held hostage. I have a picture of her, and I recognize where this picture was taken."

Meg pulled out her cell phone and passed it around the group. "You'll notice the sign on the building across the water from the girl. The girl, by the way, is named Kelsey Daniels. The sign says *Marine Salvage*. A couple of years ago, we used some warehouses near the docks as a staging area for supplies when we came to serve the community after Hurricane Alice. This picture looks like it was taken there."

One of the men raised his hand. "I'm familiar with that area. It's about fifteen miles north of the city. I remember several warehouses around the docks, but they all look the same."

Meg nodded and continued. "I think I've been in the building near this one. I think I remember looking across the water and seeing this sign."

Agent Fitzgerald stepped forward. "Men, we don't know that Kelsey is in that warehouse, but we must go in assuming they're holding her there." He turned to Meg. "Mrs. Davenport, will you go along to identify the building? You'll need to stay in the van, but you can save us valuable time if you go. Mrs. Garcia, you can stay here and wait on us."

"I'm sorry, Agent Fitzgerald. I can't just wait here while you guys drive off. I'll go crazy."

"This could become dangerous," the agent began.

"But you're taking Meg, so it must not be too dangerous. You even said the warehouse is empty."

The FBI agent paused. "I suppose you can go along as long as you both stay in the van. We'll park away from the building, so you'll be safe."

The four men jumped into the back of a cargo van. Agent Fitzgerald motioned to the back door, and the two women climbed in behind the other agents. Benches lined the van's sides, and a communications center was nestled into the front corner behind the driver's seat. Agent Fitzgerald climbed in behind the wheel. Twenty-five minutes later, the van eased into a parking lot and came to a stop. A voice came over a small speaker on the side of the communications desk.

"Men and ladies, the warehouse isn't far from this location. Mrs. Davenport, I've decided you and I need to make a visual of the warehouse on foot and then return to the van. The rest of you need to wait for my signal."

Meg got out of the van and followed Agent Mike into the back of a warehouse across from the one Meg saw in the picture. They walked up to a window in the front office, and Meg identified the place where she thought Kelsey was being held. She saw the bench where Kelsey sat for the picture and a door to the right of the bench. Something lay on the bench, but Meg couldn't make it out in the dark.

After they returned to the van, Agent Mike told the two ladies to wait for them. They'd clear the building and return to the van. Meg and Ann sat in silence while the five men suited up with weapons and flak jackets. They crawled out of the van and slipped into the night.

"So," Ann began, "we're just supposed to sit here and be quiet while they go off to prove the warehouse is empty?"

"It seems lame, but this van is the safest place."

Meg and Ann sat silently and became concerned when the FBI agents didn't return. Meg looked out the front window again. "I'm starting to get concerned."

"Me too. What can we do?"

"We could return to where Mike took me," Meg suggested. "It's safe. We can see the warehouse through a window in an office."

"You mean another warehouse is open?"

"Yep. I didn't think about it then, but the back door wasn't locked."

"You know Agent Fitzgerald won't be happy with us."

"What if they're in trouble? No one would know."

"What are we waiting on?"

Meg and Ann positioned themselves near the office window in the warehouse across the narrow drive from the bench in the picture. They waited at least five or ten minutes and wondered why the agents weren't coming out. Meg considered crossing the drive and going into the warehouse.

Shots rang out through the night, and Meg noticed a few bright lights coming through a window in the other warehouse.

The shooting stopped in a few minutes, and silence again enveloped the night.

"What happened?" Ann whispered. "Why aren't the FBI guys coming out?"

"Maybe they all got killed," Meg suggested. "If so, what about Kelsey? We can't just let the bad guys take her."

"You can't go in there, Meg. That's suicide."

"I won't go in. I'll go look in the window."

"No, Meg. That's too dangerous. We're not even supposed to be out of the van."

"Just sit tight. I'll be right back."

Meg eased out of the warehouse's front door to Ann's quiet objections and hurried across the drive. As she squatted in front of the plate glass window, she thought this office window might not offer visibility to the rest of the warehouse. She was about to return to Ann when the door to the warehouse opened, and a man stood in the doorway facing the interior. His arm was around Kelsey's neck, and his gun pointed into the warehouse.

Meg saw an old pully lying on the bench near the door. She leaped for the bench and grabbed the pully. The man began turning in her direction, but she swung the pully with all her strength and drove it into the man's head. His gun flew back into the warehouse, and his body crumpled to the floor.

"Kelsey!" Meg cried out as she wrapped the girl in her arms. "Oh, Kelsey. You're safe."

Two FBI agents ran out from the darkness. One grabbed the gun on the floor, and the other pulled the kidnapper's hands behind his back.

"Where's Agent Fitzgerald?" Meg wondered.

"He's been shot, and so was Agent Mullins. We've got to get an ambulance."

The other agent pulled out a radio and called for help. A helicopter arrived on the scene in just a few minutes, and other cars pulled up shortly after the call. Medical personnel hurried into the warehouse with stretchers and had the two agents on the helicopter within ten minutes.

"Are they going to be okay?" Ann asked the agent who held the door open for the medics.

"We think so," the man said. "Agent Fitzgerald's shot up, but they seem to have him stable. We'll know more after a while. Let's get Kelsey to our headquarters. We need to get some information from her."

Meg kept her arms around the trembling girl. "And what is your name?"

"I'm sorry, Mrs. Davenport. I'm Special Agent John Boles. I'll be stepping in for Agent Fitzgerald."

Meg took Kelsey's arm and began walking toward the van. "Kelsey, where are your parents? Do we need to contact them?"

"Mom and Dad are out of town. Let's not call them yet. My dad has been in treatment all day. The last thing he needs to worry about right now is me."

"Thank God you're okay," Meg sighed as they sat inside the van.

"Is Kerrick okay?" Kelsey asked.

"I hope so," Meg confessed. "I certainly hope so."

Chapter Thirty-Two
The Taste of Freedom

The door closed as Kerrick lay down on the bed, and he waited for Miguel to walk away from the door. He heard faint talking, so he moved toward the door, making as little sound as possible. When he placed his ear against the door, he heard Miguel say something that sounded like he was leaving the house. In a few minutes, Kerrick heard the car out front start up and drive away.

He tried the doorknob. *Aren't doors locked from the inside?* He felt around the knob and discovered two things about the doorknob. First, someone had installed it backward, and second, it had a keyhole. *For some reason, they used an exterior doorknob.*

Kerrick looked around the dark room and noticed several personal items sitting around. *I wonder if this is Miguel's room. Here's someone's travel kit. Maybe I can find a razor blade to use as a weapon.*

He rifled through the small bag and discovered that Miguel must not shave. He found a toothbrush but no razor blade. He tiptoed over to the window and tried to lift it. To his surprise, the window moved easily. *I can't believe it's open. Since this room is Miguel's, no one thought about ensuring the window was secured.* He eased back toward the door and pressed his ear against the wood. He thought he heard a female voice, but he wasn't sure. He didn't remember seeing another woman in the group. *If we're going to get out of here, the time to do it is now. Miguel is gone. Maybe Fernando went with him.*

Kerrick placed one leg over the window ledge and slipped into the night. He went down the back of the house to the window leading to the room where he knew Lacy was being held. The bottom half of the window consisted of three large panes. He had carved out most of the spackling around one of the panes earlier, so within seconds, he finished the task. He carefully removed the large window pane and looked into the room. It was empty.

When he unlocked the window from the inside, it still wouldn't budge. He inspected the outside of the window and discovered nails driven through the frame. He knew he didn't have much time, so he removed the spackling to the final two panes of glass and broke the wooden mullions. Kerrick went through the window headfirst and got into the room without making too much noise.

He heard footsteps coming down the hallway and slipped into the bathroom. The door to the bedroom opened and closed, and he could tell that someone had locked Lacy back in her room. He had no idea why they took her out. *I bet Ray took her to the kitchen to get something to eat.*

Kerrick heard Lacy approaching the bathroom. He grabbed her from behind when she stepped through the doorway and covered her mouth. She tried to wiggle out of his grasp and attempted to kick him, but he held her fast.

"Stop fighting me and listen."

Kerrick could hear curse words coming out from behind his hand. "I'm guessing that Meg's rules don't apply here."

Lacy bit his hand, and Kerrick almost cried out. "Don't you say a word about my aunt. You are scum, and she's the finest person I know."

"Lacy, listen to me. I know you hate me, but you don't know the whole story."

"I know you're a traitor, and you had it out for me from the beginning. I trusted you. I even thought I loved you. You betrayed me."

"You don't know the whole story," Kerrick repeated.

"I know enough."

"What I've done is wrong, but I didn't have a choice. Miguel promised to kill my father and my sister if I didn't tell him when Jon left the compound. That's it. That's all I was supposed to do. I had no part in kidnapping you. He kept sending me pictures of my sister to threaten me so I'd continue giving him information on Jon's location."

"Like I believe that."

"Believe it or not, those pictures are my sister. Her name is Kelsey. As of tonight, they've also kidnapped her and have threatened to kill her and you if I don't cooperate."

Lacy stared into Kerrick's eyes. "How do I know if you're lying to me?"

"Believe me or not. That's up to you. I need to get you out of here, and we're losing precious minutes arguing."

"What about your sister?"

"I'm hoping Jon somehow freed her. He told me he would get me some help and find her. Please listen to me. We've got to get out of here while we have a chance."

"How are we getting out?"

"I came through the window. I'm surprised you didn't notice it was broken."

Kerrick led Lacy back into the bedroom and helped her to climb through the broken window; he quickly followed. Once outside the house, he reached out his hand for her to take, but she folded her arms across her chest. He put his finger to his lips, moved down the back of the house, and motioned for her to stay close.

Kerrick considered his options. He remembered his last trip to the island, and the image of two vehicles in front of this house entered his mind. He decided it would be best to take the extra jeep and make a run for the boat. He stopped to look back, and Lacy bumped into him. He glanced around the corner of the house and saw the jeep.

The jeep was a beacon of freedom. If they could get into the jeep, they were free. In his mind, he remembered the last time Miguel kept the key in the switch. He hoped the key was still in the ignition.

Kerrick placed his lips on Lacy's ear. "When I count to three, let's run to the jeep. It's important that we not make a sound."

Lacy nodded, and Kerrick held up one finger. He added a second and then a third. They raced toward the jeep. Because the vehicle had no doors, they easily jumped inside, and Kerrick wrapped his hand around the key. Before he started the vehicle, he looked to the south in the direction of the gate, and to his horror, he saw headlights coming their way. He switched on the jeep, turned north, and started the steep climb in the opposite direction. He looked behind them to see another vehicle coming up behind them fast. He mashed the gas pedal to the floor.

"That's got to be Miguel," he shouted.

"Where does this road go?"

"I don't know, but we need to go in the other direction. I hope we can turn around up here somewhere."

When the road leveled out, it appeared as if the road just ended. Kerrick pictured the island's northern end and realized a cliff must be ahead. They barreled straight toward it. He tried to put on the brakes but just heard a grinding sound—metal on metal.

"It's a cliff, Lacy, and the jeep won't stop. Jump. Jump now!"

Lacy jumped from the moving vehicle, and shots rang out from a machine gun. Kerrick felt something sharp hit his shoulder, and his head jerked forward and hit the steering wheel. When he opened his eyes, the jeep bound down a steep incline. He had to get out before it was too late. The jeep flew through the air, dropping rapidly through space.

As the vehicle began to turn, Kerrick pushed away into the expanse and plummeted toward the sea. He had visions of jumping from the superstructure on *The Discoverer*, but this fall was at least three or four times as high. He made his body as straight as possible and hoped the water was deep. He plunged into the dark water feet first and sank at an alarming speed.

****

Lacy leaped from the moving jeep, and her body crashed onto the sandy ground. Pain shot up her twisted leg as she rolled over several times and came to a stop. "Jump, Kerrick! Jump."

Lacy watched in horror as Kerrick slumped over the steering wheel, and the jeep plummeted over the cliff. *No. Oh, my God. He's been shot. Kerrick!*

Lacy tried to get up to run to the cliff's edge, but her leg gave way. *My leg! Something's wrong.* She started dragging her body toward the cliff, but Fernando was on top of her and pinned her to the ground.

"Where do you think you're goin? We haven't had our fun yet."

He jerked her hair, and Lacy screamed in as much anger as pain. When he pulled her to her feet, her leg buckled, and she collapsed, crying out in pain

"I can't walk. I've hurt my leg."

Fernando picked her up and walked toward the cliff. Pain shot up her leg and enveloped her entire body. *Is he going to throw me off?* She looked toward the water but could see nothing. The jeep was gone. *Kerrick is…is dead.* Fernando turned and walked back to his jeep. He put Lacy in the back seat and told Miguel that the boy was dead. Lacy wept as Miguel turned the jeep back toward the house.

"Fernando. I want you to get a flashlight and go back up there. You need to make sure the boy is dead."

****

Kerrick struggled for the surface. He kicked and pulled, lungs burning. *I'm not going to make it. I'm going to drown, and they're going to kill Lacy. I can't give up. I can't.*

With his final effort, his head broke the surface, and he gasped for air. The night was pitch black, and the air was dank, even putrid. His right hand hit rock, and he grabbed hold of a ledge. Pain shot through his body when he tried to pull himself up with his left arm. He found a toe hold and managed to climb out of the water. *Where am I. This must be a cave. It's pitch black in here, and the smell. It's horrible!*

He thought his eyes would adjust to the darkness but could see nothing. He had no idea where he was or how to get out. This had to be a cave. He must have come up underneath the island.

"How am I going to get out of here?" he wondered aloud.

His head was burning. He rubbed it with his right hand and felt a stinging sensation on the left side above his ear. *That idiot shot me in the head and the shoulder. I've got to swim out of here with one good arm, and I don't even know the right direction to swim.*

His hand brushed something that felt like maybe driftwood or some trash. *No, it's wood.* He knew that sitting on the ledge wasn't helping Lacy at all. He had to get out. He had an idea.

He picked up the stick and slid back into the water. Though he couldn't see anything, he could feel the stick floating away from the rock. *Is the tide going out?* He took several deep breaths and went underwater. He kicked as hard as he could and pulled with his good arm. When he surfaced, he looked up into a star-filled sky and noticed a light shining down into the water. He swam back toward the cliff and hugged the rock. The light disappeared.

I've got to get to Jon and Jose. They'll know what to do. Jon said they were on the south side of the next island in the chain. Maybe I can get back to my boat.

Kerrick swam around the island's edge and became nervous about the trail of blood he knew he must be leaving. The memory of the sharks filled his mind.

After a while, he saw a bit of sand on the rocky shore and climbed out of the water. The island rose at least fifty feet from the sea, maybe more, so he knew he had to go further around the island to not re-enter Miguel's compound. He inched along the rocky shoreline at a snail's pace for a while and then decided to take his chances. He climbed some rocks to a sandy terrain and broke into a trot.

Thirty minutes later, he saw the dock where the Chris Craft floated unmolested. The bleeding from his shoulder had slowed, and his head wound had crusted over.

He jumped aboard the boat and started to climb to the wheelhouse, but then he thought about the large target he'd offer Miguel. *On top of that, he thinks I'm dead. I don't want him to know I'm alive.*

Kerrick went aft to where a rubber raft was strapped to the deck. He released the straps and lowered it into the water. Even though a small motor hung off the back of the boat, he paddled away before cranking it. Once he felt no one could hear the motor, he pulled the rope, and it came to life.

About a few hours before sunrise, he motored around the island and saw the *New Beginnings* anchored in a cove. Tears came as he pointed the raft toward the Carver yacht.

Chapter Thirty-Three
Backup

"Tell us again what you know about the island," Jose insisted. "We've got to find a way to get to Lacy without Miguel knowing."

"I've told you everything," Kerrick said for the third time. "I didn't mention that Miguel said he'd put extra guards at the fence."

"We'll either have to climb the cliff or get on the compound through the fence," Jon conceded. "With extra guards posted, I'm afraid of being spotted if we try to go through the fence. The cliff might be our best shot. I don't know any other way to do it unless we bore up from underneath."

Jose sat in silence for a moment. "Tell us again about the cave."

Kerrick relived the nightmare of being surrounded by the pitch black of the cave's interior. "I have no idea if it was a true cave or a cavity under the island's edge."

"Let's think about it a minute," Jose cautioned. "Didn't you tell us a saltwater pond was behind the house? Sort of like Ocean Hole?"

"That's true."

"We know the only way a saltwater pond can exist is if saltwater can somehow get to it."

Jon sat up in his chair. "There must be a tunnel."

"That's what I was thinking. It's possible that Kerrick came up in that tunnel."

"Maybe," Kerrick agreed, "but I got out of the water and sat on a dry ledge."

"It's possible you sat on a raised portion of the tunnel that dropped back into the water. You didn't check it out to see whether the cave continued or stopped."

"True. I suppose water could have been behind me."

"It's also probable," Jon suggested, "that the whole cave is full of water when the tide comes in. That area may be dry only at low tide."

"Okay," Jose said as he stood to his feet. "We've got to go on that assumption. It would be a great way to get to the house without being seen. Kerrick, you've got to take us around to that spot. Can you handle it?"

"You said the bullet went clean through my shoulder. If I can keep this bandage in place, I'll be all right."

Jose outlined a plan for the three to take the compound. They had no idea how many men were in Miguel's group, so Jose emphasized the importance of the element of surprise. Twenty minutes after getting aboard the *New Beginnings* and being patched up by Jon, Kerrick stood at the back of the boat as Jon lowered the raft back into the water. The three men climbed into the raft with two scuba tanks, masks, fins, spear guns, and flashlights. Jose also slipped two pistols into a waterproof bag to take along.

Kerrick guided them around the island, and Jon hoped that no one would hear the motor. He wished they could have gone in without the motor, but they didn't have time to waste.

"I think this is it," Kerrick whispered. "I remember looking up and seeing the nose cavity of the skull. It's almost like I went into the mouth."

"Okay," Jose said with confidence. "Give us twenty minutes. If we don't come back, it means we made it through, so I want you to high tale it to the other side. First, get aboard the Chris Craft and see if you can find any weapons. Next, find a vehicle and park about a quarter of a mile from the compound. Get into a position where you can see the gate, but remember, they must not know you're there."

Jon saw Jose's training begin to show. He knew his friend was once a part of the elite Spanish Operations Command, so he felt confident of Jose's skills. While Jon didn't know much about this organization in Spain's navy, he knew it was comparable to the Navy Seals of the United States.

Jon didn't know how to pull off a rescue operation, so he trusted his friend. He also wondered what happened to the Coast Guard. He had told Meg to call them and have them head toward the island. So far, no help had arrived.

Jon spat into his mask and reached out his hand. "Kerrick. I understand why you did everything. I don't hold it against you. I want your conscience to be clear if I don't return."

"Don't talk like that, Jon. You're going to make it."

"Let's hope so."

Jon slid over the side of the raft into the dark water. Before submerging, he looked up and saw they didn't have long before daylight. He followed Jose deeper toward the island's base before they both turned on their underwater lights.

The opening of the mouth gaped before them like a sinister grin. Jose led the way forward, and Jon immediately saw that they were entering a tunnel. It was now high tide, and the entire tunnel was full of water. After a few minutes, they came to another tunnel that intersected the entry tunnel like a cross. Jon looked at Jose, who pointed straight ahead. It was weird that he imagined the trelleborg, but the crossing tunnels reminded him of the old Viking fort.

They kicked forward, and Jon felt the tunnel was beginning to go up. The further they went, the narrower the cave became. Jon dropped behind Jose at one point so they could swim single file. As Jon took his place behind his friend, he looked at his watch. They left the raft a few minutes past 5:00, and now it was 5:25. It was difficult for Jon to predict how long they could remain underwater, but he felt confident they were passed the point of no return. If they continued swimming forward, they would have to come out in the pond in the next thirty minutes or less or they would run out of air. He knew Jose shared his determination to rescue Lacy as he kicked hard to keep up with his friend.

Jose stopped and motioned for Jon to remove his tank. Jon realized the cave was getting so narrow that his scuba tank would keep him from moving forward if it remained on his back. The two men proceeded forward by pushing their tanks ahead of them through the tunnel.

Forward progress was difficult and slow. The tanks were heavy, and they couldn't hold their tanks in their hands. They made progress by pushing the cylinders along the floor of the tunnel. Jon became a scuba diver as a teenager and dove in several caves. He couldn't remember ever being afraid, but now, the possibility of drowning in the cave filled his mind. He couldn't let this thought blossom into fear.

Jon felt long eels slithering against his body, and at one point, something large swam out from a hole in the wall and bumped into his side. The thought of the possibility of a shark being in the cave entered his mind, but he knew the tunnel was too narrow for such a threat.

Relief filled him when he saw Jose veer to the left. *Is the tunnel opening up into a larger cave or is this the pond?* He looked up and saw the early morning light filtering into the water from the surface. They swam to a rock wall on the pond's edge, and Jose motioned for Jon to leave his tank on the bottom.

Jon took a deep breath, dropped his regulator from his mouth, and ascended. Jose swam beside him. They broke the surface without a sound and breathed in the refreshing morning air. The pond was just like Ocean Hole with straight, rock sides dropping to a depth at the edge of the pond of about twenty feet. When Jose pointed to a break in the rock where they could climb out of the water, the two men moved toward the opening.

****

Kerrick pulled the rope with his good arm, and the little motor came to life. He didn't know how long Jon and Jose would take to the pond, but he knew they'd somehow make it. They left the raft over twenty minutes ago, so he hoped they were safe. He looked at his watch again. He had to get to the compound as fast as possible.

He rounded the island's northern end and turned the raft south toward where he had docked his boat only hours earlier. *It seems like an eternity since I tied up last night. I should be there in thirty minutes.*

As he headed down the island's eastern side, he thought he recognized the fence marking the boundaries of Miguel's compound. A new idea came to him that would cut a lot of time from his trip and put him in place to help Jon and Jose.

He pointed the rubber raft toward shore and ran upon the soft sand. The boat snagged on a rock, and he heard the air rushing out of a gaping hole in the bottom. *Oh well. I don't suppose I need this anymore*. He pulled the deflating raft further up onto the sand and climbed the short rise hoping to see familiar territory from his approach the previous night. He remembered running through the brush and approaching the fence about a few hundred yards from the gate.

He spotted the tall, chain-link fence and hurried toward it. He walked a few steps before noticing a spot at the bottom of the fence that appeared bent outward. *This spot looks familiar.* He ducked as a spotlight slid down the length of the fence. A jeep passed before turning back toward the main road.

****

Jose pointed to the broken window in the back bedroom of the house. Jon shared Jose's belief that Miguel would no longer keep Lacy in that room, but the window provided a great way to get into the house.

Jose placed his mouth against Jon's ear. "You go around to the front door, and I'll enter through the window. Let's synchronize our watches. At 6:00, I want you to burst through the front door. We cannot know for sure how many men are here. It's best not to shoot our guns and risk bringing in their reinforcements."

Jon nodded in agreement and took one of the pistols and his spear gun. He had a quick flashback to when he shot one of Alvaro Lopez's men with a spear gun when he and Meg escaped Lopez's island fortress. Making very little noise, he moved against the back of the house.

When he came to the bedroom Kerrick told them was Miguel's, he looked through the painted windows. Kerrick told him earlier about the scratches in the paint, so he peered through the room into the kitchen. One man sat on a couch in plain view, and Jon saw feet sticking out from the side of the room. *I bet those are Lacy's feet. It looks like she's wearing a splint. The man seemed to be* talking to someone else on the other side of the den, but Jon couldn't see the person.

When Jon got to the front of the house, he didn't see Miguel's jeep, but a motorcycle sat near the door propped up on a kickstand. *Does this mean Miguel's not here? I suppose one of the other men may have the jeep.* He kept his eye on the second hand and counted to six o'clock.

Chapter Thirty-Four
Time to Move

When the second hand moved the final time, Jon planted his foot on the doorknob with all his strength, and the door burst open. The spear gun dropped from his grip, so Jon reached for the pistol he had placed inside his unzipped wetsuit. As the man on the couch raised a semi-automatic pistol, a knife flew from the direction of the hallway and stuck into the bicep of the guy's extended arm. His gun dropped from his hand.

The man screamed out in pain. "Ray! The hall!"

Earlier, when Jon looked through the window in the back of the house, he could tell another person sat in the room but couldn't see him. Now, Ray stepped forward, reaching for something in his belt. Jon leaped forward and drove the butt of his pistol down on the man's head. Ray staggered backward, but to Jon's amazement, he didn't go down.

Blood spewing from his arm, the other man lunged for his pistol. Jose rushed into the room, and when the guy turned toward him, Jose drove his palm upward into his nose. The man screamed in pain and collapsed on the floor. Jose went airborne with a roundhouse kick, and Jon heard the sickening crack of what he knew was Ray's neck.

The fight was over in less than a minute, and Lacy's captors lay still on the floor.

"Jon!" Lacy cried as she tried to get up from the couch. She grimaced in pain when she put weight on her leg and collapsed backward.

Jon moved toward his niece as Jose checked the two men on the floor for a pulse. "Lacy, are you all right?"

"I hurt my leg earlier. Kerrick tried to rescue me, but he...he went over the cliff. They shot him, Jon. I think he's..." She lowered her head as tears spilled down her cheeks. "I think he's dead."

Jon sat beside Lacy and wrapped the girl in his arms. "No, Sweetheart. He's not dead. He's with us, or he was with us. He survived the fall and made it back to *The Discoverer*."

"He's alive? I can't believe it. I saw him go over the cliff. How is that possible?"

"He was shot in two places, but the bullets didn't damage much. He managed to get out of the jeep and dropped into the water. He came to us on the island south of here."

"How did he know you were there?"

"After they caught Kerrick sneaking up to the back of the house, Miguel made him call me to ask for the ransom. I don't know why the guy chose not to listen to both sides of the conversation. I told Kerrick where we'd be waiting, and Miguel had no clue we were around. It was that simple."

"He wanted ransom? All of this is about money?"

"He didn't ask for money. He wanted your medallion."

"My medallion? You've got to be kidding."

"No, I'm not kidding. It must have a clue to something valuable. It makes me wonder if he knows something we don't know."

"He might have the other medallion," Lacy said. "All along, we've thought another medallion gave the rest of the clue."

"That's possible," Jon agreed. "After we met up with Kerrick, he took us to the front of the skull, and we swam through a tunnel into the pond behind the house. It was just like we guessed about Ocean Hole on Eleuthera. A tunnel from the ocean feeds the pond.

"That's unbelievable. What do you mean about the skull?"

"The northern cliff of this island looks like a huge skull."

"I had no idea."

"Once Jose and I got into the water, Kerrick took the rubber raft around the island. He was supposed to get back to the docks and find transportation. I imagine he's not too far from the compound now."

"Is that Miguel?" Jose wondered as he pointed to the guy that had been sitting on the couch.

"No. I think his name is Paco, or something like that. The other guy is Ray. Paco's the one who put this splint on my leg. Miguel and Fernando left a little while ago in the jeep. Paco came up from the gate and whispered something to Miguel, and Miguel told him to stand guard for a while."

"So, how many men are on the compound?" Jose asked.

"I have no idea," Lacy admitted. "I just met Paco; he wasn't as cruel as the others, though that's not saying much."

Jon took Lacy's hand. "Did they…uh…did they hurt you?"

"No, but they sure had plans for me. Ray couldn't keep his hands off me until I kicked him."

"Good for you," Jose said.

"If I hadn't hurt my other leg, I could have done some real damage. I suppose that wasn't a smart thing to do, but Paco got a good laugh out of it."

"He won't be doing anything else," Jose promised. "They're both dead."

Lacy turned her head, and Jon knew she couldn't bear to look at the men. He scanned the room to see where he might drag the bodies to get them out of view.

"We've got to stop Miguel and Fernando," Jose insisted, "but we need to get Lacy somewhere safe first."

"Too bad there's only a motorcycle out front," Jon said. "I don't think you can handle riding on that."

"I saw a jeep up the road," Lacy remembered. "When Kerrick and I were trying to get away, we went up the road toward the other end of the island. We went around a curve a little from the house, and I saw an open shed with a jeep parked in it."

"Let's get going," Jon insisted, reaching down to pick up Lacy.

"If you can find a stick, I can walk by myself."

"You don't need to walk on that leg," Jon said. "You've got to quit being so hard-headed, Lacy."

Jon picked up Lacy from the couch, careful not to hurt her leg. They walked out the front door and started up the small rise. The dirt road took a right turn at a small grove of trees, and Jon saw the shed on the right side of the road. The jeep was parked under a lean-to roof that went off the back of the shed.

Jon sat Lacy down in the back seat, and Jose walked up with a tall stick he found on the side of the road.

"We have two problems," Jon concluded. "First, we've got to get through the gate."

"What's the second?" Jose asked. "I'm not too worried about the gate."

"Where's Kerrick? I don't want to leave this place and discover Kerrick has returned to the compound. On top of that, we've got to stop Miguel and the other guy. What was his name?"

"Fernando," Lacy said.

"Right. Fernando."

Jose laid the stick across Lacy's lap. "If you've got to walk, use that. Jon and I will return to the house and wait for Miguel and Fernando to return. Lacy, you stay here in the jeep. I hope you won't have to drive the thing, but it's an automatic, so you could drive back to the dock if necessary."

"Why would I need to drive back to the dock?"

Jose looked at Jon and back at Lacy. "Every fight doesn't always turn out well. If, for some reason, we don't come back for you, I want you to point the front of this jeep toward the other end of the island, blow through the gate, and never look back. I'll leave a pistol with you, too."

"I don't know anything about a pistol," Lacy gasped.

"You just point the gun and pull the trigger," Jon advised. "We'll be back, though, so you won't have to worry about using it."

"Don't you need a gun?"

"I've got one," Jon said. "It's back at the house. I should have brought it with me, but I was carrying you. I didn't think about it."

As Jon and Jose neared the house, they noticed movement coming from the direction of the gate. Jon saw headlights.

"We better climb through the window," Jose suggested. "I think a jeep is heading our way."

"I think I saw two jeeps coming," Jon added.

Jose led through the busted window, and Jon crawled in behind him. He heard the muted voice of someone calling in on a radio to Ray, so he knew Miguel knew something had gone awry. Jose motioned for Jon to stay inside the hallway while he hurried across the den and into the kitchen.

A jeep pulled up in front of the house, and two men jumped out. Jon peeked around the corner and looked toward the large window at the front of the house. He saw through a crack in the curtain at least one of the guys had what looked like a German MP5.

His mind went back to several years ago when a friend invited him to visit the Atlanta Police Department. His buddy, Sam Manning, was the captain of the SWAT team. Sam introduced Jon to the weapons in the SWAT team's arsenal and to his favorite, the German-made MP5. Jon knew nothing about weapons of this caliber, but he remembered that machine gun.

He looked around the hallway and saw the spear gun he'd dropped earlier. He grabbed it as the door opened and began trying to arm it by pulling back the two rubber slings.

One guy wearing jeans and a stained tank top eased into the door with his machine gun pointing into the room. He must have seen one of the dead guys lying on the floor in the kitchen because he turned in that direction.

He managed to get a few rounds out of his rifle before he dropped to the floor with a knife in his throat. A second guy came in shooting toward the kitchen, and Jon got him with a spear. It all happened so fast that he only had time to pull back one of the rubber slings, but the spear had plenty of force to go into the guy's body. The man dropped the rifle and fell to the floor, holding his stomach.

Jon grabbed the guy's machine gun and stood ready near the front door. He heard a jeep pull off outside and head north up the dirt road, and his mind instantly went to Lacy.

"Jose! You okay?"

"I'm fine. He winged me, though. Good thing he doesn't know how to shoot."

"Someone just took off up the road in a jeep."

"I heard. I hope Lacy stays down. Let's go."

As Jon and Jose jumped into a jeep still running outside the front door, they heard a vehicle start up just around the curve in the road.

"That has to be Lacy," Jon shouted above the engine. "Why didn't she just stay under the shed?"

Jose pulled forward onto the dirt road. "Something's wrong. She wouldn't have chased a jeep for no reason."

"Kerrick! They must have caught Kerrick."

Chapter Thirty-Five
Happy Birthday

Meg wrapped a blanket around Kelsey's quivering shoulders. The evening was not cool, but Kelsey's nerves were on edge. With Agent Fitzgerald on his way to the hospital, Agent Boles was responsible for questioning Kelsey. Meg convinced the FBI agents to allow them to return to Kelsey's home so she could shower and change into clean clothes. They also agreed to complete their questions at the house for Kelsey's comfort.

Meg pulled out her cell phone as the van drove away from the warehouse. She saw a missed call and a voicemail from a strange number. *I wonder what that's about.*

She pressed her voice-mail button and held the phone to her ear. As the message played, the blood drained from her face.

"What's wrong, Meg?" Ann asked. "You look like you've seen a ghost."

"I've got to call the Coast Guard. They can't find Jon because they went to the wrong George Town. It seems that the dispatcher never heard me say *Exuma*, and they sent a cutter to the Cayman Islands."

"Oh, no. George Town is the capital of the Caymans. Right?"

"Yes. What a stupid mistake. I don't know how that could have happened. That means Jon and Jose have no backup."

Kelsey looked up in shock. "What about Kerrick?"

Meg pressed the number for the missed call and waited for someone to answer on the other end. She had the name and number of a supervisor, so she hoped to resolve the problem without further delay. A woman's voice came on the other end, and she explained to Meg that a lot of interference made Meg's earlier call difficult to understand. She said the call ended abruptly, and the dispatcher thought Meg must have hung up.

Meg recalled the phone call she'd placed to the Coast Guard earlier that evening. She remembered a lot of interference and the abrupt ending of the call. She thought the dispatcher hung up, so maybe the woman never heard Meg say *Exuma*.

"How long will it take to have a ship south of Great Exuma?" Meg asked. "This is critical. I think my husband is on that island now. He left Eleuthera last night, and it's past 6:30."

"I'm sorry, ma'am. We have a cutter near Nassau now, so they could be on the south end of the Exuma islands in a couple of hours."

"A couple of hours?" Meg blurted into the phone. "That's not good enough. My husband's life is on the line, and we assume my niece is there too. Can you send a helicopter?"

"I'll see what I can do, Mrs. Davenport. I'll call you with an update."

Meg stared in disbelief at her phone as the line went dead. How could they make such a mistake? The men who had Lacy were extremely dangerous, and her husband was not a trained fighter. Jose was the one with the training. All she could do was hope and pray.

****

When Jon and Jose pulled past the shed, the jeep was gone. For some reason, Lacy got into the driver's seat and chased after the other guy. Jon figured Miguel drove up during the fight and decided to flee toward the end of the island. He must have Kerrick in his vehicle, and Lacy saw him.

The road leveled, and Jon saw Lacy's jeep skid to a stop. *She must be driving with her left foot.* She almost fell out of the jeep as she worked to hold herself up with the stick Jose had given her. Jon noticed Jose's pistol in one of her hands.

A larger man held a knife and had Kerrick around the neck. He'd tied Kerrick's hands behind his back. When the man saw Jon and Jose leaving their jeep, he pulled Kerrick back to the cliff's edge.

"Fernando," Lacy cried as she pointed a quivering pistol at him. "Stop."

Fernando positioned himself behind Kerrick to use his body for protection. He held the huge knife to Kerrick's throat. Lacy hobbled toward them while Fernando warned everyone to stay back. Jon and Jose stopped within fifteen feet of the cliff's edge while Lacy got closer.

"You're not going to accomplish anything by killing Kerrick," Jose said. "Drop the knife, Fernando."

"If you give me the medallion, I'll release Kerrick at the docks…if you don't follow me. This can still end well for you. Just don't do anything stupid."

"I don't have the medallion," Jon confessed. "I'd have to go back to George Town to get it. I was already here when Kerrick called me last night. We can go to George Town together."

"That's too bad," Fernando warned. "I'm not stupid. I know what you'll do if I let Kerrick go."

Jon saw a helicopter moving toward them at a fast rate of speed. *That's got to be the Coast Guard. It's about time.*

Fernando noticed Jon looking out toward sea, and he took a quick glance in that direction. "Too late. You shouldn't have called the Coast Guard. You blew it, my friend. You're all a bunch of fools."

Blood began seeping out of Kerrick's neck as the knife sliced through his first layer of skin. Kerrick's knees bent slightly, and he thrust himself back into Fernando. Lacy screamed as Fernando and Kerrick flew backward off the cliff and fell toward the sea.

Kerrick's momentum pushed him further out than Fernando, but his body began to flip repeatedly. Fernando, however, was much closer to the cliff's face, and his body crashed on some rocks jutting out just below the cavity that served as the nose of the huge rock skull. His body bounced a couple of times and fell the rest of the way into the water.

Kerrick managed to go into the water feet first, but one of his legs appeared to hit the water awkwardly. Jon was out of his shoes before Kerrick went under, and he dove from the top of the cliff.

"Uncle Jon!" Lacy screamed in disbelief as Jon flew headfirst toward the ocean's surface.

He tore through the air and briefly thought about whether the water was deep enough for such a dive. When he hit the water, it felt like crashing into a plate glass window. His outstretched arms somewhat broke the surface of the water, but his head pounded with the force of his entrance. He pulled toward the surface, came up for air, and swam to the spot where Kerrick went underwater. He breathed in deeply and dove toward the bottom.

****

Lacy couldn't believe what had just happened. How could her uncle or Kerrick survive such a fall? Of course, Kerrick had already gone off the cliff once and managed to survive. Holding onto her stick, she hobbled up to the cliff's edge, and Jose grabbed her arm to steady her.

"Hold on, now. You don't need to go over, too."

She peered over the cliff, and to her amazement, Jon surfaced below. After two strong strokes, he dove under the water again. She looked up to see the Coast Guard helicopter approaching the island. They must have seen what happened because they dropped toward the water and hovered about twenty feet in the air. She saw a basket swing out the side door and drop toward the ocean. A diver dropped from the other side.

Lacy almost fainted with relief when Jon returned to the surface with Kerrick in his arms. *Is Jon giving him mouth-to-mouth resuscitation? No, God. Please don't let Kerrick die. He's been through so much. Please let him live. I love him. I don't care what he did. I love him.*

Tears spilled down her cheeks as her legs gave way. "I...I can't stand anymore, Jose."

Jose eased her to the ground and pulled her back from the edge. As the helicopter rose, she saw a basket swinging. A winch pulled Jon and Kerrick toward the open door, and the diver came up on the other side. *They have to be okay.*

Instead of landing, the helicopter flew north.

"Where are they going?" Lacy asked in disbelief.

"I assume they're going to the clinic in George Town or maybe Nassau."

"Oh, God. No. That must mean Kerrick is bad."

"Let's get back to the boat. We can call the Coast Guard and find out what's going on. Before we leave, I need to rewrap your leg. It's got to be immobilized."

"What about Miguel and the other men on the compound?" Lacy asked as Jose unwrapped the strips of cloth from her leg.

"There's no telling where any of them went. Maybe we'll never hear from him again." Jose repositioned the two pieces of wood on each side of Lacy's leg and tied the cloth in place. "Is that snug? It doesn't need to cut off your blood supply, but it needs to keep your leg from moving."

"It's fine."

"I've got some Ibuprofen back on the Carver."

Jose scooped Lacy up in his arms and carried her to the jeep. Thirty minutes later, they were aboard the *New Beginnings,* motoring north. Jose dialed a number on the sat phone, and Lacy looked back at the docks. No sign of Miguel's boat. She heard Jose say Meg's name. Although Lacy could only hear Jose's side of the conversation, she realized the helicopter was flying to Nassau.

"What did she say?" Lacy asked as soon as Jose disconnected the call. "I know they're going to Nassau, but is Kerrick okay?"

"She didn't know, Lacy. I'm sorry. She said that she just got off the phone with someone with the Coast Guard, and we should head to Nassau. It'll take us a couple of hours to get to the marina."

Lacy leaned back in the soft chair on the opposite side of the bridge from Jose. How could all of this be happening to her? She couldn't lose Kerrick now. Why hadn't he been upfront with her about his sister? Jon could have helped him. *What if he's dead or hurt badly? What if he's crippled now for the rest of his life?*

"Lacy, he's going to be all right. It didn't look like he hit any rocks, and Jon got to him in time."

"You don't know that for sure."

"What's that saying?" Jose asked. "Don't borrow trouble."

Lacy leaned back in the chair and closed her eyes. Five minutes later she jerked upright "Oh, my God,"

"What is it?"

"My mom! Today's my birthday. She's coming."

Chapter Thirty-Six
Princess Margaret

"I don't need an x-ray," Lacy insisted. "I just want to see Kerrick!"

Jon pushed Lacy through the double doors in the Princess Margaret Hospital emergency room. "Lacy, I told you ten times that you can't see Kerrick right now. He's in surgery. If it's any consolation, he asked about you before they took him back."

"Jon, I'm fine, really! I just bruised my leg a little. All I need is an Ace bandage."

Meg rolled her eyes at her husband. "Lacy, you and I both know your leg is broken. You can see Kerrick when he gets out of surgery. We need to know the condition of your leg."

"And what will that mean?"

"If it's only a fracture, then all you need is a cast," Meg said. "If it's broken and depending on the severity of the break, it could mean surgery."

"I don't need surgery," Lacy pleaded. "I just need…"

"I know," Meg interrupted. "You just need an Ace bandage."

Once the x-ray technician completed her task and rolled Lacy back to the curtained-off patient's room, the emergency room doctor came in holding an x-ray. Jon stood to greet him. The doctor had been formal but cordial with Meg and Lacy earlier, but Jon had not been with them.

"Dr. Davenport. I'm Dr. Simmons. Our suspicions were confirmed with the x-ray. Lacy's got a compound fracture. It's a pretty bad break."

This doctor was treating Lacy like a preschooler. *Hello. By the way, I'm in the room and almost legal. I'm at least a year closer to legal today than yesterday.*

"I've consulted with the orthopedic doctor," he continued, "and he thinks she'll need surgery. If you'd rather, we can immobilize it so she can return to Georgia. I don't recommend waiting. But if you prefer to get her home first, I understand. If you want us to proceed with the surgery today, we can fit her in this evening."

"Doesn't anyone care what I think?" Lacy blurted. "It's my leg, and I do have an opinion."

"Does it have anything to do with an Ace bandage?" Jon grinned.

"Okay. I admit I was not viewing my situation with the proper perspective earlier. It's ridiculous to put off surgery. I can't fly back to Georgia like this."

"Okay, Lacy," Dr. Simmons smiled. "We'll process the order and take you back as soon as possible. When's the last time you've eaten anything?"

Lacy wrinkled her brow. "I don't know. Maybe twelve hours. Not sure."

"Long enough. I'll have the orthopedic come by to talk with you when he's available, but he asked for an MRI before surgery."

It seemed like an eternity before an attendant took her back for the MRI, and Lacy about lost her patience with waiting on news about Kerrick. When she returned, Jon told her the operating room nurse called him while she was gone, and Kerrick was out of surgery. She felt some relief, but now it appeared she may have her own surgical issues to face.

Before the orthopedic surgeon could come back to talk with Lacy and the Davenports, Jon pulled out his iPhone and found information about the doctor on the internet.

"He graduated top in his class at Johns Hopkins and has great reviews," Jon reported. "The information online didn't say why he left a practice in Jacksonville to come to Nassau, but his background seems stellar. He was the team doctor for the Jaguars."

"Dr. Davenport?" a voice came through the curtain before it parted.

A young, good-looking man walked into the little room. Lacy couldn't quit staring at him. He was gorgeous. *Okay, so men aren't supposed to be gorgeous. He can't be a doctor. He's got to be a movie star.*

"I'm Dr. Williams. I'm the Orthopedic, and I happen to be on call today. Dr. Simmons and I have been reviewing Lacy's case. Hello, Lacy."

"Hi," Lacy tried to smile, but the pain in her leg showed on her face. "So, do I need surgery?"

"I'm sorry to tell you, but you need surgery. Your bone is broken just above your ankle. We'll need to perform a procedure called Open Reduction and Internal Fixation."

"What does that mean?"

"We'll put your bone back into the proper position and then hold it in place with a metal plate and screws. You'll be in a cast for a while as it heals."

"Uh, well," Lacy hesitated. "Have you done a lot of these kinds of surgeries?"

Dr. Williams laughed. "I know I look young. I'm forty and graduated from John Hopkins almost fifteen years ago. I did my residency at the Mayo Clinic in Rochester. I had a practice in Jacksonville, where I worked with several sports organizations."

"We saw that you were the doctor for the Jaguars," Meg interjected.

"I was the team doctor, and I enjoyed it. I left Jacksonville because I got tired of the rat race. The pace here on Nassau is a lot slower. If you want me to do the surgery, I can do it this evening as long as you haven't eaten anything since midnight. I understand if you'd rather wait and go back to Georgia."

"I haven't eaten since yesterday, and I'm starved. I had some water this morning but haven't had anything else to drink. I'd rather go ahead and have the surgery."

"Are you in agreement with that, Dr. Davenport?"

"If that's what Lacy wants, let's do it."

Lacy pulled herself up in the bed as the doctor left the room. "Jon, while I was back having an MRI, I started thinking about everything that's happened. I had a memory of the park back on Eleuthera. When I came out of the restaurant, I ran into Mr. Phil. You know. Mr. Phil Register. He's the old man we met for dinner several times, and we went to church with him. Anyway, I met him, and we sat down on a bench in a park near the restaurant to talk. Some guys came up to us, and Mr. Phil stood up. I don't remember anything else."

"Lacy," Jon cleared his throat. "When Jose and I came through the park, we saw Mr. Phil. Well, he…the paramedics think he may have had a heart attack. He didn't make it."

Lacy felt the blood drain from her face. She lay back on the bed in near shock. After several minutes, she spoke up in a quiet voice. "He didn't die of a heart attack."

"Jose didn't think so either."

Tears began to spill down Lacy's cheek. "He tried to save me. I'm sure of it."

Meg pulled Lacy against her as she wept over the loss of her friend. "You know he loved you, Lacy. I'm sure of it."

"He died for me."

"Well, he's in heaven now. I'm sure of that, too. I'll make a few phone calls and find out about his funeral."

When the nurse came to cart Lacy off to surgery, her tears had dried up, but her heart lay in pieces. That precious old man loved her; because he loved her, he died for her. It was almost too much to bear. *He didn't even know me, but he loved me.*

Almost four hours later, Lacy could hear talking in the room, but she didn't want to open her eyes. Someone was calling her name.

"Yeah," Lacy croaked.

"How do you feel?" Meg asked as Lacy felt her aunt rubbing her bare arm.

"Like I've been run over by something big." She opened one eye to a bright room and squinted in pain. "Do the lights have to be on?"

Jon jumped toward the switch, and Meg pulled the curtains. Lacy opened her eyes again and could see Jose and Ann in the room. Another person stood behind Ann. Her eyes roamed around the semi-private room, and she thought it odd that no curtain separated her from the person in the bed beside her. Though she couldn't see the entire room, it must have been small because the beds were side-by-side. She felt a warm hand grab hers, and she realized the hand belonged to the person in the bed next to her.

"Hey, Lacy," Kerrick croaked. "I'm so glad you're okay."

"Kerrick?" Lacy jerked up, causing pain to shoot through her leg. She fell back against her pillow. "Oh. That hurt like…that hurt like crud."

Kerrick laughed and then grimaced with his own pain. "Yeah. Crud hurts."

"How are you?"

"I'm fine. They did surgery on my leg. When I fell off the cliff, I grazed a rock with my leg on the way down to the water, and then I landed funny."

"Thankfully, just your leg hit it," Jon said. "Fernando wasn't as lucky."

Lacy shuddered at the memory of seeing Kerrick push himself backward and off the cliff. She didn't see Fernando hit the rocks, but she saw him floating face-down in the water.

"I'll be out of commission for a little while," Kerrick concluded. "They still need to put a cast on my leg."

Tears began to roll down Lacy's face. "Why didn't you tell us? I mean, why didn't you tell us about what Miguel and Fernando were doing to you? You could have been killed."

A beautiful girl stepped toward Lacy's bed, her face was familiar. "He did it for Mom and Dad and me. It wasn't right, but he was trying to save our family."

"Kelsey? Are you Kerrick's sister?"

"In the flesh."

Lacy thought of the last picture she saw of Kerrick's beautiful sister. She almost reacted to the flesh comment and decided Kelsey might be sensitive about that topic. *I'm so stupid. I can't believe I almost brought that picture up.*

Jon stepped toward Lacy's bed. "Kelsey has quite a story, too. One of Miguel's men kidnapped her, but thankfully, she's okay."

"Yeah. Thanks to Meg and the FBI. They got me out. I'm glad you're okay, Lacy."

"Me too. I'm just glad this nightmare is over."

"Happy birthday," Kelsey said as she pulled out a bouquet of flowers from behind her back. "Kerrick told me it was your birthday."

"He should have told you I was skipping it this year."

"He said something about that, but I figured you'd like some flowers."

"Thanks, Kelsey. You're so thoughtful." Lacy took the bouquet of assorted flowers and put them to her nose. "They're beautiful. Thanks so much."

"I'll put them in some water," Meg offered. "The good news is you don't have to stay in here too long. As soon as you feel up to it, you can leave."

"I don't want to leave Kerrick," Lacy insisted. "When can he leave?"

"They want him to spend the night," Meg replied.

"Can I spend the night with him? We have some things to talk about."

"Don't you think your talk can wait?" Meg asked. "You've got five boys who are dying to see you."

"Doesn't insurance do the twenty-three-hour thing for the same price? I mean, it won't cost any more for me to stay overnight than to leave right now, will it?"

"Probably not," Jon admitted. "If you want to stay, I suppose we can work that out. Letting people of the opposite sex share a room is beyond protocol."

"I don't think we'll get out of bed, Uncle Jon. Y'all don't have to worry about us."

"I don't know," Jon teased. "You've given us the slip before."

"It'll be fine," Meg agreed. "If you're going to stay, we may leave in a few minutes."

Someone tapped on the door and stepped into the room. "Is it okay if I come in, Dr. Davenport?"

Lacy recognized the voice of her friend. "Miss Debra! How did you know we were here?"

"I ran into Dr. Davenport downstairs while you were in surgery. I told him I'd come up. Hey, Kerrick. How are you two feeling?"

"We're fine," Kerrick insisted. "We need to quit meeting like this."

Debra laughed. "I'd say that you are accident-prone, Kerrick."

"It appears that way."

"It looks like you have plenty of company," Debra said. "I just wanted to stick my head in and say hello. I'm sorry about your accident, but I'm glad you're both okay. I had a strong feeling to pray for you last night, Lacy. I prayed for you all night."

"Thank you, Miss Debra. I did a little praying myself."

"I hope we can catch up soon. I want to hear your story."

"I imagine I'll return to see Dr. Movie Star soon."

Debra laughed. "All of the single women on the island have their eyes on Dr. Williams."

"He's single?" Lacy couldn't believe that he wasn't married. She felt Kerrick take hold of her hand again.

"Sure is," Debra smiled, "but I don't think you are. Let's have lunch when you come back to Nassau."

"Sounds good. I have your number, so I'll call you. Thanks for coming by." Lacy opened her mouth to a large, unguarded yawn. "Excuse me," she said as another yawn escaped. "I'm wiped out."

Debra stepped back toward the door. "I'll see you two soon."

"It's getting late," Jon acknowledged as Debra left the room. "We need to get back to the boys. We'll see you two in the morning."

As the group filed out of the room, Meg stood beside Lacy. She leaned over and kissed her forehead. "Happy birthday, Lacy. I love you."

"I love you, too, Aunt Meg."

"Your mom called."

"Let me guess. She got tied up and can't come down."

"I'm sorry, Lacy. I really am."

"Don't be. I would have been more surprised if she came."

Chapter Thirty-Seven
Defining the Future

The next morning, Jon pulled the rental van into the parking lot, and he and Meg walked toward the hospital entrance. Meg looked at the hospital with gratitude and discomfort. *I'd be happy if I never have to see this hospital again.* Two times in about a month was two times too many.

Jon took her hand. "So, do you think Lacy and Kerrick made up?"

"They probably talked a while, but I don't think there was much making up to do."

"I don't know about that," Jon said. "Kerrick was quite deceitful. Lacy might have a hard time getting over that."

"True, but I think she'll understand. After all, Kelsey's life was at stake."

Meg opened the door to the room, and Jon followed her inside. They were both sound asleep, and their hands and arms were as intertwined as possible through the rails of their beds.

Jon whispered in Meg's ear. "I think that's as close as they could get to one another. It's a good thing they're immobilized."

Meg walked over beside Lacy and rubbed her arm. "Good morning, sleepyhead. You ready to get out of here?"

"Huh...oh," Lacy opened her eyes and yawned. "Hey, Meg and Jon."

"Good morning," Kerrick added. "Sorry. We didn't get a lot of sleep last night."

"I guessed that might happen," Meg grinned. "It took an act of Congress to convince the powers that be to allow you two in the same room. I hope you had enough time to work through your issues."

"We at least started," Kerrick smiled. "I'm ready to go back to work."

"We're going back to Rock Sound," Jon informed them. "I'm sorry that your work for the summer is over. Neither of you can do much for a few months, so you can stay in the house with Randal.

"If anyone else gets hurt, we're going to have to get a bigger house," Meg teased.

Lacy yawned again. "Sounds boring."

Four hours later, Jon pushed Lacy toward the house in her wheelchair while Jose followed close behind, pushing Kerrick. As they neared the house, the door opened to the choruses of the boys shouting, "Surprise."

A huge banner spanned the wall on the back of the large den that welcomed them home. As Lacy and Kerrick settled in on the two couches, the boys gathered around, wanting to hear the whole story.

Ann came in from the kitchen and then hurried to the bathroom. Her hand was on her abdomen, and she was as white as a sheet.

Meg walked in through the front door. "Okay, guys. Give them some space. We need to eat first, and then our two heroes can tell their stories. Lacy, I'll fix your plate, and Jon will get yours, Kerrick."

As everyone filed back into the den with plates of food, Ann rejoined the group and sat beside Jose. "Before we begin our little reunion," Ann interrupted, "we have an announcement to make."

Everyone in the room looked toward the loveseat where Ann and Jose sat holding hands.

"Let me guess," Meg suggested.

Everyone in the room, except Kelsey, said in unison, "You're pregnant."

Ann was aghast. "How did you know?"

Meg placed her index finger on her cheek. "Well, let's see. Throwing up four times a day was one clue."

"I thought I hid it pretty well. Lacy knew, but she was the only one."

"We're so excited," Meg said as she got up and hugged her friend. "There's nothing quite like being a mom."

"We're excited, too," Ann agreed. "I hope to have a little boy. I don't think I'll know what to do with a girl."

"Oh," Meg grinned, "I think you'll do just fine with whatever you have."

The boys spent the next couple of hours dragging the story out of Kerrick and Lacy. Jon and Jose added a few comments along the way.

"That's amazing," Barry concluded. "I had no idea this summer would be so...so..."

"Action-packed?" Ann suggested.

"Yeah. Action-packed."

"They should make a movie about this," Tae insisted.

"Yeah," Randal chimed in from his wheelchair. "They could call it *Skull Island*."

"I think there's a movie coming out with that name," Ann recounted. "Seems like it has to do with King Kong."

"Did you ever figure out why the jerk wanted Lacy's medallion?" Aaron asked.

"Not really," Jon replied. "We think Miguel has the other one with the clue on it. I suppose we'll never know."

"So, what do we do now?" Barry wondered.

"We get back to work," Jon said. "What did you expect?"

"I didn't know," Barry confessed. "With Randal, Kerrick, and Lacy out of the picture, we're missing a few people."

"Nonsense," Lacy insisted. "Kerrick and I have just joined the cheerleading squad. Randal's well enough that he's able to help a little."

"She's right," Jon added. "We still have three weeks before you guys return home. You never know what we'll find."

"Didn't you clean the stuff we brought up from the other side of that deep tunnel?" Kerrick asked.

"We did," Jose replied, "and it was nothing. We think it's possible the ship could have sunk in that area, however."

"Speaking of work," Jon interrupted, "I think we should get the boys back to *The Discoverer*. We want to start out early in the morning. I want to finish up in the bay and then follow a possible line that would have taken the galleon around the edge of the island to the spot below the tunnel. I'd like to see if we find any sign of a debris trail."

The next three weeks passed by a lot faster than Lacy anticipated. She even grew fond of Kelsey, and they only spent a few days together before she returned to Jacksonville.

Mr. Phil's funeral was something Lacy would never forget. His family decided to have the funeral service at the park where he died because the funeral home and the church were too small for the crowd they anticipated. The park was packed with people.

The music was moving, but several people stood to tell stories about Mr. Phil. Lacy tried to tell her story, but she began to cry and couldn't finish.

She said between sobs, "All I can say is that I love Mr. Phil, and I'll never forget him."

The scripture the pastor read would also be forever etched into her mind: "Greater love has no one than this, that someone lay down his life for his friends."

Lacy found herself dreading the day the summer ended. She didn't know how she would react to all the boys returning to their homes. The debriefing sessions each night became a lifeline for her and Kerrick to the day's events.

The most exciting day of the final three weeks was when Aaron found a few pieces of broken plates. This find led Jon to spend several extra days combing the area, where they found a string of artifacts, including cannon balls, another arquebus, and a brass plate.

The final night arrived, and Jon had Chef Marceau come to the house in Rock Sound to prepare a celebration dinner. Jon asked each of the boys to share one thing that meant the most to them about the summer, and every boy agreed that the one thing was not a thing but a person: Lacy. Lacy wept as the boys took turns hugging her. She couldn't bear to see them leave.

"You boys mean the world to me," Lacy said between sniffs. "You've taught me some important lessons about life and love."

"Kerrick's the one who's taught you about love," Tae teased.

"If Kerrick doesn't treat you right," Barry added, "you call me. I'll get the boys together, and we'll come down to Miami and give him a lesson or two."

"And then you can marry me," Randal beamed.

Lacy blew her nose into a tissue. "I'll keep that in mind." She hopped over to Randal and kissed his cheek.

The boys howled with laughter and demanded to be next. The evening continued with a lot of stories and laughter. Jon ended the evening with a challenge to the boys to ensure the summer wasn't wasted.

"Boys, you're not leaving the same as you were two months ago. You must realize this time wasn't about doing something cool during your summer break. It's about life. I've seen enough in you these weeks together to believe the best in you. I expect to hear great things from each of you. Just remember that your future has everything to do with your choices. You can choose to define your future."

Lacy was sad she and Kerrick wouldn't be able to return to Miami with Marcy and the boys. She and Kerrick had an appointment on Nassau with Dr. Williams and lunch with Debra. She hugged each boy and kissed them on the cheek as they left for the night. Marcy's flight back home was to leave from Miami, so Lacy agreed to stay in touch.

Because he was still restricted to a wheelchair, Randal would have to wait until the following morning to get aboard *The Discoverer.* Lacy and Kerrick had to leave for Nassau early the next morning, so they told Randal goodbye before bed.

"You know my family's going to be moving," Randal told Lacy. "Thanks to Mr. Jon."

"I heard that," Lacy admitted. "I'm so excited. Meg told me your mom planned to buy a house from Uncle Jon."

"Yeah. It's out in the suburbs. He's the best."

"I'm sorry I won't get to see you off in the morning," Lacy said. "I have your e-mail, so I'll stay in touch. Remember to respond to my Facebook friend request."

"I will, Lacy. Good night."

Lacy stopped at Kerrick's bedroom door. "I don't think I can cry anymore for a month."

"I'm going to miss those boys," Kerrick agreed. "What about us?"

"Uh, well," Lacy stammered. "What about us?"

"I don't want our relationship to just be a summer thing either. Maybe we should take Jon's advice."

"What advice was that?"

"Instead of letting the future define us, let's define the future."

Lacy placed her hand on Kerrick's cheek. "I'm game." She pulled his face toward hers and kissed him. "See you in the morning."

After their day on Nassau, Jose took Kerrick and Lacy back to the marina, where they docked the *New Beginnings*. To her surprise, Jon, Judy, and Ann sat in chairs on the back deck of the yacht.

"Carla's asleep in the cabin," Meg whispered as she stepped out of the galley, "so you guys be quiet."

Jon offered his chair as Lacy hopped aboard the boat on a set of crutches. "I decided to give the crew a month off, so Captain Buffington dropped us off here. I figured we could all head back to Pirate's Cover together."

When they returned to the Davenport compound, Judy and Meg got right to work on dinner. They grilled hamburgers while Jon dropped some French fries into a deep fryer.

Dinner around the table felt a little funny with such a small group.

"I've been thinking about my medallion," Lacy said.

"Really?" Meg sat forward in her chair. "What have you been thinking?"

"I've been thinking I never got it back from the jeweler."

Meg got up from the table, grabbed an envelope containing Lacy's medallion, and gave it to her niece. "Here you go. I had Diego pick it up."

"He's such a good man," Ann added. "You were lucky to find someone so dependable to care for your property."

"We are thankful," Jon admitted.

Lacy pulled the medallion out of the envelope and stared at it. "Thanks so much, Meg. You know I'll cherish this for the rest of my life."

"I suppose we can assume Miguel has a medallion that contains a clue," Jon said. "The medallion the little girl from Sweden had didn't seem to say much."

"Don't you have a picture of that one?" Lacy asked.

Meg grabbed Queen Ella's file that contained pictures of the medallion. She laid it down on the table for the group to see.

Ann pointed to the picture of the little Swedish girl's medallion. "A cross in a circle. I guess that's referring to the King's conversion."

"It makes me think of the trelleborg," Meg suggested.

"That's strange," Jon said. "I had that thought when we were swimming through the tunnel beneath Skull Island."

"Why?" Meg asked.

"Jose and I crossed intersecting tunnels when we swam from the ocean to the pond. For some reason, it reminded me of the trelleborg."

"I'd love to visit the Trelleborg Museum one of these days," Ann said.

"We better go before the baby comes," Jose suggested.

"I'm so sad this is our last night together," Meg said. "Lacy, what are your plans? I mean, about the future?"

"I'm considering transferring to the University of Miami in January."

"Really?" Meg winked at Kerrick. "I didn't think there was anything special about their exercise science program."

Lacy blushed. "Maybe not, but there's someone special at the University."

Jon flew with Kerrick and Lacy back to Miami on a private charter the following day. Saying goodbye to Kerrick was difficult, but she knew they had plans to be together over the Labor Day weekend. She was grateful they had a lot of private time earlier for the real goodbyes. Before climbing aboard the Delta flight for Atlanta, she hugged Jon and Meg tightly.

"You've changed my life," she offered. "I love you both so much."

"We love you, too, Lacy. You know that you have a home with us anytime."

Lacy waved goodbye and sat in a wheelchair that a Delta attendant rolled up behind her. Once aboard the plane, she got out of the wheelchair and hopped over to her window seat in first class. She smiled as she thought about the benefits of having a broken leg.

As the plane began taxiing down the runway, she remembered her summer and touched her medallion. *It's been a crazy summer. Who would have thought a small medallion with one little word could cause so much trouble?* She laid her head back against the seat and closed her eyes. Her mind raced over the events of the summer. She thought about Mr. Phil. She'd never forget the sweet, old man who tried to save her life.

She thought about the discussion from the previous night as images of trelleborgs, medallions, crosses, and tunnels filled her mind. She jolted upright in her seat and said out loud: "Beneath! That's it. Beneath! I've got to call Jon."

She pulled out her cell phone, but the flight attendant told her she'd have to put it away until they landed in Atlanta. *Oh, well. I suppose the secret has been hidden for hundreds of years. It can stand to remain a secret for a little longer.*

What's Next?
Book 5 in the Davenport Series

Summer may be over, but the adventure is just beginning.

When Lacy Henderson discovers that a golden medallion from her aunt contains a hidden clue to long-lost Viking treasure, she becomes convinced she knows where King Harold Bluetooth's fortune lies buried—deep beneath the waters of the Bahamas.

There's only one problem: she's not the only one searching.

Determined to uncover the truth, Lacy returns to Coral Cay—the island of the skull—to reunite with Kerrick Daniels and the Davenports for one final dive. But treasure hunting is never just about gold, and the closer Lacy and Kerrick grow, the more she realizes that love may demand a risk greater than any ocean dive.

In this gripping continuation of the series, adventure, danger, and romance collide beneath tropical waters where every discovery comes with a price.

Some treasures are worth the hunt. Others may cost you everything.

From the Author

Thank you for reading my book, *Ready to Love Again*. If you enjoyed it, will you please take a moment to leave a review on Amazon? If you have missed reading any of the previous books of the series, you'll find descriptions on the following pages. You can pick them up from Amazon or your favorite retailer. In the opening pages of Book 1, I offered the prequel to the series as a free gift. If you would like a free pdf copy of a story about Jon and Meg as teenagers, visit my website and click on the "free gift" tab (judahknight.com).

I would enjoy dialoguing with you about any of my books or about the one I'm currently writing. You can reach me through my publisher (www.greentreepublishers.com), through the contact page on my website (judahknight.com), or through one of the social media links listed below. I look forward to hearing from you soon.

I think you can probably tell from some of the story where the adventure goes next. I'll give you a hint. I'll be spending some time in central and southern Mexico doing research for Book 5. I look forward to sharing with you some of the rich history of the Mayan people.

Thanks again for taking the time to read my book, and I'll see you in the next adventure.

Judah Knight

Follow me on Twitter:

http://www.twitter.com/judahknight

Check out my website:

http://www.judahknight.com

Have a discussion with me on Goodreads.com:

http://bit.ly/1m5heLe

The Davenport Series

THE DAVENPORT SERIES BOOK 1
2ND EDITION

THE LONG WAY HOME

JUDAH KNIGHT

THE DAVENPORT SERIES BOOK 2
2ND EDITION

HOPE FOR TOMORROW

JUDAH KNIGHT

THE DAVENPORT SERIES BOOK 3
2ND EDITION

FINDING MY WAY

JUDAH KNIGHT

The Davenport Series - Book 4

Ready to Love Again

Judah Knight

The Davenport Series - Book 5

Love Waits

Judah Knight

The Davenport Series - Book 6

No Greater Love

Judah Knight

CHRISTMAS CAPTIVE

JUDAH KNIGHT

Prequel: A Girl Can Always Hope

In *The Long Way Home*, we learn that the two main characters knew one another as teenagers, and Margaret Robertson (Meg Freeman in *The Long Way Home*) had a crush on her brother's best friend, Jon Davenport. Read the fun short story of one awkward middle schooler's attempt to capture the impossible catch. This book is available as a free gift on the author's website: judahknight.com.